THE LONG MEMORY

THE
LONG MEMORY

HOWARD CLEWES

THE REPRINT SOCIETY · LONDON

FIRST PUBLISHED 1951
THIS EDITION PUBLISHED BY THE REPRINT SOCIETY LTD.
BY ARRANGEMENT WITH MACMILLAN & CO. LTD. 1953

PRINTED IN GREAT BRITAIN

CONTENTS

CONTENTS

BOOK ONE

THE RETURN

CHAPTER ONE

I

ON A bright afternoon early in November, some
eighteen months ago, Philip Davidson walked along
the track which follows the bend of the river east of
Gravesend where the lonely marshes sweep up into
Higham Bight and the white towers and turrets of the
cement works at Cliffe rise out of the mist like those of a
legendary citadel, bald and inscrutable. A man called
Jackson saw him there, and spoke to him.

I had asked to be kept informed of Davidson's movements, and so as soon as I heard where he had gone I
ordered a car and drove down from Westminster to have
a look at the place.

There are two ways of reaching Morocco Bay from
Gravesend. You can follow the river's edge on foot, as
Davidson had done; or you can drive along the crest of
the low hills and then, turning left, follow the new road
down across the marshes; the road was built during the
war for the construction of the defence obstacle which juts
out into the river from St. Mary's Bay. At the end of the
road you get out and walk.

Morocco Bay is about a mile from St. Mary's. It faces
Blyth Sand, which is in fact a mud flat stretching from
Lower Hope Point to Yantlet Flats and the Isle of Grain,
and is covered by a few feet of water at high tide. It is a
sad, forgotten place—hardly more than a creek, and it has
been used in the past as a burial ground for old barges,
which are as a rule long-lived; indeed so long do they
last that when they are finished they are scarcely worth
breaking up; so the owners, to save the cost of breakage,

are wont to run the hulks into the reeds at high tide,
towing them there at night (since the practice is illegal)
and, having stripped them of their identity, to leave them
there to rot away. In the course of time the horizontal
timbers spring and warp and fall off or are ripped off by
scavengers who saw them up for use as fuel; so that at last
only the spines of the ships are left, buried in the mud, and
the verticals, which rear up above the reeds like gargantuan
ribs, turning slowly white in the sun and the wind; you
would think the place a graveyard of elephants which
had come there one by one to die, or a beach where a
school of whales, thrown up by the sea, had expired on
their backs.

As I got out of the car and set off along the river bank I
wondered if Flood had had a word, as he had promised,
with the local police; I was well beyond the Metropolitan
boundary, and local forces are not too glad to have
Deputy Assistant Commissioners working in their territory
without so much as a tip of the hat; I winced at the
possibility of a sarcastic memorandum from the local
Chief Constable to the effect that, while Commander
Lowther was of course always welcome in this area, he,
the C.C., did not remember having requested . . . etc.,
etc. However, I did not expect to be seen, and put the
matter out of my mind.

The banks are low and laced with wandering gullies
of still water. Where the mud is dry it is cracked and
fissured and like rubber to walk on; now and then there
are little beaches of bright blue mussel-shell and river
flotsam, and the wet mud whispers and mutters as it dries.
The river flows heavily by out beyond the flats, and the
ships are low and black under the purple haze of the
Essex shore. Ahead of me as I walked I could see the
reeds which fringed the little bay and, above them, the
prows of the barges. Davidson evidently had had the
place in mind for years; nobody else would have found it,
or wanted to go there; he had gone straight to it.

Some kind of habitation can be made of nearly any type of barge or lighter; you have only to build a roof across the stern-frame—an old tarpaulin will do, and I have seen it done with a few lengths of plank or corrugated iron. Spritsail barges are the best, however, for then you have it all complete with a cabin and bunks and even a kitchen stove. So until they fall apart or are pulled to pieces the hulks in Morocco Bay are mostly lived in by old men, watermen or bawley-men or lightermen, who, having no other home and being too old even to be nightwatch-men, have settled like hermit crabs in them and made themselves as comfortable as may be. You can tell which are occupied; there is a length of drainpipe projecting rakishly from the roof of the cabin in the stern, with a ribbon of blue smoke swirling about the chimney like a ring-master's whip, and probably a couple of shirts or a jersey flapping from a line slung across the deck.

I turned up the collar of my coat against the wind and stood in the reeds trying to make up my mind which of these wrecks was Davidson's; there were only two or three which seemed to be habitable, noses in the reeds, sterns in the mud, huge as ships always are on land. I watched them for a long time, for I had no wish to come face to face with the man just then. Somewhere, far up-stream, a dredger was working; I caught the squeal and rattle of the dredge faintly on the wind. The tide was rising and the water swung restlessly about the great green keels of the hulks.

It would be the one nearest the river, I thought, and the only reason I had was that it seemed less frowsty than its neighbours. There was a ladder against the beam. I waited fifteen minutes and then went aboard.

The door of the cabin was slightly ajar and, pushing it open, I looked in.

There was a blanket on the bunk, neatly folded. There was an old pan on the stove, but the fire was dead. On

the window ledge there was a razor and a shaving brush.
I saw a mug on the table with a minute thread of brown,
of dried tea, running from the rim to the base, where a
mouth had drunk.

Immediately behind me a man said: "Looking for
something, mister?"

I spun about and stammered, "No no, nothing
particular," and felt like a guilty schoolboy.

He had a straggling, bristling moustache and red-
rimmed eyes that watered copiously and continuously.
A shotgun lay across his arms. "I been watching you," he
said. His voice shook and cracked. "You got no business
aboard this ship."

"Is it yours?" I enquired. This would be Jackson, I
thought.

"Belongs to me."

"And these things?" I was angry, but more with myself
than with this old man. "Whose are these?" I indicated
the shaving tackle and the blanket and the mug.

"They ain't yours," said Jackson shrilly.

"Then whose are they?"

"'Tain't nothing to do with you. Belong to a friend of
mine. One of my friends."

"What's his name?"

"I never asked."

"Where has he gone?"

"Didn't ask that, neither," Jackson said.

I saw his little blue eyes move over me, blinking; he
compressed his lips and the bristles stood out like quills.
And presently, as the expression on his face changed,
I knew he had recognised me for a policeman; it always
unnerved me; but by the same token I knew this old man
had had much to do with policemen: the recognition is
usually mutual.

I said cruelly: "When did you come out?"

The ruin was complete. The belligerence evaporated.
He began to plead: "I haven't done nothing. It's twelve

years since I was in last. I haven't done nothing. Honest.
I don't want no trouble . . ."

"It's all right, don't worry." I felt myself a bully.
"Where do you live?"

He pointed to the adjacent hulk.

"And you know the man who lives here . . ."

He looked away, over the river.

"Tell me about him."

"He's a friend of mine," he muttered. "He ain't done
nothing wrong."

Clearly it was going to take time; I wanted to get off
the ship lest Davidson should return and find me there.
"Let's get out of here," I said, and motioned towards
the ladder at the beam. We went down and through the
reeds and aboard the hulk he lived in, into the little
cabin. It smelled sourly of ancient life, but it was warm
and comfortable.

There, after I had assured him he was doing his friend
no ill, Jackson told me how he had first met Philip
Davidson.

2

He had been out in the marsh with his gun, in the
afternoon. He had seen Davidson a long way away, as
you can see people in that country, leaning on the wind
coming towards him, small and lonely on the flat green
earth.

Where they met there is an old fortress called Shornmead. It is deserted and derelict; the courtyard, which is
circular and open to the sky, is littered with broken glass
and pebbles, and the doors in the walls bang to and fro in
the wind. During the war it was manned and then later
occupied by prisoners; the names of the offices were painted
on the doors and are still legible: *Küche: kein Eintritt* and
Abort and *Schuhmacherei* and one or two in English like

C.A.S.L.s Stores and *Battery Office*. Jackson had been standing on the slope outside, under the walls among the brambles and the rusty barbed wire, near the river's edge.

"He was walking like a feller a bit blind," Jackson told me. "As if he was feeling his way with his feet. His hands was in his pockets. Had 'em clenched, you could see the bulges. Kept looking at my shotgun."

"Did he speak?"

"Yes. Wanted to know what I was shooting. So I told him—duck. Then he asked me if there was many about and I said there's more when there's a bit of frost."

"What did he look like?"

"Look like? Oh . . . big feller. Bushy eyebrows. Big. Tired. Couldn't hardly lift one foot after the other. . . ."

I left it at that. "Did he say anything else?"

"Asked me if that was the Ovens . . . the buoy." You could hear the bell tolling, even from Shornmead, far away under the Essex shore. "So I says yes, that's her."

And Davidson, then, had nodded briefly and walked on with his fists clenched tightly in his pockets. Jackson had watched for a little while, with the shotgun resting across his arms.

It could not have been easy for Davidson, that first encounter, but he hadn't bolted. He had asked his questions of a stranger, useless questions to which he must already have known the answers, forcing himself to it, and then, with the shotgun at his back, had walked away.

I dragged from Jackson what had passed; for the old man had followed Davidson all the way from Shornmead to the bay. Presently he was talking quite freely. When there was nothing more to be learned I got up and went out on to the deck of the barge. But Jackson had not finished; he followed me anxiously.

We stood on the smooth boards. The wind came bustling across the low country, rippling the pools and veins of water between the islands of turf and stiff marsh grass. On the horizon beyond the bows of the barge you could see the distant rubble-dumps like a range of blue hills, where at one time the débris of the city had been tipped. Inland a little, by itself in the desolation, there was a ruined ware-house, and later I went over to have a look at it. It was not as a matter of fact a warehouse; nor was it ruined; it was only half built, having supports and a roof, but no walls. God knows who built it or what it was intended for, or why they stopped when it was only half finished; it might have been a cattle shelter or a place for drying pelts, or simply a barn. At all events there it stood, rusting slowly away. And the slats of corrugated iron which formed the roof had worked loose, if indeed they had ever been screwed down, so that now they beat against one an-other when the wind stirred, like iron hands applauding or the gossiping of long metal tongues. The clamour was there all the time I talked to Jackson, over and above the melancholy tolling of the buoys and the bitter hiss of the wind in the reeds.

I was certain he had not come to this place by chance; as soon as he was let out of prison he came straight here, having chosen it because he knew it well and because it was excellently suited to his purpose. Often enough, as a boy, he had explored these marshes; his father, Mark Davidson, gave him a sailing dinghy, I remember, and on summer afternoons he would put into the reeds and climb about the wrecks or lie on the warm timbers and read or search the sky for larks; in summer the air is full of the shrill sustained hysteria of their song. And here, too, a mile or so upstream, he had run up under the lee of William Driver's spritsail barge that afternoon and had spoken to Fay, who was Driver's daughter. It was through her that he had been led into his association with Spenser Boyd, of whose murder, after the firing of the barge, he was con-victed. Davidson had been twenty-four then, and the year 1932. He served seventeen of his sentence of twenty years.

He came back to the river after his release because Fay

Driver and little Pewsey, who had been Boyd's hanger-on, had both been river people, and this was where he would find them again. These were the two who had shared the crime with him, who had given evidence against him, whose statements had led to his conviction. When the barge had caught fire they had been there, in the cabin. They knew it all. Their faces flickered through the endless nightmare of the trial and the years that followed. I thought: now he can begin the search for them; and there is nothing we, the police, can do, but wait. Nothing.

I stood in the door of Jackson's cabin and stared across the serene desolation of the bay. The sun dropped a bar of light between the scudding clouds and I watched it sweep over the river and the levels and on towards the distant city. Here Davidson would be left alone; he would need that. A man who has spent so many years in hard labour is, if he survives at all, a broken pitiful creature whose first necessity is a hole in which to hide, for he has an over-whelming fear of people and the bustle of life; he needs a crevice in which to spin a cocoon about himself, where he can keep about him for a little while the four walls which for so many years have been both his prison and his stronghold. Too often and too easily a man of Davidson's calibre will founder in freedom itself; he loses his purpose and his identity in the shapeless torrent he swims in. I wondered if Davidson knew it. It is a hard thing to resist.

Jackson said: "Mister. . . ." He touched my arm.

"Yes?"

"He's a friend of mine."

That would be all right, I told him.

CHAPTER TWO

I

I SET off along the river bank in the direction Jackson had pointed; there was a café, he said, beyond the road, by a small landing-stage; that was where Davidson was likely to be.

As I walked, and it was quite a long way, I pieced together in my mind the rest of that first encounter as the old man had described it. He had stood back out of sight in the reeds and watched Davidson climb aboard the barge lying nearest the river. There was not much of it left. The horizontals in the bows had gone; the boards encircling the well amidships had sprung; there was water in the bilge, for the keel was buried in the mud which at high tide would be covered. But the shell of the cabin in the stern was sound enough. There were two bunks and there was a stove from which the flue had been torn away.

Davidson had left his bundle in the cabin and then had returned to the deck, to stand in the pale sunlight and stare across the land at the rubble-tips, huge on the horizon, and at the shining misty river. Then Jackson had called him from below the beam:

"Hey." And again: "Hey you."

I knew the effect the familiar peremptory summons must have had. Davidson had come to the rail and looked down on the old man with the shotgun in his arms, holding himself back from the instinct to submit utterly and immediately; he stood swaying.

"You got to pay rent for that," Jackson had said. He

had a harsh, strangled voice, an old man's voice, but vigorous and aggressive.

And Davidson had asked at last: "Whose is it?"—wrenching at the words.

"Belongs to me."

And then, with a sudden blind plunging courage: "By what right?"

"By right of it belongs to me."

I had interrupted Jackson's story at that point to ask him: "Did he move? Did he come down?"

"No. Just stood there with his fists clenched in his pockets. Swayed a bit, that's all. Shaking like a leaf, he was. So then I says again: You got to pay rent, see?"

And at length Davidson had asked: "How much?"

"Five shilling," Jackson told him. "Five shilling a week." The man on the ship had nodded. "Very well."

"Fridays," Jackson had said. "Every Friday. You got the money?"

Davidson had taken his hand from his pocket and felt for a wallet. He had held out a ten-shilling note, saying: "Take it. Two weeks."

It was then for the first time that I began to understand Jackson, for when I asked him if he had taken the money, he looked away, embarrassed. "No," he muttered. "I told him to keep it. Told him I didn't want it. . . ."

"Why?"

"Ah, nobody pays rent. What do I want with rent? All they have to do is know it's mine. Belongs to me." His eyes watered profusely. "It would be a nice thing," he said with a sudden, almost comical defiance, "if I couldn't let a friend of mine have it, now wouldn't it?"

I agreed. "Did you tell Davidson that?"

"Told him he needn't pay rent—yes."

I sometimes wonder if Davidson realised his mistake. He accepted Jackson's hospitality. It was a trick, of course, and the old fellow must have played it quite often—a bait

to catch a friend. Davidson had put the note back in his
pocket and Jackson, pressing home his advantage, had
said: "Like a cup of tea?"

But Davidson had shied away. "No. No."

"It's made . . . hot."

"No." He had turned abruptly and gone into the cabin.
He was bewildered and frightened by the turn the
encounter had taken. When Jackson went aboard the man
was sitting on the bunk rubbing his outspread hands to
and fro across his knees.

He must have heard the shuffling footsteps on the deck
and then the sibilance of the old hand on the door, for
when Jackson looked in he cried at once:

"Why can't you leave me alone?"

"I brought the tea," Jackson said. He stood in the doorway with the mug of tea in his hand. He looked down at
the hard, lined face and blazing blue eyes.

"I don't want it! I told you I don't want it!" The hands
on the knees were shaking.

"It's no trouble . . ." To me he tried to explain:
"I thought maybe it was just that he didn't want to give
trouble. I told him it weren't any trouble. . . ." He had put
out his loneliness and his capacity for hurt like antennae,
feeling for a fissure in the wall. And Davidson had resisted
fiercely, a little wildly perhaps, knowing even then that it
was too late: already he was beholden to this damned
old man, and involved in his pathetic friendliness.

"So I left it there," Jackson told me. He moved his
shoulders. "Put it on the other bunk in case he felt like
it later."

But he had not left. He had lingered in the doorway of
the cabin, watching Davidson untie his bundle, taking out
the blanket and the shaving kit and the few things he
owned, one by one. Presently, brightly, he had asked:

"Well, what d'y'plan to do, mister?" He watched the
high wide shoulders; he could see the line of the cheekbone
and jaw, set and tensed. The silence was unbearable.

"There's fishing—some, not much. There's a bit of totting, round the dumps. There's toshing, upalong . . . too far. maybe, too far upstream, 'round the docks. Then there's a feller got a bawley, goes after shrimps. And there's those as don't specialise."

Jackson himself was a totter, I learned. He told me without pride, but steadfastly: it was a profession like any other. He picked the dumps for scrap-iron and bicycle frames and junk, wheeling the stuff to the junk-merchants' yards in an old perambulator.

I asked him. "What did he answer?"

"Nothing. Wouldn't speak. Not till I asked him what they'd put him away for. . . ."

"You asked him that?"

"Any harm in it?"

"How did you know he'd been in prison?"

Jackson looked at me, blinking his red-rimmed eyes. "Knew as soon as I saw him," he said. "You can tell, specially just after they've come out. Tell it in the way they look at you, the way they walk. Mind you," he said, "I was only in twice myself. Once in 'thirty-five and once in 'thirty-seven. When I was combing, that was, up in Limehouse Reach. Six months I got." Clearly the sense of grievance still lingered. "For a couple of sacks of coal, the first time. Second time it was pomegranates—two cases. Pomegranates," he said bitterly.

I nodded, wondering who had run him in. I had left the Thames Division by then. But I remembered the toshers. They used to comb the mud-banks exposed by the ebb, living, ostensibly, on their findings; more often than not, however, the stuff was pilfered from lighters left overnight for unloading or from the wharves; the toshers were expected to surrender their prizes to H.M. Burning Ground, below Greenwich, known by the watermen as Condemned Hole, where they would receive a small cash award, but very little of value ever found its way there.

"Go on," I told Jackson. "What did he say?" I wanted to know how Davidson had taken that question.

But he had neither flown into a rage nor melted in the terrible urge to self-pity and tears which are the scourge of the ex-convict. Evidently he had stood very still for a moment and then, over his shoulder, had asked quietly: "What the hell is it you want?" In a moment then he had begun to clear the cabin, busying himself about the webs on the windows, kicking the ashes over the floor towards the stove, rubbing his fingers across the ceiling till the flaking paint-work fell like snow on his shoulders. When he stopped and looked about him, Jackson had nodded and said:

"There's a lot of things you're going to need."

"I'll manage."

"You'll need the flue for the stove." Jackson wooed him gently. "You'll need the lid for the grate yonder. There's a table. A poker." For Jackson had them all: had taken everything movable from the cabin and had stored them away in his own barge. "The barrel, for to catch the rain. A pan or two." As he told me what he had said he smiled, remembering his triumph, like a card player recalling the hand he had once laid down. "Couple of blankets. A saw for to cut timber, make yourself a fire . . ." Jackson had them all; the trap was well baited.

Davidson had sunk on to the edge of the bunk and was running his open hands to and fro across his knees.

"Nobody pays," the old man said softly. "Not if they're friends of mine."

Davidson sat still. Then he put out a hand and, with deliberation, swept the mug of tea off the bunk and out over the boards at the old man's feet. The mug clattered and lay still; the tea spread across the floor, steaming.

2

But the next morning when Davidson stepped out of the cabin into the cold white sunlight he saw a little heap of tools laid out along the beam at the head of the ladder: the chimney flue, a pan, the lid of the grate, a poker, a handsaw. And he had to have them: he couldn't live without them.

He picked up the handsaw and went into the bows. He ripped up a loose board and, setting it against the beam, began to saw it into lengths, working fast.

"Hey."

Jackson stood among the glistening reeds. For a few minutes he watched the frantic rise and fall of the shining blade. Then he called:

"Sawing up the ship?"

Davidson wrenched at the sticking saw.

"Belongs to me," Jackson said. And then: "Well, that other stuff won't burn, that's a fact." He nodded towards the rows of white tusks rising above the reeds. "Like concrete, they are." His eyes returned to the saw. "So I reckon it will be all right, for a friend."

Davidson stopped. "You have a good many friends," he said between set teeth. His head shook a little.

"A fair few." It was a lie; Jackson had none; he was very lonely indeed.

For a moment Davidson had stared at him; then he had returned to the work. When the board splintered and snapped he had torn up another in a silent frenzy; he was immensely strong, with heavy calloused hands and a belt of muscle across his shoulders that gave him almost a stoop. Listening to Jackson's story I knew what Davidson must have felt as the tide of that old man's pathetic charity came lapping relentlessly about his ankles, so that from now onwards, till the end, every step he took must cause a kind of splash in another man's life. Well, let it, let it. He had but one thing to do; nothing would stop him.

Let there be ten thousand Jacksons, and neither they nor any like them would or could keep him from it.

The wind moved, and far away across the marsh the warehouse roof awoke like a languid brazen claque and gently applauded. Jackson watched him.

CHAPTER THREE

I

I WALKED along the bank towards the café. It was here on the dull grey waters of Sea Reach that the squall had forced Davidson, that Sunday afternoon in July, to run for shelter under the lee of William Driver's barge. The old vessel lay at anchor in the roads a mile or two east of Gravesend.

Medhurst, who is dead now, was sent down from the Central panel at the request of the Chief Constable. He was put in charge of the investigation and I, as commander of the Thames Division patrol boat which, in November of that year, had come upon the blazing barge and picked up Fay Driver and Pewsey, was attached to him as pilot, assistant and general deputy. Medhurst was a kindly fellow, bluff and hearty, very much a policeman of the old school who, though sticking to an established formula, was competent enough. I always liked him, and indeed it was to Medhurst that I owed my transfer and subsequent promotion. Together we were able to prepare a fairly coherent account of the events leading up to the catastrophe: from Fay Driver's statements, Pewsey's, Mark Davidson's, and from young Philip himself. The rest, the more intimate detail, I learned from Fay.

The squall was nothing very alarming: hardly more than enough to ruffle the river's placid temper for a few minutes. Davidson had been reading; later, when the tide deposited the scarred and blistered dinghy on Yantlet Flats, we found his books in the locker in the stern—a volume of Swinburne and the *Oxford Book of Verse* and some others. When he felt the rain and saw the clouds coming up be-

24

hind him he dropped the book he was reading and, hoisting all the sail the craft had, made for home. But he was fairly caught. Passing Denton's wharf he saw the spritsail at anchor and ran up under her lee and, lowering the excited canvas, hung on to a fender till the flurry of wind should have spent itself and the rainstorm lift. When he looked up Fay Driver was watching him from the beam above his head; she had a raincoat across her shoulders. Presently she called:

"Shouldn't you come aboard?"

He was wet to the skin. "Thanks," he cried.

He tied the dinghy to the fender—it was an old motor tyre—and clambered up the shabby flank of the spritsail. It was of the type known as hay-stacks, or stackies. Fay lived in it, in some squalor, with her father, William Driver; it was often to be seen where Davidson found it that afternoon; when he was sober enough to wish himself drunk again William ferried hay or straw from landing stages on the Essex coast to the wharves of the brickworks and riverside hauliers far upstream, but while he had money he would lie up off Gravesend and spend his time ashore, looking, so he described it, for freight.

William was a feckless individual with a liquid eye and blurred features who accepted his own imperfections, and they were formidable, with immense fortitude. "When you've got a character like mine," he told the police, "you're sunk before you start. It's been the ruin of me all my life, my character has, same as Joanna"—his unhappy wife and mother of Fay—"had her gallstones. She couldn't help it, could she? No more can I." And indeed the notion lent him a certain resilience; there is little to be made of a man who admits cheerfully to any infamy, but nor on the other hand is he destructible.

I never knew Joanna; she died as she had evidently lived, under the burden of William's inertia, having watched him fritter away his business—at one time he had owned three such barges—despite her efforts to hold it together. One thing only she had kept for her own, and that was her daughter. Everything Joanna had and was she devoted to Fay; every penny she could prise from her husband's pocket she spent on the girl's education. She had better have saved her money, for it was those few years at a cheap boarding-school which lay at the heart of Fay's un-happiness and of the havoc it caused in more lives than hers alone.

For they gave her ambition. She learned to want better things than William Driver's spritsail, both for herself and, in a way it wasn't hard to understand, for her dead mother, whom she had adored and whose life she knew to have been drudged away for her daughter's sake. Fay had it on her conscience, and indeed one liked her the more for it. But strain and hard intent sat ill on her slender shoulders. One felt immediately that she had a fine lusty capacity for enjoying life and for laughing at it; given her head she would be wild, even a little reckless, but warm and friendly and generous, like her long brown limbs and sandy hair and freckled face and wide full lips. Yet she was con-strained and wary and cunning, and even when her natural irresponsibility broke out, as it sometimes must, it had a flavour of defiance and guilt. Davidson blundered into the web.

She led him into the cabin and said briskly, "You'd better take off those wet clothes, hadn't you? You're soaked. What's your name? I've seen you before, in your little boat. Here's a towel." It did not strike her that she was suggesting anything bold or immodest.

He was astonished to find such a girl in this place. His eye moved round the cabin, over the walls from which the paint had been scrubbed years ago, over the scraps of broken crockery on the shelf, the addled blankets slung between the bunks, and then back to her. She smiled gaily. "I'll look the other way," she said.

So he took off the wet clothes and she hung them to dry before the fire. She felt his embarrassment and constraint and, feeling it also on her own shoulders, attacked it. He sat uneasily on the edge of the bunk wrapped in a towel and tried to match her bright adventurousness. "I ought to introduce myself," he said; he told her his name. But it was hard to match it; there was something forced and unnatural in her manner. "Do you live here?" he asked her.

She knew he was referring obliquely to the squalor of the little cabin.

"Yes, I live here," she said. "It's fun, isn't it?"

"Yes. Yes."

Gradually the brittle self-consciousness wore away. They sat and talked, she of her mother, he of his father and of his work. At last he said: "I can't imagine what they'd say if they saw us sitting here like this . . ." He drew the towel about his shoulders.

"What's wrong with it?" she asked.

"Well, it's a bit unconventional, isn't it?"

"Oh, what do we care?"

But the next time their eyes met they both understood, and the constraint returned to his manner and the defiance to hers. She went to the clothes at the fire to turn them, and suddenly when she looked at him over her shoulder there was a challenge in her light brown eyes. She liked this man with the golden hairs along his forearms and the blue eyes and long, sensitive face. Had he moved towards her of his own volition, she might have resisted, but he didn't; and while she would have accepted her own restraint, his she would not; she would always throw off the hand that held her back.

2

In the evenings he would wait on the river bank till her father had sculled himself ashore and shuffled away in the dusk to saturate himself with liquor somewhere, and then row out to the barge where Fay would be waiting. She would wave; above her there would be the tall mast and the soft pearly twilight. But as he dipped the oars in the still water he would tell himself that this time it would not happen, he would see to it; he would remember what he had seen in her eyes the first time he had left her, and every time thereafter, and swear to himself they wouldn't make love tonight.

It was a sad little farce, that which he and Fay used to play out together in the cabin of Driver's barge, and later I, too, became familiar with the cues.

For she would always agree: tonight they would not love one another; but he must not come near her; he must keep his distance. And so for a little while they would sit and think of things to say, with but one thought in mind. But when he prepared to leave and took her gingerly in his arms to kiss her she would wind her arms about his neck and look up at him, knowing her power, unable not to use it, yet hating herself, and say: "Did you very much want to make love to me tonight, Philip?" and move her narrow hips gently against his, till he could resist her no longer. And then she would cry out: "No, Philip, please not. Philip, I'm afraid . . ."

But it was neither simple mischievousness nor witchery. She was afraid. Her protest was a policy, an insurance against the sequel. They would lie on the bunk and play upon one another as if on instruments, goading their bodies up and up the spiral of desire, till in a frenzy of possession they melted like snow in a fire and toppled from the summit and came rolling, tumbling down into the waiting abyss. When he stirred she would be watching him with something like hatred in her eyes, cast down and envenomed by the sense of guilt and desolation which, helpless to resist as it came blundering in upon herself, she had tried to burden him with also, with all of it, so that she could hold him to blame for her misery and find in his remorse a certain relief. Heavy with responsibility he would leave her and scull himself home across the starry water.

3

Mark Davidson's fleet of tugboats, I remember, showed four green rings and a red star on black funnels, and Mark had an office in Gravesend, on the Royal Terrace Pier: the Bantam Tugboat Company, Ltd.

As I recall Mark he had stiff, reddish hair which grew bolt upright from his scalp and lent him the aspect of prodigious ferocity. In his business he was indeed a hard, harsh man well-known in London River for his ruthlessness and bad temper. I think it was largely shyness, however, for those who knew him well spoke of him as gentle and kindly.

We, the police, felt very sorry for him when Philip, his son, was arrested and charged with the murder of Spenser Boyd. It broke him utterly; he died two or three months after the trial, and his business, left in the hands of a distant relative, fell to pieces and was sold up. The old man had worshipped his son, and Philip his father. Mrs. Davidson was long since dead, and so the two of them were thrown very much into each other's company; on the whole they asked no other. Mark was an entirely self-made man and was no doubt, as such men are, unnecessarily hard on his son, but Philip, who liked the work, took it in good part; he was training to take his father's place, of course, and though he looked more like a poet than a Thames tugmaster he knuckled down to the job and did it well.

Philip in those days was tall and slight and contemplative, with peculiarly bushy eyebrows which lent the unlined face something of the expression of an older man. And indeed, though he was boyish and a little dreamy, I would guess that he was a good deal more mature than Mark ever realised, for the old man persisted in regarding his son as no more than an eager youth, as if, absentmindedly, that were the last stage he remembered his son having grown up to, and Philip, to please his father and I suppose preserve the relationship they had both delighted in for so long, played the part with a will. But the deception, until he climbed aboard William Driver's barge that Sunday afternoon, was quite artless; if he sometimes gentled the tyrant with a touch of mockery, it was always with love.

4

Philip was led into his association with Spenser Boyd who, by arrangement with William Driver, began to use the barge as a pierhead in the September of that year, only because Fay would not let him lead her out of it and was clearly piqued by his efforts to do so. They quarrelled bitterly about it, more bitterly on his side, perhaps, than on hers, for I fancy she knew he was right; what she needed was not a series of sound reasons for having nothing to do with Boyd—these she could supply herself; she wanted a command, an ultimatum—something stronger than her own love of devilment; she would probably have been glad of it.

"But the fellow's a blackguard," Davidson told her. "You can see it a mile off. You mustn't have anything to do with him."

"How can I help it?" she said. "If my father has said he could use the barge——"

"Then let him, but you don't have to get mixed up in it. I'll come and fetch you, we'll go to the pictures or something . . ."

"Oh, why should I? It's rather exciting, as a matter of fact." She laughed at the anxiety on his face. "Oh, Philip, you're such a big fool. It's quite harmless really."

"Do you know what he's doing?"

"Of course."

"He's smuggling criminals out of the country—men wanted by the police."

"Well, it's fun to watch. In any case it's not as solemn as all that."

Certainly there appeared to be little solemnity in the business. Boyd's geniality was very infectious. He laughed all the time and his hanger-on, Tim Pewsey, who knew him well enough to be afraid of him, played up to his gay clowning. For Boyd had a trick of appearing to parody infamy in such a way that it all seemed rather a good joke, a harmless escapade, and his own activities about as dangerous as a schoolboy's raid on an apple orchard. At that time he was already inclining to stoutness and had a full, pallid face, curiously flat and wide, with small, black, shining eyes which, set on the surface, reminded you of those of a child's teddy-bear, of glass.

"Fay, I wish I could make you see . . ."

"All right—marry me," she said and laughed again at his discomfiture. "That'll make me see."

"I will, Fay. I've said I will."

"When?"

"I've told you: when my father——"

"Poor Philip. I do tease you, don't I. Come on, let's go and swim." And immediately she forgot the whole affair and swam, diving time and again from the beam of the barge till she was exhausted, and he with her. Everything she did she gave herself to utterly, as if to outstrip the nagging pursuit.

Boyd had been somewhat disconcerted to find Davidson and Fay on the ship. He had arranged to rent the vessel from William Driver, whom he had picked up in a pub in Gravesend, once or twice a week in the evening; nothing had been said about these two; he had understood the ship to be entirely at his disposal. The first encounter had not been pleasant; the time-table, however, had been fixed and it was already too late to cancel and rearrange the shipment of the fugitive he was handling that night. Boyd managed the situation adroitly. He knew he was safe enough with Fay, and to Davidson he said with a fat little smile and a jerk of the head towards the girl:

"The old man know?"

For he knew Mark by reputation and he knew the son by sight. Evidently he thought it wiser to involve Philip deeply, letting him see and know all, than to set him loose with a little knowledge only.

When Davidson flushed then he knew it was all right. "Righto, sonny," he said, "I won't let on. I was young once myself," and uttered a shrill bark of laughter and slapped his plump thigh and struck a self-derisive attitude, for he was only twenty-eight himself, albeit older in appearance.

Davidson took Fay's arm. "Come on, Fay, let's get out of here," he said. And that, for Boyd, was a dangerous moment. But Fay was intrigued and excited and wanted to stay to see the fun. So Davidson also remained, reluctantly and uneasily, because he felt responsible for her: one did not throw off a burden because one's shoulder ached.

"Think you'll be bored?" Boyd asked him. "Don't you worry, we'll keep you laughing. Won't we, Tim?" he said to Pewsey. And Pewsey capered about the cabin in his white sweater and rubber shoes and shadow-boxed and clicked his teeth; he was short and brown and alert, with thinning fair hair and a broken nose which nestled between his chubby cheeks like a ball of putty that a glazier had clapped down and forgotten. They were an odious pair, typical enough of the riffraff infesting the river in those days of the depression. Pewsey was weak and stupid rather than evil, but Boyd was cold and clever and dangerous.

He developed an odd liking for Davidson during those few months, though they did not meet often; whenever he knew for certain that another "deal" was to take place at a given time, Davidson would avoid the barge and take Fay with him; but it was not always possible to know, and so from time to time he was a witness of Boyd's activities. And Boyd apparently looked forward to his company and was disappointed when Davidson was not there; when Philip was present, then he would go to some lengths to please and entertain him, showing off to him, recognising in Davidson somebody a cut above the ordinary. Davidson hated him, but Fay, thrilled and excited, tended to scoff at his uneasiness. His efforts to restrain her were, as always, a challenge; she wanted to stay and participate—the idea of breaking the law appealed to her sense of adventure; yet she also wanted him to insist, to drag her away—inwardly she was frightened and guilty. But he did not insist; he tried to reason with her; and so she would hang on, assuaging her own conscience with the comforting, if spurious, notion that, should there be trouble, then it wouldn't be her fault: Philip should have insisted.

But already it was too late. Davidson should have gone to the police, and he knew it. Now, having held his tongue once for Fay's sake, he was for ever committed. If he spoke now, if he went to the police to tell them what he knew, he would have to tell them everything, even about himself and Fay, and he had no stomach for the rôle; if he spoke he must destroy the love his father had for him, and, himself sinking, drag Fay down with him. His silence counted heavily against him at his trial. Good and true men are ruthless in their judgment of one who believes he owes more to those who love him than he owes to society.

In November of that year Spenser Boyd undertook to arrange the escape of a man named Delaney.

CHAPTER FOUR

I

I KEPT a diary at that time, scribbling something in it each night after Mrs. Galloway, in whose house in Battersea I lodged, had gone to bed. The daily round seemed interesting then, and my own job with the Thames Division of considerable importance; I wanted to preserve something of its sheen, for myself and for my children when they should materialise. Whether because the work was commonplace or because I, the author, was a dull dog, is hard to say; the fact is, however, that the document stands as one of the dullest ever ground out by man. Somehow in the writing I contrived to divest my life, which was not without colour, of every vestige of interest and reality, setting down the unimportant detail with a curt, jejune toughness that is quite infuriating, and leaving out altogether all that was human and illuminating. I have read and re-read it a thousand times since then, exploring its arid wastes for the secret I felt it must hold. I kept it under lock and key latterly, lest anybody else, chancing upon the little pile of shabby exercise books, should open them and drop in a flash on the phrase, the weakness, the revelation which eluded me.

I was commanding a patrol boat in those days with the rank of sergeant, and the diary contains a good deal of entirely irrelevant data about the work. The first entry relating to Philip Davidson is dated 7th November 1932. I remember the night very well.

We were moving in the direction of Gravesend at a cruising speed, Dombey, Higgins and I. It was about eleven-thirty. There were no stars; there was a slight mist,

which was thickening, coming in from the Nore; we could
see the water we rode in only by the reflection of the street
lamps on the south bank. We came down Northfleet
Hope and somewhere off Bowater's noticed a queer glow
in the mist ahead. It seemed to flicker. I told Higgins to
give the boat all the speed available.

To see more clearly I stood up and leaned forward,
elbows on the cabin roof. It was always the best place to
stand in those boats; you had a sense of excitement and
exhilaration; the spray leapt up into your face when the
boat bumped the swell and you could hear the hum of the
engine and the water swilling about frantically in the bilge
and the deep chuckle of the exhaust when she dipped her
stern under.

We were level with the Town Pier before we realised it
was a ship on fire—a small vessel, but well alight; the
flames rose a clear hundred feet in the air. As we came
closer we saw the red heart of the thing, which was the
cargo of straw, throbbing in the mist, and when the wind
veered a fraction the flames all leaned over as if they were
about to lose their balance and fall off altogether and we
saw the mast, tall and thin and black, and the diminutive
stack projecting from the roof of the cabin in the stern. It
was a spritsail, a Medway barge. We could see the semi-
circle of odd craft gathered about her and, beyond in mid-
stream, a big Dutch schuyt on her way out; she had slowed
and was sounding her siren vigorously and the flames shone
along her long flat flank; but in a few seconds she had
vanished, into the darkness beyond the high bright flames.
Then there was nothing more than the fire and the reflection on the water. We could hear the crackle of burning
straw and the soft thunder of the flames, and presently
noticed the strange black rain of burnt vegetation which
was falling all over the river, fluttering down quietly out
of the night. The other vessels, the tugs and bawleys and
launches of one kind or another which had been passing
or had put out from Gravesend to lend a hand, were like

a half circle of boys round a bonfire with the flames playing on their faces.

Pewsey and Fay must have shoved off from the beam of the barge a few moments before we came up. We saw Pewsey, who was sculling furiously, silhouetted in the stern of the boat. But it was not till the first of the fire-floats had arrived and sent a column of glittering water arching across the sky that we saw the man on the beam of the spritsail. He staggered out of the blazing cabin and climbed up on to the rail. We saw him drop into the river.

I told Higgins to take the boat in as close as he could and we all three got down behind the housing as we felt the heat. The man was swimming, but feebly. There were clouds of steam drifting out across the water from the Medway's waterline. We had to lean out over the stern and pull him up by the hair and then by the shoulders and then by the seat of the trousers and he came in like a half-filled sack of potatoes and lay heaving on the boards.

Dombey covered him with a blanket and kept him down till we were out of range of the blistering heat . . . not that he made any effort to move, till Dombey took hold of him; then he let out a screech and, having begun, went on screaming at intervals, with a kind of detachment. He was burned, how badly we couldn't tell, and slippery with sodden black straw and blood; there was a wound of some sort on the side of his head; Dombey put a dressing on it.

Then we moved after the skiff. We did not know whether there was anybody left on the barge, but in any event there was nothing to be done by then. I remember Fay's outline and the weight of her hand as she came aboard. She was whimpering softly.

A few minutes later the mast of the barge cracked and slowly fell across the deck with a splash of angry sparks. Thereafter the vessel settled rapidly. I took a flashlight and had another look at the fellow we had fished out of the water. The girl was bending over him and I heard her saying, "Please don't die, please don't die, oh, Philip, what

have I done . . ." He seemed quite a young man, somewhere about my own age, I remember thinking, perhaps
a year or two younger, but slightly built whereas I was
thickset even then. His eyes were blue in the light of the
flash-lamp. While I was attending to the dressing on the
side of his head the barge went down with a gulp and a
resonant melancholy belch.

A day or two later, it must have been 8th or 9th November, I stood on the deck of a float with Medhurst and
one or two others and watched a Trinity House diver
go down to the wreck.

It was a grey, misty afternoon. We stamped our feet on
the boards to keep warm, watching the ferry-boats swinging out wide against the fierce ebb as they plied to and fro
between Gravesend and Tilbury, and listened to the
shipping calling mournfully down the river. Presently the
diver signalled and was hauled to the surface.

So the body, or what remained of it, was found, caught
in the twisted metal framework of the gutted cabin; it was
charred to a cinder and then had been subjected to the
erosion of the estuary tides, which are fast and strong; still,
there remained enough for recognition. Scraps of the
leather jacket which Boyd habitually wore were found
adhering to the back of the torso; the belt buckle was his;
so also the wrist-watch. Anything light and movable had
been swept away by the current, but the poker was
brought to light, with, on the handle, both Boyd's and
Davidson's oily fingerprints. The skull was stove in, but
the shape of the head was clear. Fay and Pewsey formally
identified the remains as Boyd's.

They described what had happened in the cabin up to
the moment of their flight in some detail. Neither of them
was at first able to name the man Boyd had killed; he
had been a stranger to them they said; nor did they know,
by their statements, what he was doing there; he had
quarrelled with Boyd and Boyd, losing his temper, had
killed the man with the poker; then Davidson had inter-

vened. They were lying, of course, in the hope of clearing themselves of complicity in the smuggling out of a wanted man. Delaney's body, in fact, had been carried away by the tides; we found a shoe in the cabin which was his and, a day or two later, his jacket was picked up in the estuary by a coastguard; some of the money he had taken from the bank in Swindon, where he had mortally wounded the cashier, was still in the pockets. We never found the body, but that was not surprising; the bodies of men lost in those waters are very rarely recovered. Faced with the evidence, Pewsey admitted his complicity; yes, he had known the man's name was Delaney, and he had known Delaney was pursued by the police; he identified the jacket.

2

The scene in the cabin had been ugly and violent. Delaney and Boyd richly deserved what they got. But that was no business of the jury's. Two men had been bloodily done to death; it was the jury's business to decide whether Davidson had killed Spenser Boyd or not.

By the time Delaney reached Driver's barge, from which he was to be put aboard an outgoing freighter, he had been on the run for five days and was in poor shape. Pewsey met him at the rendezvous—Denton's explosives wharf—and rowed him out to the spritsail where Boyd was waiting. Davidson also was there, with Fay; he was upset and angry with himself that he had been trapped again, but Boyd, pleased to have him there, was in high spirits.

I think it was Fay who spoke of the chill which entered the cabin with Delaney. Suddenly with his arrival it was serious, no longer a mere escapade, and Boyd's clowning was garish and unfunny. Suddenly she realised she was watching a man run for his life, and was herself involved. For Delaney was in no mood for gaiety. He was unshaven and his eyes red-rimmed; his breath rasped in his throat. He was a heavily-built man, something of Boyd's age and weight; and he was desperate. He stood in the door of the cabin and stared at the people in there. Where was the ship, he said; he wanted to know where the ship was: the one he was to go aboard. Boyd patted the man's shoulder and said it was on the way downstream; everything was all right. Delaney shook off the hand. There was the matter of payment, Boyd ventured. . . .

They watched while the man fumbled in his pockets for the money. His hands were shaking and he dropped a wad of notes.

The figure Boyd had asked was two hundred pounds. When he saw how much money this man had he put up his price; five hundred, he said, was the figure he had agreed. But Delaney would not pay. Boyd chaffed him and, reaching forward, tried to put his hand, slyly but openly, into the man's pocket. Delaney pushed him off and Boyd fell back on to the stove, which was red-hot, and let out a cry as his hand burned. When he got up he had the poker.

He hit out in a blind rage and Delaney went down. According to Pewsey the man was dead before he reached the floor, for the poker crushed his skull like an eggshell. And then a number of things happened at once. Fay screamed and Pewsey shouted: "Christ, now look what you've done!" and Davidson tried to intervene, for it was plain that Boyd intended to hit the man again, for he was astride the body raising the poker above his shoulder. Davidson grasped the poker and shouted.

Almost at once it became less a matter of wresting the weapon from Boyd's grip than of holding on to it so that it should not be used against himself. His face was an inch or two from Boyd's, which was as white as the belly of a fish, and the poker waved like a flail above their heads. Then it struck the lamp and down it came and a flaming river of paraffin ran across the floor and under the cabin door. Pewsey was shouting and trying to stamp out the flames, stumbling over Delaney; he opened the door and the cabin was lit with a bright yellow light, for the deck-load of straw had taken fire; there was a wall of roaring flame across the deck. Pewsey ran and Fay followed him, believing, she said later, that Davidson and Boyd would see their grave danger and desist. But both she and Pewsey, as they paused in the doorway, saw that Davidson had got possession of the poker; he had raised it above his head.

They waited in the skiff under the lee of the barge. Pewsey was on his feet in the boat, shouting frantically; he waited, he said, three or four minutes, till his clothes and Fay's were singeing in the heat. But there was no answer from the cabin.

3

The case against Davidson was quite straightforward. It was passed to the Director of Public Prosecutions, in whose office there was at that time a clever and ambitious young barrister named Oswald Flood. It was partly as a result of his handling of the Davidson case, though he did not appear in court, that he was offered employment in the headquarters of the Metropolitan Police. He accepted, and was soon making a name for himself in Scotland Yard. He rose high; at the time of Davidson's release he was one of the five Assistant Commissioners, with his own depart-ment; I, by another and more devious route, plodded up the ladder, drifted into administration, and was appointed his Deputy. I knew it was as far as I would ever get. Flood's ambition, however, was as limitless now as it had been then; he had prepared the case for the Crown with the cool, bland competence which later was always associated with his name.

Against that weight of evidence Davidson's own account of what had taken place in the cabin between Fay's and Pewsey's flight and his own plunge into the river was hopelessly, fatally inadequate. He did get possession of the poker, he said, and if he raised it, as Fay and Pewsey claimed he did, then he did so only to keep Boyd at bay. His story was that Boyd lunged at him with his foot and, doubling up as the blow took him in the abdomen, he felt the poker wrested from his hand. He raised his arm to ward off the blow and was struck on the side of the head; he lost consciousness. Certainly there had been a wound in his head; Dombey had dressed it. But there was nothing else to confirm the story. He said he knew nothing more till he felt his clothes alight. The cabin was full of smoke. He stumbled out and dropped over the side of the ship into the water. And that was all.

His own involvement with the activities of Boyd and Pewsey over a period of months counted heavily against him; that neither he nor Fay had actually assisted made little difference in his favour. To all intents and purposes he had been one of them.

It was not irrelevant, either, that there was a good deal of anxiety in the public mind at that time about the resurgence of crimes of violence, arising out of the depression. There were millions of men without work. Suppose they all took to settling their grievances with pokers? The police, too, were anxious; the Royal Commission of 1928 was still fresh in the public mind and though it had allayed a good deal of uneasiness, the competence of the force was always liable to be called into question again.

As it happened it was all plain sailing. The jury needed only forty minutes to reach a unanimous verdict. I was in the court when the judge passed sentence—it was later commuted to twenty years' penal servitude on the grounds that a degree of self-defence was allowable—but when the words were spoken it was Fay I looked at, not Davidson. She was sitting white and rigid.

The doubt came very slowly, with the years, out of the chafing of one person against another.

4

Three months after Davidson's conviction I asked Fay to marry me. "No," she said. She recoiled and shook her head violently. "No. . . ."

I was very persistent, however. To put the worst possible construction on it—the right one, I fear—I felt I was doing something rather laudable; certainly I was very sorry for her. But then when she refused, then suddenly I wanted her. Then I was in love.

I had found her in a wretched condition. Soon after the trial she left her father and got work in a glove shop, and found lodgings in a Paddington mews. I had been attracted to her, as were most men, from the first, and I hadn't lost sight of her. So I began to take her about, mostly from pity, I suppose, at first. She seemed to have taken the whole weight of the disaster on to her own back, and she was floundering under it badly, mute, numbed and lonely. She seemed afraid of me—of everybody indeed, and yet curiously resigned; she would have preferred, if anything, to be left alone. But I forced myself on her, taking her to the cinema, the theatre and, when I could afford it, to bright and cheerful restaurants. And slowly, with the passing months, she found again her gaiety and love of life. One evening—we had been to a variety theatre of some kind, I remember—she slipped her arm through mine as we came out into the cold night air, and gave it a little squeeze; it was the first truly warm and impulsive thing she had done and I had the feeling, which was as heady as wine, of being both wanted and owned; I looked into her bright laughing face and was immensely touched.

It took a long time to discover the reason for her refusal.

Finally she told me lightly, but I knew she meant it: because she was bad, she was bad. I remember laughing with relief, for I had thought the fault lay with me. I dealt with the argument as best I knew. But there were others. One by one I coped with her objections, till at last it came to her worry about me—about what my superiors would say: I was a police officer and I shouldn't marry a girl who had been involved in a case of the nature of Davidson's.

To tell the truth, I was rather apprehensive about that aspect of it myself. The police, if they knew, would certainly frown on the idea, at least to the extent of its interference with promotion. "Very well," I told Fay; "we'll marry in secret—tell nobody." She wanted to know how long I thought we could keep such a secret. "As long as we want," I answered extravagantly.

So I over-rode her refusal. I persisted, and at last she consented. It was as if she were relieved: I had taken the weight on to my own shoulders: well, she seemed to say, I have warned you; now it has nothing more to do with me. And I recall her saying, on one occasion: "I wish my mother was here. She'd be very pleased with you," and she hugged my arm. I was very happy. If, in the bleak silence of my room, I felt a faint uneasiness, I ignored it; the bond was made; I was full of the splendour of pity and love and pride.

The secret, at any rate of her maiden name and her connection with Philip Davidson, was well kept. I grew into the habit of avoiding any mention of her to my associates; they knew I was married, of course, and one or two of them met her at minor functions of one kind and another; but my superior officers, those to whom it might have been of importance, knew nothing; why should they? Still, it never really sank out of mind and as Mick, our son, grew up, it was even accentuated. It had no name and no shape: it was a doubt. It grew, I think, simply out of Fay's reluctance ever to speak of or in any way refer to Philip Davidson or the fire or the conviction; she would stiffen a little and turn away; after a time I found myself doing the same thing. Yet, despite the fact that we never spoke of him—or perhaps because of it— his shadow grew. We skirted it; we walked round it, like an area of forbidden territory.

CHAPTER FIVE

I

IT was Oswald Flood, the Assistant Commissioner, who told me of Davidson's release: as pretty an irony, in the circumstances, as one could wish, for it could mean only one thing. He suggested, that morning, that we should walk back from Blackfriars, where we had attended a conference, leaving Peabody and Harris to return in the car. I caught the flicker of speculation on Peabody's face, and indeed the invitation surprised me too, for Flood was not wont to seek the company of his juniors without good reason.

When the car had left and we had set off, he said without preamble:

"By the way, Philip Davidson came out last week."

For a moment I could not utter a word.

"You remember Davidson?"

"Of course." I kept my gaze on the vacant glass eye set in the scarlet rump of the tram which went rocking past us beyond the trees.

"Didn't you know?"

"No." I heard the grinding brakes and the peevish stutter of the bell.

"Well, anyway, he's out."

The sun shone brightly. Four or five dusty seagulls were quarrelling over a crust of mildewed bread on the parapet. Beyond, the river flashed and the gaunt warehouses on the south bank frowned in their own shadow.

Flood, tall and shambling and angular, loped along on his curious rigid legs, eyes on the ground, hat tilted back, like a country cleric considering a fresh phase of his attack on an incestuous parish, or next Sunday's text. Presently he must surely begin: "Let us now turn to . . ." in his suffocated tenor voice. No, no; I was too well acquainted with that desperate benevolence of manner; it meant really very little, except perhaps that he knew he was, if successful, disliked and friendless. I had watched him grow old; I knew him as well, I suppose, as anybody knew him. But he was always a stranger—a clever and ambitious man; a man with a deadly, knowing brain, but a brain whose approach was oblique, so that you were aware of its direction only at the point of contact with your own. The rest was guesswork.

My head was swimming. It was not the news of Davidson's release which mattered; that much, assuming the man's survival, I had always known must happen sooner or later. But I certainly had not expected to hear of it from my own A.C.; anybody but Flood. The release of a prisoner was far below his level of interest, and indeed outside his department. He was saying: "As an old waterman yourself, no doubt you'll remember the business."

"Fairly well."

"Something to do with a fire in a barge, hadn't it?"

"That's right."

"Yes. Hit a man over the head with a poker, didn't he?"

"Yes."

"Wasn't it you who picked him up?"

"It was." The case had passed through his hands: did he really think I had forgotten that? He knew all about it. I glanced at his bald, bleak face; it was impassive.

And then he said: "Wasn't there a woman mixed up in it?"

So I was sure: he knew, he knew. "Yes," I said.

"What was her name? Fay something, as I remember."

"Fay Driver."

"Ah, yes. Driver." It dawned on me that he must always have known, for years and years. All the time I had thought it a secret he had known. It was like an explosion, a sudden dazzling flash in one's eyes.

"What became of her?"

Calamity brings with it a certain exhilaration. When the world rocks you rush in dismay to shore it up, but when it topples you stand in the ruins and giggle; the dust is a paralysing drug.

"I married her," I said. "I thought you knew."

A faint frown passed over his face; he had expected evasion, I suppose. "So you did," he said, "so you did." He cleared his throat. "Is there any record of it?"

"Not now," I told him blithely; this was madness. "I burned it."

It was idiotic, a kind of truth game, a brandishing of one's own ignominy, as if that way there lay sanity, or expiation; the Assistant Commissioner had been burrowing in my record of service and of my wife he had found no trace because I had burned it. "In 1938," I told him. "I sent Atkins out on a bogus errand of some description while I ran through the file and took out everything relating to my wife."

He looked a little baffled. "Their absence was very conspicuous, Lowther," he said.

"Was it?" The conversation had acquired a wavering, insubstantial quality for me; it was like a dream at dawn, which presently would end.

"I confess I don't see what you expected to gain by it, Lowther. What was your object?"

"Well, I don't suppose the powers would have liked the idea much, even though I was small fry. So I kept it dark. And when Medhurst went I dug out a few tell-tale papers and burned them." Now I had begun to lie; it was not Medhurst's retirement which had prompted the action; I burned the papers when I came back from Holland that year, after I had talked to the skipper of the schuyt.

Flood stared across the river. "You amaze me," he said in his cold tenor voice. "After all these years." He shook his head slightly. "So much trouble for so little reason. What was there to hide? She was acquitted, wasn't she?"

"Oh, yes."

"Wasn't there any other reason?"

"No. Should there have been?"

"My dear Lowther, a man doesn't go to those extremes without good cause."

"It seemed enough to me."

"Simply because she had been mixed up in the Davidson affair. . . ."

"Yes."

He said again: "Well, you amaze me." He cleared his throat with a long sustained yarr and we walked on in silence for a moment. "Tell me," he began at length; "why did you wait till Medhurst left?"

I said: "I have an idea Medhurst knew. There was no point in destroying the papers while he was there."

"Then why did you tell me?" he enquired gently.

"About my wife?"

"Yes. Just now."

I said, "You already knew. As soon as you mentioned Davidson I knew you must know about it." I was glad to have said that; perhaps now he would come into the open.

"Oh, I don't see that it follows, Lowther." He was rather pained. "Davidson's release would naturally be of interest to you. As an old waterman . . ."

"So you said."

"It's of no importance to me, I do assure you. If you considered your marriage a mistake and wished to conceal it——"

"I have never considered it a mistake." I felt myself growing red.

He said quickly: "Of course not. I'm not prying into your private life, Lowther. If you will drag it into your business life, however . . ."

"On the contrary," I said. "I have done my best to keep it out of my business life."

We went on towards Westminster. I still did not understand his purpose. Why had he told me of Davidson's release? Flood was never casual, notwithstanding his efforts to appear unconcerned. Was it simply that he wished to tell me he knew my wife's identity? He said nothing more till we crossed the road. Then he asked:

"What do you think of doing about Davidson?" When I looked at him in surprise he moved his bony shoulders and explained: "I'm thinking of the Press. Old lags sometimes get a paragraph or two when they finish a long spell. It seems a pity, in view of all the trouble you've gone to. . . ."

"You think they might make a song about it."

"It's possible."

"I doubt if they'll go to the extent of digging out the original witnesses."

Flood said: "Unless of course he gets himself into serious trouble again. Then they might."

"What sort of trouble? Why should he?"

"Oh, one never knows. A sense of grievance. . . . I was thinking it might be worth your while to have him watched for a week or two, till he settles down."

"What for?" I asked flatly.

"Just to head him away from mischief. He was a difficult prisoner, you know."

"The fellow's free."

"Oh, quite. One couldn't actively interfere, of course. Still, in certain circumstances. . . . Did you see the governor's report?"

"No." I hadn't known there was one.

"I think perhaps you'd better. I'll send it along to you this afternoon."

We turned in under the arch. He eased his long red neck from the collar of his coat. "The sun's quite warm for November," he said, "isn't it?" He raised his bald, shuttered face. "Quite warm."

CHAPTER SIX

I

ONLY Maureen, the Irish maid, was in when I reached Chiswick and home. Her footsteps came pattering along the passage from the kitchen as soon as I let myself in. Mrs. Lowther was out, she said, gone out to tea and not yet home, and Mick himself was out, too, gone to the cinema. So I had an early dinner and took the governor's report upstairs to the study—a spare room we hadn't known what to do with, so I had taken it and put in a desk and a carpet and an old armchair and a few photographs of Mick at school.

The report was quite brief, consisting of four foolscap sheets only. It outlined Davidson's turbulent career in prison, his attempts to escape and his attack on the warder which had docked three years off his remission of time for good behaviour. It suggested he should be watched; the reasons were set out in a concluding paragraph.

I remember getting myself a drink when I had read it, and then two or three more in quick succession. I went over to the window and stared down into the quiet lamplit street. When I looked into the mirror over the mantel the face I saw was that of a stranger, grey and drawn, and the pupils of the eyes were oddly distended. I thought: it must be the gin. Presently I sat down and began to read the report again.

Somewhere in the silent house a door slammed, and then I heard Mick moving lightly from room to room. Now he was tinkering on the piano directly beneath the study and the distant tintinnabulation came up old and sweet through the floor. Then he was on the stairs and

I was trying to look pleasant and natural as the fair round head was thrust into the room.

"Hallo," he said, "who're you hiding from?" The grin left his face as he looked at me. "Something up, Dad?"

"No no. Good film?"

"Oh, pretty awful."

"What was it about?"

"'Bout a policeman." He grinned.

"You don't say? How did your essay go down today?"

"Oh, fine."

"How many did you get?"

"Three."

"Out of how many?"

"Ten." He grinned suddenly.

"Doesn't sound very many."

"Well, old Croxton only got four."

"It's about time you beat Croxton at something, Mick."

"Oh, he's just a swot."

I remember looking at him and thinking absently: I wonder if he's all right . . . Am I so close to him that I cannot see? I tried to recall the problems I had had at his age. He was sixteen. Sixteen . . . oh God, yes. . . .

"Everything's all right with you, Mick, isn't it?"

He looked at me, puzzled. "Yes. Fine." I thought he flushed slightly. "Fine."

"You must tell me if it isn't, any time . . ."

"Yes."

"Done your homework?"

"Just going to."

So we made our curt, embarrassed conversation, fumbling for the articulacy we were both afraid to find, Mick lest he should see what I thought of him, I lest I should show it: a kind of anguish.

He went out and I turned back to the report. I wondered if Mick was going to be involved. No; whatever sort of a wilderness the rest of us had made of our lives, nothing of it would touch Mick. Whatever we did, I thought, he would be all right. But I knew it was a lie even then.

2

The report was an astonishing jumble of perspicacity, soldierly obtuseness, psychological jargon (plainly borrowed) and bald fact, as if the author, uneasy in deep water, had made haste now and then to reassure himself of his foothold on firm, dry, familiar land.

Philip Davidson, the governor said, still clung to his belief in his own innocence. He was apparently convinced that two people had testified falsely against him, and was bent on their destruction. Exactly what the governor intended to convey by his choice of words it was hard to know. Later he spoke of Davidson's determination to make those people suffer as he had suffered, and since Davidson considered himself, no doubt with good reason, a broken and useless husk, it was quite on the cards that he meant: to kill.

The notion was certainly dramatic; it was even fantastic; but it could not be ignored altogether. Nobody knows exactly what happens to a man's brain in seventeen years of penal servitude. In this instance, the governor said, the fellow's obsession had gone some way beyond an assumed purpose; he had dedicated himself to that single, simple conception, and indeed had held himself together by it for so long now that without it he would lose his reason completely. The governor thought it worth adding, in parenthesis, that he had known other men who had suffered from similar fixations, but none who had so utterly identified himself with his idea.

And then he, the governor, said something which brought to my mind the suspicion that the report was in fact the work of two men, and that somebody else—no doubt an adventurous and over-speculative young prison psychiatrist—had supplied the data and the governor was merely re-phrasing it. He said: as other men go inevitably towards death, so Davidson was moving towards the destruction of a man named Pewsey and a woman named Fay Driver. That, I thought, flatulent though it was, didn't come from the governor.

He, whoever it was, went on to explain that this yearning of Davidson's was as integral as another man's need for food, and that there would be no peace for him— he expected and even wanted to find his own death at the same time—till it was satisfied. It was particularly important to note that Davidson was not interested in vindication: he believed it far too late; the establishment of his own innocence, supposing such a thing to be possible, would never and could never give him back what he had lost; innocent or guilty, he was finished; life had no more to offer him. This, the governor added, clearly taking the reins again, rendered Davidson only the more dangerous; he, the governor, had done his best to knock a little sense into him, but the fellow persisted with his folly. He should be closely watched.

Such was the gist of the report. The glimpses it afforded of the character of its author were mildly piquant; the rest was a bombshell, but not to the extent it might have been; the shapeless, anonymous doubt I had always had was by this much confirmed. It came a little closer. It came into the room and stood at my side; its presence was grimly familiar.

3

I lay in bed and watched Fay's face in the mirror beneath her raised arm. She stood at the dressing-table and brushed her hair, throwing back her head under the caress of the brush, looking at herself beneath lowered lids. It took me a long time to get the words out, for I knew what they would mean to her; but at last it was said.

She stopped. Her whole body stiffened. There was a moment of frozen silence. I saw her eyes on me in the glass, wide, touched with panic and then, as her throat moved and she swallowed, with resentment, as if I had used a forbidden weapon without warning.

"Released?"

"Yes."

"When?"

"Last week."

She pulled herself together. The curtains closed again and the brush began to move. "Well!" she murmured; "would you believe it?" She leaned forward to examine her chin; her hand trembled but her voice was recovering its strength. "It seems only yesterday he went in. How long is it?"

"Seventeen years."

"Gracious, is it really?" Rhythmically she stroked her hair with the brush.

She was thirty-eight then. Lines were beginning to appear at the corners of her eyes and sometimes her lips were too tightly compressed, but she was still a beautiful woman, with wide shoulders and big bosom and humorous brown eyes; people liked her immediately; her voice was pleasantly husky, rarely strident, and though she would openly joke to her friends that she was nothing but a bargee's daughter, it was patently absurd and I doubt if they believed her; she had the natural poise of a handsome, happy woman; all the tortuous, tedious complexes of youth had gone. Her debt to her mother was, in a sense, paid; she loved her home and her son; she never spoke of her gratitude, but it was there.

The relationship we showed our friends, however, was not quite the one we had reached in our own home. For the first few years we had been very happy; it had seemed more tactful and sympathetic not to mention Davidson's name to her at all, in that time. But then, when I tried to make her speak of it, she refused, and her refusal irked, for

I felt it unnecessary. And presently it met and joined my old uneasiness about Davidson, still so vague that I had no name for it, and the two became one, taking a dim shape: a doubt that would not be dispelled. I remember feeling angry that she would not deal with it, for it worried me; so the anger grew into suspicion. And then, after my trip to Rotterdam that year, I too began to avoid any mention of Davidson and the past, lest she should see in my eyes or hear in my voice what I dreaded to think, or, worse still, lest in some way she should confirm it.

We could not forget it. It was always there, with us, just below the wary surface. Sometimes I would see her harden as perhaps the conversation took an unexpected turn in that direction, and withdraw into herself defensively as if in some way I was threatening to take away all that she believed I had given her. It became rather a farce, for there are few secrets you can keep from the person you have lived with for seventeen years; you learn to exchange your thoughts almost without speaking, and despite your will. I think we both understood very well. Yet we clung doggedly to our ridiculous defences.

And now I had shattered them we seemed to take up the battle as if there had been no change, as indeed there was not, and clashed with words instead of silence.

"I'm glad he's out," she said. In a way it must have been a relief to her. "What's he doing?"

"I couldn't say. I suppose he'll go back to the river."

"Has he any money?"

"I shouldn't think so. There's a report from the governor of the prison."

"Is there?" She wrinkled her nose and sniffed. "Bobby," she said, "have you been drinking?"

"I had a drink."

"I thought I smelled gin." I caught the vigilant eyes on me in the mirror. "What does it say?"

"It says . . ." I heard my own voice a little way away, carefully indifferent. "It says Davidson is likely to attempt the destruction of the witnesses who gave evidence against him."

"What does he mean by 'destruction'?" she asked at last.

"I suppose he means kill." The word was grotesque in this soft, pink bedroom. "Do away with."

"Oh, my," she said. She scrutinised her eyebrows in the glass. "At midnight?" she said satirically.

"It looks rather as though he means it."

She smiled. "It doesn't sound like Philip," she said, "does it?"

"No doubt he's changed."

"How does the governor know, anyway?"

"Governors get to know something about their prisoners sooner or later," I told her. "They get it from the doctors and warders and padres. Spies, sometimes."

"Well, I suppose it's to be expected," she said. Her voice was calm now, and casual. "Don't they all swear to get even with the witnesses and judges and jury and everybody?"

"Not usually," I said, "after so long. They start that way. But they don't often keep it up."

"Why not?"

"They forget. They go to pieces. There's very little left of a man after seventeen years of that, you know."

She put down the brush and opened a small white pot and began to apply the cream to her face. "But enough left of Philip," she said.

"Just enough, apparently."

"Good for him. And I'm one of them."

"Yes."

"Poor old chap, Somebody ought to talk to him. Is he all right in the head?"

"Hard to say, at this stage."

"Does it mention me by name—the report?"

"Fay Driver."

"Well, that's something," she said. "For you, I mean, isn't it?"

"I don't think it makes all that difference."

"I was thinking of the people at the office. It's a good thing the report didn't call me Mrs. Lowther, that's all." I saw her eyes flick at me in the mirror. "You've kept me under cover long enough."

"Oh, yes," I said: "that." I wondered whether to tell her that at least Flood knew—that it had all been so much wasted subterfuge.

"Promotion," she said; "that's what I . . ."

"Yes," I agreed. Promotion; that had always been an excellent reason; for Fay, too; she took a jealous pride in my ponderous advancement. "However," I said, "if Davidson means to make trouble, one name's as good as another."

She said: "Well, you'll look after us, won't you, Bobby?"

I watched her apply the cream to the corners of her eyes. "You're not at all afraid, are you, Fay?"

"Afraid?" She looked at me now, over her shoulder. "With you and the whole of the Metropolitan Police to protect me? Afraid of poor Philip?"

"I meant, of me, Fay—afraid of me."

"Oh, you." She laughed softly in her throat. I was beginning then to hate this simulated venomousness of hers; it was so unlike the woman beneath; I wished she would stop it. "Why, what are you thinking of doing?"

I said: "I'm a police officer, Fay."

She asked lightly: "Bobby, what is it you are hinting at?"

"The possibility of Davidson's innocence."

"Who says he's innocent?"

"Nobody."

She set down the pot of cream with a slight click on the dressing-table. "I can't see how it affects me," she murmured. She began to pin up her hair. "Unless you intend to let him run about shooting all the witnesses. . . ."

"No, he won't be allowed to do that."

"He might go and hit Mickie or somebody."

Yes. I had not forgotten. I knew exactly what she meant.

"You know, the trouble with you, Bobby," she said, patting her hair, "is that you're such a *responsible* old thing. You really give yourself a hell of a life with it."

"Do I?"

"Well, don't you? Yet you know perfectly well that when it comes to the point . . ." She turned, smiling. The strips of metal gleamed frostily in her hair; she looked oddly boyish with it pinned close to her head like that. She sat on the edge of her bed and kicked off her slippers.

Then she was asking: "What did you say Philip had a bee in his bonnet about?"

"He seems to think some of the evidence was phoney."

"Oh dear, oh dear. . . ." She got into bed and pulled up the eiderdown. "Is that in the report?"

"Yes."

"But really," she began warmly, "the judge and jury and police and even his own barrister . . ."

"Yes, Fay."

"He's crazy. He's dangerous. Is he being watched?"

"He will be."

She settled down between the sheets. Then at last she said with a light indifference: "Who's looking after it? You?"

"Yes."

I saw her smile faintly, satisfied. Her smile at that moment was, as I look back, almost decisive. Up to then I had been feeling sorry for her, sorry that she should have to assume this mask, the false nose and moustache of villainy, frightened by her own helplessness and inward uncertainty into this outward show of callousness. I understood exactly what she was trying to do, and what moved her; it was her passion for her home and for Mick and all that went with them; she was using every weapon she could lay her hands to.

But that confident smile was hard to stomach. Suddenly it grated. She felt safe because the matter was in my hands; I would see to it that Davidson made no trouble, because she, Fay, was my wife, because if Fay were in some way betrayed, my son would pay, because I was afraid for myself and my career.

I heard her say: "Ready?"

She switched out the light and I heard her draw the sheets about her neck. Then it was quiet. The lamp in the street below the window threw a pencil of yellow light through the gap in the curtains across the ceiling. A long time later she murmured:

"What are you thinking about, Bobby?"

"Oh—Davidson."

"What about him?"

"He may be innocent."

"Really, darling, if you think it's possible why didn't you do something about it long ago?"

"I did," I said. "Once."

4

We went, that year, to Scheveningen, near the Hague, for our summer holidays, Fay, Mick and I. It was hot and sunny and we sat all day on the beach in hooded basket-chairs which looked like up-ended cradles, and I taught Mick to swim.

It was while we were there that the idea of a trip to Rotterdam, which had been in my mind a long time, hardened into a resolve. I told Fay I had a job to do—a contact to make with the Hollandsche Politie, and had to go to Rotterdam for a day or two. Afterwards I regretted it, for the weather was lovely and I thought of long train journeys without enthusiasm; however, it was too late to withdraw the lie then, and so one morning I set off, reaching Rotterdam in the early afternoon. I went straight to the offices of the port authorities and asked them help me to trace a man called Schrey—Captain Schrey, skipper of a schuyt running between Rotterdam and the Port of London. I told them who I was, but explained that my trip was entirely informal; Captain Schrey was an old friend.

He was in fact the master of the vessel that Dombey, Higgins and I had seen on her way downstream the night we picked up Davidson. I had reported the ship's proximity to Medhurst and Schrey had been contacted and questioned by the Dutch police, who were very helpful. However, it had been little more than a formality. Schrey's answer, as was to be expected, had been that he had seen nobody get away from the burning spritsail. There had been no reason to doubt him, and there the matter had rested. But during the years of nameless unease, while I turned the story over and over in my mind, chewing it this way and that way, there was always this small core of hardness, a grittiness which would not be swallowed. Its name was Schrey.

I was lucky that afternoon. The port authorities knew him by name, and they knew his ship. Moreover she was in now. They gave the name of the dock and I took a taxi and went straight there. I found the schuyt among several others of the same type, in a small quiet dock off the river. There was a gangway running up to the beam. I stood looking at it for some time, wondering what the devil I was going to say to the man. He would probably throw me off the ship.

However, Schrey, when I found him, was courtesy itself. He was a big, stout fellow of middle age, rather pink and glossy, with the comical, mobile face of a clown. He spoke a little English. I contrived to avoid mentioning my name, and he took me up to his cabin, offered me a shot of schnapps and then, over the table, asked what he could do for the "yunk man", as he called me. I drew a breath.

"Captain Schrey," I said, "do you happen to recall a

certain night a few years ago, when you were taking your
ship down the Thames . . . There was a barge on fire, a
mile or two east of Gravesend. . . ." I was watching him
closely. It was very interesting. Without moving a muscle
of his face, without the flicker of an eyelid, he gave me the
impression I had brought up a subject on which he was
sensitive. I went on: "A friend of mine was lost in the fire.
We never found him. . . ."

"Ah. And the yunk man is looking for him."

"Yes."

"But why should you come to me?" he said.

"Well, I've always thought there was a chance he could
have got aboard your ship. . . ."

He shook his head sadly. "The fire I remember," he
said. "But your friend . . ."

"His name was Delaney."

He smiled sympathetically and raised his plump hands
an inch or two from the table. "Nobody could board my
ship without my knowledge, yunk man. I am sorry."
He refilled my glass. "The police, too. They had the same
idea. They come and talk to me."

"Oh, well. There it is."

He leaned towards me a fraction and said: "Forgive,
I did not hear the name. . . ."

I said: "My name is Boyd."

"Ah. Mister Boyd." He looked me straight in the face
and smiled. His eyes were full of humour.

So I left as I had arrived: with nothing but a suspicion
and a scatter-brained theory. Schrey asked me how I had
discovered his name; I told him, the press. He smiled all
the time. Schrey was a companion of my mind for several
years. I believed him to be a liar, but there was nothing
to be done.

5

I listened to the chimes of the clock in the living-room beneath. After a while I must have dozed off, for when I heard the clock again it was half-past three. I lay on my back neither awake nor asleep.

I said softly: "Are you awake, Fay?"

She stirred. "Mm?"

"Fay . . ."

"Yes?"

Then I was asking her: "Was it Boyd, Fay?"

"Was what Boyd, dear?"

"The body you identified—you and Pewsey."

She lay silent for a moment. Then I heard her begin to laugh.

"Well?"

She said: "You've been wanting to ask me that question for years, haven't you? Go to sleep. . . ."

Before the clock struck again I knew what I had to do; it was quite clear.

CHAPTER SEVEN

I

AS SOON as I arrived in the office I called Harris up
and asked him if he could lend me a youngster for a
few days for a job of my own. He sent Detective-con-
stable Bletchley.

Bletchley was one of the young men who, having
pounded a beat for a year or two, had applied for posting
to the C.I.D. and, having appeared before a Selection
Board, had been put into plain clothes as what we called
an "aid"—a very junior probationer. Bletchley had been
to one of the minor public schools and, I rather think,
believed himself a cut above the average. Certainly he
was fluent enough; I dare say it was because I had been
brought up, or hauled up, in the old tradition that I found
his manner irritatingly familiar. However, he seemed to be
about right: I thought he would make the right kind of
hash of the job I had for him. For that was what I meant
him to do. He was too junior to be held greatly to blame
for what would follow.

I told him something about Davidson. "Have a look at
the files. He got twenty years for murder in 1932. He came
out last week."

"Probation, I suppose?"

"Yes. Get the reports from the stations and find out
where he is. Then I want you to go and have a look at the
place."

"What exactly is it you want to know, sir?"

Was there something faintly disparaging in the question?
I didn't really care. "We'll get around to that in a moment,
Bletchley. First, I want to know where he is and what sort

63

of a place it is, who his neighbours are, what he's living on and so on and so forth."

He nodded, smiling. I could all but hear him thinking: dear old Lowther, ironically: nothing will make old Lowther jib: dear old friendly old dull-as-ditch-water Uncle Lowther.

I said: "Get all you can on him."

He nodded perfunctorily.

"Don't go and ask him yourself, of course. Don't talk to anybody if you can help it. I don't suppose there will be any newspaper men hanging about, but if there are—well, no doubt you've been taught what to say: nothing."

He nodded and smiled. "What's Davidson been up to, sir?"

"Nothing yet. Nothing more than threats, anyway. There may be nothing in it. Just a matter of checking up."

He asked: "Who's he been threatening?"

"The witnesses who gave evidence against him at his trial, or some of them. It's an old story, but it won't do any harm to keep an eye on him. If he means mischief we'll put a spoke in his wheel." The boy was watching my face. I could see that he was puzzled: this was hardly my job. "You can start as soon as you like," I told him.

"Suppose he does mean to cause trouble, sir?"

"Then it will be up to you to stop him, Bletchley."

His face straightened. "Oh. Quite a job."

"Quite a job. Too big for you, Bletchley?"

"Oh no, sir, I'd love to have a crack at it." He asked rather wistfully: "I suppose there are no more details?"

I felt sorry for him suddenly, so I told him a little more, but not very much: he would have to make his own blunders. With his fresh face and fair hair he reminded me somewhat of my son. Everything I looked at that morning reminded me of Mick. But I went on with it.

Bletchley was going to try to stop Davidson. He was hopelessly inadequate for the job; he would fail. And out of Bletchley's failure would come the enquiry which sooner or later must bring the whole wretched edifice tumbling about our ears. There would be ruin. . . . Fay's and my own and my son's, Pewsey's, perhaps even Flood's, though Flood I was not yet certain of. Mick would understand one day. I was sure that he would see it. It was a matter of principle. I said it aloud in my office: It's a question of principle. I wished only that it sounded a little less damned sanctimonious.

2

The slow mid-morning hours dragged past; I waited for Flood's summons. It was a relief when, a few moments before midday, the secretary put a head round the door and told me the Assistant Commissioner wished to see me.

"Right. Thank you."

I put the governor's report under my arm and walked along the gloomy corridor to Flood's office. I tapped on the door and entered and he looked up.

"Good morning, Lowther. You weren't busy, I hope?"

"No no." I dropped the report on his desk. "There's the report on Davidson," I said, and sat down.

"Ah yes, I wanted to talk to you about that. Have you read it?" He raised his colourless eyes.

"Yes, I've read it."

"You're not looking too well, Lowther. . . ."

"No? A little tired."

He nodded. "Well, and what do you make of it?"

"It seems pretty clear."

"Oh yes." He smiled faintly. "It's clear enough. That isn't quite what I meant."

So now we begin, I thought wearily. Now everything must be oblique. Now we must sidle to and fro like a couple of hostile crabs, looking for the weak spot, feeling, sensing, till at last we have one another's measure.

"Well, let's look at it." He leaned back in his chair. "First, Davidson will have to be watched, that goes without saying."

3

I nodded. "I've put a man on to him."

"Who?"

"Bletchley."

"Who's he?"

"One of Harris's new boys. Seems quite a good lad."

Flood frowned. "Sufficiently experienced, do you think?"

"Oh yes, I think so, for a job of this kind. There's nothing frightfully difficult about it."

"Well, you know, we mustn't take risks, Lowther. We ought to be sure."

"Risks?"

He cleared his throat and moved an inch or two further forward in his chair. He began: "I don't take this very seriously, I must admit. . . ." He tapped the report under his hand. "Nevertheless, if we are to act on it, and I don't see how we can ignore it . . . if we are, then I think we'd better have it done well. And I'm not at all sure that an inexperienced boy . . ."

"Had you somebody particular in mind, then?" I asked him.

"Well . . ."

Suddenly I realised what was coming. I had a moment of panic. "Oh, I'll keep an eye on him," I said quickly.

"Yes, but Bletchley . . ." He frowned and nibbled the tip of his finger. "I don't like it, Lowther."

"There are others," I pointed out.

"Yes. It occurred to me . . ." Clearly he disliked intensely to have to be so direct. "It occurred to me that the man best qualified for the job——"

I said abruptly: "I'm very busy, sir. I'm up to the neck."

He smiled, evidently relieved. "We have been thinking along the same lines, I see."

"Sir, I'm extremely busy. There's the report on the Dalston Junction rowdies, we're reorganising postings department . . ."

"Of course, of course. That presents no great difficulty,

Lowther. I would see that you are relieved of some of your work for a week or two."

"But really, it's junior routine stuff."

"Oh, do you think so?" He raised his eyebrows and rubbed his small hooked nose. "I'm surprised. Checking up on an old lag in the ordinary way, yes, I agree, anybody can do it. But wouldn't you rate Davidson a little higher than that?"

"No, sir, not very much."

"It seems to me the circumstances are exceptional."

"It's junior C.I.D. work."

"C.I.D. aren't so familiar with the man's history as we are, Lowther."

I said slowly: "Because I happen to have a personal interest in the affair doesn't seem to me to justify my taking a hand."

"Oh, come. My dear fellow . . ." He made a gesture of deprecation. "We are a family, Lowther."

I winced a little at that. That was going a shade far, I thought, even for Flood.

"You and I have worked together a good many years," he said. "You made it pretty clear to me yesterday that you were worried about Davidson."

"Yes, I did."

"I'm trying to help you."

"You're very kind," I said. It was hopeless.

"What else did you expect me to say? If Davidson is out to make serious trouble and there's an enquiry and the press get hold of it . . ."

"Yes, I know."

"It may also have escaped your attention," he said with a touch of frost, "that the problem—the possible exposure of your problem, shall I say—wouldn't reflect too well on any of us. We don't want another enquiry."

"I understand perfectly."

"Well, there it is."

I said: "Are you making it an order?"

"I think it would be better if you handled it yourself, Lowther, I must confess."

I nodded. And, looking back, I remember that all I felt at that moment was a miserable, merciless relief. My noble cross came tumbling down. I heard Flood saying something about the interests of law and order; and then about simple duty. Yes and yes. So we would all be protected from Philip Davidson and from the just consequences of what we had done to him because the Assistant Commissioner wished it and ordered it. One had only to obey and life was really very easy. Bletchley would not try to stop Davidson and fail; he would be called off; I would do it myself and somehow succeed. There would be no enquiry; no hullaballoo in the press; nobody would know that Fay Driver had married the sergeant who fished Davidson out of the river; nobody would discover that a monstrous wrong had been done. And there would be no ruin, except a little in one's heart.

But Mick would be all right. He would not learn hatred and contempt for his parents. He would not find himself saddled at the beginning of his life with a name he would be ashamed of. He would be all right. Those were my instructions; this was my duty. So now I could build myself yet another bridge across the stream of ignominy and assure myself at frequent intervals that I would, I really would, have allowed Bletchley to fail, but for the call of duty. . . .

"There's one thing," I said, "that I haven't got straight." He looked up, waiting. "Am I supposed to be taking care of Davidson for my own sake, or because it would embarrass the police if the press took up his case and my wife's identity came out, or because you——"

He broke in urbanely. "You will be doing your job, Lowther." He continued: "Let me know if there is anything you need. I'll warn the local Chief Constable you will be in his area. Would you like police protection for your wife?"

"That won't be necessary."

"It could be justified."

"No."

"What about the other man—Pewsey?"

"Isn't it better he should know nothing about it?"

"There's no need for him to know. Just tell the local stations to keep an eye on him. Is he still in London?"

"I'll find out."

"Yes, do."

I stood up and went over to the window playing with the keys in my pocket. Flood also rose, stretching, and, glancing at the clock on the wall, plainly waited for me to leave.

I said: "It's a hell of a thing, isn't it?"

Flood paused; like that, with his bald head thrust forward and his arms outflung as he pulled on his overcoat, he had for an instant the air of a vulture, incalculably wise and depraved and practised, in the moment of alighting.

"What is?"

"The whole affair."

He landed, folding his wings. "Oh, I don't know."

"Well, to begin with," I said; "the way you are pushing me into this . . ."

Very pleasantly he said: "Hadn't you better go back to your office, Lowther?"

"I'd rather like to have it out here and now," I told him, "if you wouldn't mind." I felt curiously hot and bright.

"Have what out?"

I had to know the exact extent of his interest; I had to know his motives; they were still obscure to me. I was a little afraid, but sometimes one's fear is a powerful stimulant. "When did it occur to you," I said, "that Davidson probably didn't do that fellow in after all?"

For a moment he stood perfectly still. Then he said: "My dear Lowther, I don't think you can know what you

are saying," which was the formal, the obvious, counter:
a fair beginning.

From the window I could see, beyond the tree-tops,
Westminster Bridge; somewhere upstream a siren barked
huskily. "I realised it last night," I told him, "—really
looked it in the face, I mean."

He made no move.

"But I think I knew, at the back of my mind, all the
time. I always have done. I simply shut my eyes to it."
When I turned round he said curtly:

"You're ill."

"No, I'm well enough."

"Mistakes of that kind aren't made nowadays," he said.

"Not often," I agreed.

"A man isn't given a life sentence without a fair trial."

"Of course not."

"There wasn't a shadow of doubt, Lowther." He was
very angry. "Judge, jury, even his own Counsel——"

"That's quite true."

"All the police did was to make the facts available. It's
the jury that decides, not the police."

"We're all responsible."

"Responsible! Really!" A tinge of colour came into his
sallow face. "The evidence was quite conclusive." He was
gripping his gloves tightly. "As I remember it the fellow
was lucky to escape a hanging."

"Some of the evidence," I said, "was—mistaken."

"You're being uncommonly exasperating, Lowther." I
could hear the breath in his nostrils. "I will not be drawn
into an argument about the evidence in a trial which took
place seventeen or eighteen years ago," he said harshly.
But he failed to ask which part of the evidence I considered
unsound and, knowing what he was feeling, knowing now
that he knew and perhaps even felt in his heart as I did,
my own anger of a sudden evaporated.

"No, there was no way of breaking that evidence down,
was there?" I said. "No way at all." He was putting on his

hat. "We weren't really to blame. We couldn't have done more, could we? Could we? Or less."

"You're talking like a fool, Lowther."

"Yes. Yes, I suppose so."

"I won't stand here and be subjected to it. If you thought there was something wrong with the case, why didn't you look into it long ago?"

"Oh, I did. I did try. I did something."

"And what did you find?"

"I drew a blank."

"Very well, then."

I nodded. "Yes." I left the window. "All I know is," I told him, "that I've very little stomach for my duty in this matter."

"We have a job to do, Lowther," he said, "and it has to be done."

"It hasn't," I said, "it hasn't. We do it because we choose to do it."

He did not reply to that. In a way I felt sorry for him. He was driven by a gnawing ambition. I knew he was likely to get his knighthood sooner or later; a re-opening of the Davidson case, with which he had had so much to do, would cause him grievous damage. But even then I did not wholly believe in his attitude. I think he was just waiting to see. I did not believe that an Assistant Commissioner, a man of the highest integrity, would truly contemplate the suppression of evidence in any circumstances. But there was one thing I wanted to say, for my own sake as much as for his; and this I would cling to.

"Well, I'll get on with it," I said. "But I think you'd better know that when, if ever, Davidson settles down and there is no more danger of his running amok with an axe, then I shall do my best to clear him and get him justice, at whatever cost."

3

I sat in the back of the car and with a vacant mind watched the road beyond the driver's head. I had no plan other than to get a glimpse of Davidson. Bletchley had returned and so I knew where the man was. I would pick up the trail. Observe. See without being seen. Hunt the hunter, like an animal.

We drove through Gravesend and took the secondary road to High Halstow and the Isle of Grain. In Halstow on the crest of the hill I sent the driver to enquire if there was a road down to the marshes and the river. Yes, there was a road, a new one, laid during the war for the building of the boom across St. Mary's Bay. So we left the higher ground and drove down to the flat green land under a roof of scudding cloud. The car bounced decorously on the uneven surface and shied a little in the buffeting wind. The road sped across the marsh to the distant river.

I was not anxious to attract attention, so when we had gone a couple of miles I told the driver to stop and wait, and I got out and set off on foot, feeling very conspicuous on the level earth, for there was nothing else but the sky and the road and, far away, the river. A ship moved slowly downstream, under Canvey Island. I listened to the sharp grinding of my heels on the road and the bumbling of the cold, fierce wind in my ears.

The other car, when I saw it, was drawn into the ditch a couple of hundred yards further on. It was an old Austin. For some reason I knew at once it was important, and, disturbed, I went towards it. There was nobody in the driver's seat, nor any means of identification anywhere; I looked in through the cracked and muddied windows. Nothing. Taking a note of the number I left the road and struck across the marsh towards the bank and Morocco Bay. Once I turned to look back at the car on the road, and I remember thinking: I don't know where this is going to end. . . .

So I met Jackson and he told me of Davidson's arrival. Afterwards I set out along the river's edge to find the café where, said Jackson, Davidson would be.

4

During the day he sat in the café and drank cups of tea and coffee. But at night he barricaded himself in the cabin of the barge. He would close the door and jam the table up against it, and then cover the windows. When he heard Jackson's shuffling footsteps on the deck outside he would put his shoulder to the table so that the old man couldn't open the door. Then he would run to the windows. And back to the door.

Presently he would light the lamp. But it was Jackson's. And Jackson's oil burned. He would put a match to Jackson's stove which was charged with fuel from the deck of Jackson's ship. Then he would sit on the edge of the bunk and run his hands to and fro across his knees and listen to the crackle of the fire and the restless lapping of the incoming tide in the bilge beneath.

Book Two

THE FLOWERING BAMBOO

CHAPTER ONE

I

THE CAFÉ belonged to a man called Gedge. He had been a pilot and had built it there, along the bank from St. Mary's Bay, because he had thought that the defence obstacle and the new road would bring custom to the place; it was used only by a handful of rubble-pickers, however, and bawleymen and salvage men and others who seemed to do nothing particular.

It stood a few yards from the river's edge, overlooking Blyth Sand, and from its windows you could see the ramshackle landing-stage running out from the bank into the water and, beyond, the wide river and the freighters, coming and going all day, and the mud-hoppers tramping out to the estuary to drop their loads into the Black Deeps and then return for more, from the dredgers working upstream. Sometimes you would see a spritsail beating across the wide windy spaces under a spread of brown canvas, but not too often; they are dying out now; there is a special mooring for those that remain, called, appropriately enough, Starvation Buoys, off North Woolwich, where you will see six or eight of them rubbing shoulders in the wake of the passing tugboats, the little copse of masts weaving slowly to and fro across the sky.

There was a board outside the café which read: *Teas and Light Refreshments: Always Open.* For a few minutes I stood outside by the river. Then I thought: well, I've nothing to lose.

Three men were sitting at a table in the corner and a girl was scrubbing the floor. There was a high counter with

a tall shining machine at one end; there were four or five
trestle tables covered with pink oilcloth, and on the wall
a photograph of Winston Churchill; and there was a stove,
softly roaring. It was a cheap, clean, unpretentious place,
like a thousand others of its kind, but warm and brightly
lit. I noticed a curtained door beyond the counter, leading
to the kitchen, I supposed, and the living quarters and the
open ground where Gedge grew his cabbages.

None of the three men looked like Philip Davidson; it
was a relief. They all raised their heads as I entered, and
then went on with their game of cards, and the little
creature on the floor, whose hair overhung her eyes like
a long-haired dog's, went on scrubbing.

Alice Gedge came out of the kitchen and stared at me
from behind the counter. She was an angular woman with
a big body and thin, bowed legs; her face was drawn and
bitter and she wore an air of perpetual dishevelment, as if
she had been interrupted in the middle of something more
important, and would pause now and then to sweep back
her hair before the mirror behind the counter and utter an
exclamation of impatience. But she had a certain laconic
humour.

"Are those cheese?" I asked, nodding towards the plate
of sandwiches she was preparing. "I'll try one. And a cup
of tea, if you please."

While I ate I watched her working, and while she
worked she looked me over. "It's pretty quiet along
here," I ventured. "You'd think you were miles from
anywhere."

"Aren't you?" she said briefly, stabbing at the
cheese.

"I suppose it is a bit lonely."

"Lonely! God . . ." She leaned on the knifeblade as it
sank through the sandwich. "Damned river," she
muttered.

"Your husband a waterman?"

"Was. Mud pilot. You'd have thought he'd have had

enough of it after forty years, wouldn't you? But no. Not him. He has to retire to this hole. Gets himself a patch of mud and digs all day and listen to the sirens. Personally they give me the willies. Moo. Moo. Like a lot of damned cows. But him, he knows half of them by sight and what's funny about the way they steer and where they come from and what the cargo is and give him half a chance and he'll tell you. I could scream."

I nodded as sympathetically as I dared.

"You a Trinity House man?" she asked.

"No."

"P.L.A.?"

"No."

"Oh. I just wondered. We don't get many strangers." Alice's curiosity, I learned, was a kind of greed; she filled her life with other people's business, real or imagined, and other people's emotions.

"As a matter of fact," I said, "I'm looking for an old friend of mine——"

She dropped the knife with a clatter and set her arms akimbo. "I know," she said. "An old friend of yours who used to be in tugboats and lives around here called Davidson. You're the second in the last twenty-four hours."

I thought: that will have been Bletchley. "Am I?"

"Is your name Pewsey?"

I stared at her; this was unnerving. "No."

"Well, this fellow Davidson was asking for somebody by the name of Pewsey. Then along comes another one asking for Davidson. Now you. Why don't you fellows arrange to meet some time?"

He had begun sooner than we had expected then; I was aware of being a long way behind. "Does he ever come in here?" I asked Alice Gedge.

"Who, Davidson?" When I nodded she moved her shoulders. "If it's the fellow I'm thinking of, yes. The question is, which are you thinking of?"

"Tall. Forty-odd." I remembered Jackson's attempt to describe him. "Bushy eyebrows."

"More than forty," Alice said. "More like fifty." And then: "Say, what's everybody want him for?"

"Nothing out of the way. Who are those people?" I motioned towards the men in the corner playing cards.

She made a face. But she told me. Willie picked the rubble-dumps, like Jackson. So did Rigfold, whose face was gentle and whose forehead was unexpectedly high; the other was Barney Scotson, who owned a bawley, which is a little shrimping vessel . . . all old watermen, like Alice's husband, the dross and dottle of the river that Alice hated, had always hated and would always hate, flowing quietly by beyond the windows there, laden with ships in the mist. They, Alice said, were nobody. People, real people—it was implicit in her manner—came from the city, upstream. And I was one of these.

She watched me carry my cup of tea to a table and sit down near the stove. I kept an eye on the door; if Davidson should come in I would get up and leave before Alice could bring us face to face; but I would have seen him.

The girl scrubbed the floor. Her skirt was pathetically short and beneath it, at the back, the thin thighs were visible above the stockings. I tried not to watch her. But then Alice, who must have seen my eyes on the girl, came round from behind the counter and, lifting her foot, tapped the girl's arm with the toe of her shoe, and when the girl looked up brushing back her hair with her wrist, said: "Over there, dear."

She spoke as if to a deaf person. "Over there." And motioned with her foot towards the counter.

The girl pushed the bucket before her across the boards and Alice, turning to me, said explanatorily: "Foreigner," with a deprecatory smile. "One's got to do something for them." She sank on to the chair facing me across the table and put her chin in her hand companionably. "Down here for long?" she enquired.

"Not very long."

"From town?"

"Yes."

"Which part?"

To my great relief the fire chose that moment to shift and fall in and Alice called: "Elsie!"

The girl got up and came towards the table. She might have been anything between eighteen and thirty. She was small and thin and there was a scarlet weal of some kind on her cheek, which could have been either a scratch or an eruption of the blood. Her eyes were wide and grey and steady, or unseeing.

"The fire, Elsie."

The girl turned and went quietly into the kitchen beyond the curtained door.

"Refugee," Alice said, turning to me again. "Come off a ship. Gives herself a lot of airs, you'd be surprised. Elsa, she calls herself. Elsa," the woman repeated with a sudden gust of contempt. "As far as I'm concerned she's an Elsie." She settled herself comfortably. "Now, what were we saying? Oh, yes . . ."

Elsa returned with a bucket of coke. Alice broke off to watch the operation. The girl struggled with the bucket to tip a little coke into the small round maw of the stove. When it spilled across the floor Alice cried bitterly: "Now look what you've done!"

Suddenly she was trembling with rage. I have never understood what it was that Alice hated so much in Elsa; she disliked women as a whole, certainly, but there was something in Elsa which acted on Alice like explosive on a smouldering fire: the dumb humility, perhaps, with its undertone of steadfastness and breeding. She struggled to her feet while Elsa waited.

"Get a brush," she said. And again, shouting into the girl's ear: "A brush. A brush." She took her by the shoulder to swing her about and then, feeling the timid flesh beneath her hand, took it in her thumb and forefinger and twisted it. Elsa uttered a little cry.

The men in the corner looked up. Gedge, a small neat man with black eyebrows and glasses, appeared in the curtained door.

"Let the girl alone, Alice," he said.

For a moment there was a silence. Then Gedge went back into the kitchen. Alice knew she had gone too far.

"The brush, dear," she said to Elsa. "A brush to sweep the floor." With her hands she made the motions of sweeping. "In the kitchen, dear." The girl turned and went out quietly and Alice ran a hand over her hair. "It's so hard to make them understand," she said, to nobody in particular. One feels one should do all one can for them. . . ."

I said: "Of course."

But then Elsa returned with a brush and began to sweep the coke across the floor towards the stove, with small timid movements. The stuff rattled on the wet boards.

"Not now, dear," Alice said. Her voice soared again. "Not now, not now."

Elsa swept the coke across the floor.

"Elsie."

The girl looked up, her grey eyes wide.

"Leave it till later, dear. I'm talking to the gentleman."

Elsa smiled helplessly and began to gather the coke into her hands and drop it with terrible carefulness into the open stove. We all waited. I think a sort of fellowship had developed among the rest of us, the three men in the corner and I, though I was a stranger to them. For it was an agony nobody could withstand. I could feel my hackles rising. I thought: if she touches the girl again . . . We were all very glad when Alice took her arm and led her through the curtained door and left her there.

"Now then, where were we?" Alice said as she returned to my table. She sat down and I saw that her hands were shaking. "Oh yes," she said gaily, "I remember. I was going to guess your job, wasn't I?"

"Were you?"

"Three guesses," she said. She leaned towards me, smiling with that appalling brightness. "You're a newspaper reporter, from town, like that other man."

CHAPTER TWO

I

TO GET the information I wanted from Bletchley was like drawing teeth. Alice Gedge had told me that he, Bletchley, had spoken to the newspaper reporter: Bletchley had told me he had seen and talked with nobody. He had been caught out in a lie, and he fought to minimise the attendant humiliation. To be caught, moreover, by Uncle Lowther, who had now the unexpected effrontery to cross-examine him, was almost intolerable.

"He was waiting for you, was he?"

"No, sir. He saw me coming, that's all. Then he hung about."

"Had you seen the car on the road?"

"Yes, sir, but how was I to know it was his?"

Its presence might have served as a red light, I suggested.

"Well, sir," he protested.

"It's your job, Bletchley. Go on. I want to know exactly what was said. Exactly, you understand?"

He moistened his lips. "He was standing outside the café, sir. And then I came along. He asked me if I happened to be looking for Davidson."

"What did you answer?"

"Well, sir, I naturally thought he was from one of the local stations . . ."

" 'Naturally', Bletchley? Why?"

"He seemed to know so much about it. So I said yes, I was looking for Davidson."

"That wasn't very clever, was it? And then?"

"Then he asked me what my paper was. I suppose he thought I was a reporter or something."

"And who did you think he was?"

"I've told you, sir, I thought he was a plain-clothes man from one of the other stations."

"Didn't you ask him which?"

He wilted a little. "Yes, sir, I asked him which."

"Did he give you an answer?"

"He said he was from a Sunday newspaper."

"Not to put too fine a point on it, Bletchley," I said, "you must have looked a bloody fool even in your own eyes then."

He swallowed. "Yes, sir."

"Well—go ahead."

"He asked me what Davidson had been up to. But I didn't tell him any more."

"Didn't you?"

"Oh no, sir. He was quite a decent chap, sir."

"Oh, I'm sure."

"He knows the Assistant Commissioner, sir, too—asked me how he was these days."

"And how was he, Bletchley, in your opinion?"

"Oh, I just said he was all right, sir." He grinned a little sheepishly, and I rather liked him for it. "He asked me how I got on with him and I said as a matter of fact I didn't see very much of him."

"Very sound, Bletchley. What did he have to say to that masterstroke of evasion?"

"Nothing very much, sir." I knew the boy was lying again. But I didn't pull him up. After all I had sent him out because I had known he would bungle the job; it seemed unreasonable to complain, now, of his having done so. "He asked me who tucks us up now, was it Superintendent Harris. . . ."

Suddenly I was on edge. "Did you tell him who had sent you?"

"Yes, sir. Well, he seemed to know everybody, sir, and I thought——"

"Did you tell him my name?"

"Yes, sir."

I recall getting to my feet and going to the window so that the boy shouldn't see my face. I heard him saying: "I'm terribly sorry, sir . . . never happen again. . . ."

"That's all right, Bletchley."

So the press was there already. There was a reporter watching every move Davidson would make. And now he knew that I was watching, too.

"You'd better go back," I told Bletchley. "Go back to the place right away."

"Yes, sir?"

"And watch Davidson." I tried to impress on him precisely what he had to do. "Watch him. Try not to let him know that you're watching him. And talk to nobody. You understand that? Nobody." The instruction was superfluous now: Bletchley had probably learned his lesson. And it seemed better to use him, whatever his faults, than to begin again with another man.

"Day and night, sir?"

"That is up to you. I want to know if and when Davidson makes a move. I want to know if he leaves the marsh. If he does, telephone me immediately." I gave him my private number so that he could call me at night, if necessary.

"Very well, sir."

"You can start now."

"I suppose there's no chance of another man . . ."

"I'm afraid not. I shall be down myself quite often, then you can have a break."

When he had gone I spoke to the Records Office and asked them to trace Pewsey.

2

It was a few minutes short of eleven o'clock when the telephone rang. "A Mr. Craig to speak to you, sir." I told them to put him through.

The man asked if my name was Lowther and then he told me his. He mentioned the name of his newspaper. It was a dry, clipped voice, quite pleasant in tone. "It has to do with a man named Davidson," he said.

"No statement."

"Just a moment——"

"Try Public Relations." I knew the P.R.O. had no information on Davidson.

"Look, I wonder if we could have a drink some time?"

I said: "I'm sorry, I know nothing about Davidson. If a statement is issued it will come through the usual channels."

"You don't happen to be free for lunch today, do you?"

"There is nothing I can tell you about Davidson, Mr. Craig."

"Well, maybe I could tell you something." The reply was a little pert, but the tone of voice was gentle and friendly. "It's really rather important."

"If you wish to make a statement about Davidson you can do so at any police station."

"Listen," he said; he was very persistent; "I don't want an interview. I'm not wasting your time. I just don't want to talk about it on the phone. Will you lunch with me today?"

It occurred to me suddenly that I might be able to shake the fellow off altogether if I saw him. I might talk him into dropping the story. It seemed a chance worth taking.

"Oh, very well." I must have sounded exceedingly ungracious. However, he suggested a restaurant in Charlotte Street and I agreed to meet him there.

When I arrived he was already there. He introduced himself and we sat down. "I don't suppose my call was very welcome," he began with a smile.

"Where did you get my name from, Mr. Craig?"

"I ran into one of your boys the other day."

I nodded, "Bletchley."

"I haven't got him into trouble?" he said.

"No no."

"He seemed a nice lad. I'm rather a louse, you know, at getting people to talk too much—had a lot of practice. He didn't know he was giving anything away."

"He wasn't, Mr. Craig."

While we ordered I had time to look at this man. He gave the impression of being somewhat worn—in himself no less than in his clothes. Soiled, perhaps, is the word. He could not have been much more than thirty-eight or thirty-nine, yet he had the heavily scored face of an older man. The eyes, I noticed, were tired and evasive, and he wrinkled them defensively while he talked.

"Mr. Craig," I said, "who put you on to this?"

"My paper. You mean Davidson?"

"Yes."

"My paper. The features editor, fellow called Asprey."

"Well, if you're expecting to get a story out of it, and I can't see what else you'd want, you're wasting your time."

He smiled slightly. "What are you drinking?"

I said I would like beer and he ordered a jug. We ate the smoked salmon in silence. Then, without any preamble, he said: "Davidson seems to think he didn't kill that fellow."

He must have known the effect such an announcement, coming from him, would have. He was lighting a cigarette.

"Doesn't worry you if I smoke, does it?"

"No. Have you been talking to Davidson?"

"We had a chat."

"Mr. Craig," I said, "I hate to eat your food and talk this way, but I wish to God you newspapermen would leave things alone."

"Oh, I did no harm," he said mildly. "As a matter of

fact I tried to put him off the idea. He's out to make trouble, I suppose you know."

"He won't make any trouble."

"I hope you're right."

"What did he tell you?"

"Well, not very much." He went on in his queer, cryptic way: "He's interested in two people, so far as he's interested in anything. Chap by the name of Pewsey. And a woman—Fay Driver." He kept his eyes on his plate. "I expect they ring a bell."

"Does that constitute a story, Mr. Craig?"

"Depends how it develops."

"It won't develop."

"I take it you've no objection to my hanging around for a while?"

"I think you're wasting your time, but it's your affair."

"You don't think they'll turn up, then?"

"Who?"

"The people he's after."

I asked him: "What makes you think they might?"

"Well, for instance," he said, "you turned up." He was bland and smiling, yet I had the impression he viewed the remark, which was venomous enough certainly, with some distaste.

"It was your car I saw on the road, was it?"

"Yes. It's pure hunch, of course," he continued. "But that's what I think. Sooner or later Pewsey and that woman will get to know Davidson is after them. If they clamour for police protection, then I'd say it was some indication of their—what shall we call it: innocence?" He waited. "Wouldn't you?"

"Not necessarily, Mr. Craig."

"Well, maybe not. It occurred to me. On the other hand, if they run like rabbits, it's just possible they'll do so because they're scared stiff."

"Honest men often run like rabbits."

"True enough. Still, such is my theory. So they wait for

him to start something. But he doesn't, not just yet, because he's trying to get used to people and noise and fending for himself. And after a couple of weeks or so these people's feet get tired of being on tiptoe, ready to bolt. It becomes rather a bore for them. And presently they get curious—can't understand what he's waiting for. So they tiptoe along to have a look, to see what he's up to. Like moths to a flame."

"You've a lively imagination, Mr. Craig."

"Oh, I don't know. Anyway, that's what I'm hanging about for. If they do turn up in Morocco Bay, and I fancy they will, isn't it going to look as if Davidson has a case of some sort?"

"What makes you think he might have?"

He wrinkled his eyes and said: "Pure sentiment."

I said: "Forgive me—I don't quite understand. Have you brought me here to eat a capital lunch and tell me this? Are you talking simply in the capacity of a newspaper reporter, Mr. Craig?"

"Well, no," he admitted; he hesitated, floundering a little. "Just as a citizen." He shifted on his chair. "The trouble is, I rather like the fellow."

"I see."

"Yes." He rolled little pebbles of bread on the table-cloth. "I'd like to see him getting a fair crack of the whip," he blurted. "I don't want to see him crucified all over again." He called the waiter before I could reply and ordered another jug of beer; the one we had was still half full.

Presently I put it to him: "Mr. Craig, are you suggesting that Davidson should be allowed to do as he pleases? It's not my business to discuss his innocence or guilt. He was found guilty. However, as a police officer——"

"Oh, sure, sure."

"I'd suggest that you leave it to the people whose business it is."

"Trouble is it's also mine," he said. "It's a story, or looks like developing into one, and I have to write it."

"Oh, come——"

"Them's my orders."

"There are plenty of other stories. Every day——"

"I've been allotted this one," he said.

So I asked him: "Would you have any objection, Mr. Craig, to telling me how you came by those instructions?"

He smiled. "Not a bit."

I came to know Craig quite well during the weeks that followed this first meeting. His failing, if you could call it a failing, was that he was the wrong man for his job; his work required him to "act tough", even callously, whereas he was in fact a very gentle and compassionate man. It was this, I fancy, that produced the worried evasiveness of manner which was the first thing you noticed about him. He knew, he knew. Once, when we were better acquainted, he spoke of it, with a bitter chagrin: "Show me a first-class bastard," he said; "show me a Heinrich Himmler; show me Old Nick himself, stooping to pat a dog or speak a kind word to a small boy, and me, I'm a total loss."

Craig had attended Davidson's trial as a junior reporter, and so when the matter of Davidson's release was raised by Asprey he had been in the position of knowing something about the case already—as much of it as he could remember, at any rate.

He had protested: Asprey insisted. For a while they bickered amiably enough. Till at last Asprey had said: "Look here, do you want this job or don't you?"

"Not if it's what I think it is."

"Then what the hell's the use of talking about it?"

"You're doing the talking, George, not me. Go on, you're loving it."

So Asprey had filled in the background. "He's done seventeen years. Went in in 1932. That's a long time. All sorts of things have happened, we've had one war, we're heading for another, everything has changed, it's a different world, we've got a nice new morality, we've got atom bombs." And here was a fellow, he had continued, a fellow of education, who knew little or nothing about it. Like a babe, only forty years old. Older. God knew how old. Did Craig begin to see what he meant? "Went in when he was a kid. Got mixed up with a girl. The girl got mixed up with this Boyd fellow—some sort of waterfront yahoo. Davidson gets into a fight with him, cracks him over the head with a poker, and gets twenty years. Now he's out—free."

And what, Asprey wanted to know, was going to become of the fellow? Where would he go? How would he live? What would he think and feel about things? Would any living soul remember him? Who would lend the fellow a hand? "Good human stuff, Craig. A pippin. Get on to it. Have a look at the files, dig out the back numbers, see what's to be done. You know the kind of thing."

Craig knew. "Something sunny."

"Sunny," Asprey agreed. "Bags of sunshine."

"Haven't you anything else, George?"

"You don't want it?"

"It doesn't sound so good to me."

"To you," Asprey said, "it doesn't have to sound good. You just write it."

It had been then, I gathered, that Craig had said: "Let's let the fellow alone, George. He's done a fair whack."

Asprey studied him bleakly for a moment. "If you don't want the job, Craig, there are plenty of youngsters," he said.

"I didn't say anything about the job. I was talking about this particular story. You couldn't publish it anyway."

"Why not?"

"Because there's a law of libel." He flared up suddenly.
"Because there's a law of common decency. Because the
chap's had a bellyful and you can't throw him to the lions
for a few columns of muck."

Asprey was unmoved. He would get the solicitors to look
it over for libel, he said. Craig might pay Davidson a few
pounds for the use of the name and an indemnity. If not,
then they would give him a number: Convict 123456.
For the rest—"Who appointed you arbiter of decency,
Craig? Come off it, old son." If Craig didn't feel up
to it, then he could say so — "But don't let's be pious
about it, for God's sake. You've done this sort of thing
before."

"Only once."

"Many a time——"

"And what happened last year? A woman put her head
in the gas oven."

"That wasn't your fault, Craig. Don't be a fool."

Craig said: "What happens if I turn it down?"

"You'll take it, never fear."

Craig nodded. "Yes, I usually do, don't I?"

"Always," Asprey said. And then, kindly: "You've
registered your protest, Craig. You tried. Nobody can
say you didn't. Now you don't have to worry any
more."

"You rotten bastard," Craig said, and Asprey laughed
delightedly. "When do you want it?"

"Soon as you like. Take a bit of time, of course, but not
too much."

"Any idea where he's to be found?"

"None," Asprey said. "I dare say I could find out."

"It would help."

Asprey nodded and Craig rose. At the door he turned
and said: "George, why is it you always pick on me for this
sort of job?"

"What sort is that?"

"This—other people's damn misery."

Asprey laughed shrilly and said: "What do you want?—
to write up your own?"

"It amounts to the same thing."

"Just so," said Asprey. "That's why I pick on you,
Craig. You're so good at it," he concluded gravely.
"So very, very good."

Craig took the lift down to the basement of the building.
He walked along the dry, dim corridors to the rooms where
the back numbers were kept, which smelled of mice and
perfumed disinfectant.

3

"So you talked to Davidson." We sat for a few minutes
over a cup of coffee. He seemed willing to tell me all he
knew and indeed I was glad to add to the shadowy picture
which was all I had of Davidson.

"A couple of days ago," Craig said.

"Did you get what you wanted?"

"No, he won't talk. How old is he?"

"Forty-one."

"Yes. He looks older, of course. Much. Hair going grey,
rather a stoop, a shuffling sort of walk, no expression in
his face and a voice that sounds as though it hasn't been
used in years. More or less what you'd expect."

"You went aboard that barge of his, did you?"

"I did. I put my head round the door and he got up
slowly from that stove thing and then asked me who
I was and what I wanted and who said I could crash
in there like that. Not so glib, but that was it, roughly.
I told him his neighbour, fellow called Jackson, had
said it would be all right. I told him I was from a newspaper.

"He didn't seem to get it at first. Then it sank in. A
newspaper, I told him—a reporter. He asked me what I
wanted. When I told him he seemed absolutely stupefied.

I asked him a few questions off the reel just to let him know the sort of muck I was after. 'You've been out of the swim a long time, you're by way of being a phenomenon, we might make quite a story out of you'. I must have put the wind up him, for I saw him look round at his boots on the floor, the blankets and shaving tackle and odds and ends, so I let him know he'd be wasting his time running for it, I'd only find him again.

"He said, 'Please let me alone,' in that voice of his—sounds as if it comes from nowhere, pulled up one word at a time. When I asked him if he was thinking of throwing me out neck and crop he said he didn't want any trouble and would I please get the hell out of it, and I told him he certainly could, if he wanted, throw me out, I couldn't stop him, or, if it came to that, he could slap me over the head with a poker.

"The next thing I knew was that I was being pinned up against the wall by those hands of his, you never saw anything like them, held there by the lapels of my coat with his face like stone a couple of inches away from mine. But he didn't do anything. He let me go and opened the door and said 'Get out' in a whisper and gave me a little shove into the darkness. I went too far and down I went into the well of that damned barge and cracked my head on something . . . it's still swollen." He touched the back of his head very gingerly and made a wry face. "It was a beauty. Then I'm not sure what happened. I've a vague recollection of being carried up a ladder on Davidson's back and then dumped on one of the bunks in the cabin. There was somebody shouting, it must have been old Jackson: 'Hey, are you all right?' and I was trying to answer, but it was Davidson's voice. 'Yes, yes, go away.' Then he was trying to bring me round, slapping my hands and one thing or another, and finally he gave me a mug of cold water straight in the face. That worked.

"The poor devil had been worried stiff. He thought I

was hurt badly. I had a headache like the crack of doom, of course, but no bones broken, so I thought I'd stick it out, I'd never get another chance like this. He thought he'd pushed me down the hole, d'you see? and he was damned grateful I hadn't broken my neck. It would have mucked things up for him, wouldn't it?"

"Might have been difficult."

"You'd have had him inside again before he could say Jack Robinson, wouldn't you?" He went on: "Well, any-way, I asked him a few questions, the usual blarney, but he still wasn't having any. Wouldn't even say anything when I asked him why he'd killed that other fellow, Boyd. Nothing. Not a word. It was like talking to a wall. He just sat there on the edge of the bunk rubbing the palms of his hands up and down his knees and waited for me to get out.

"So I had one last shot. I said: 'Tim Pewsey . . . Fay Driver.' Just like that. Like dropping pebbles into a pool. That jolted him. He looked up slowly and gave me a stare that made the hair on my neck stand up. Then he was saying: 'Who sent you?' I fancy he thought I'd come from the prison or the police or something. I told him I was from a newspaper and hoped it had got him going, but it hadn't, it hadn't. He closed up again. I plugged away for a while but there was nothing doing. I told him it was a funny thing, I'd seen it happen before: a crook gets a clever Counsel to defend him and they both know he's as guilty as they come, but of course they put in a plea of not guilty, and then the defence does such a wonderful job that it convinces the culprit himself, till he really believes he's as innocent as a child in arms and couldn't possibly have done it. So he goes to quod with a chip on his shoulder you could build a bridge with and dreams for years of justice and how he'll get even with everybody when he comes out. And so on. Nothing. I must have talked for an hour, but I couldn't find a bait he'd take. Till finally I was squatting on my heels down in front of him, begging him to answer—did he kill Boyd, did he kill Boyd . . ."

"Did you get an answer?"

"I got one word. No. That's all I could get out of him." He flicked the pellets of bread across the table.

"Would you say he is unbalanced, Mr. Craig?"

"No. I'd say he's part child and part man. He's living in a world of his own and he won't come out and he won't let anybody in. But it's voluntary. He's not crazy."

I nodded.

It was then that Craig looked up and asked me: "Did he do it?"

"Mr. Craig, there are not many miscarriages of justice. A man accused of a crime of that nature gets more than a fair hearing."

"Yes. Yes, of course." Then, lightly but carefully, he said: "You see, sooner or later I have to write some stuff about Davidson. At the moment, of course, there's nothing very much to say. But you never know. If he were to get Pewsey or"—there was always a split-second's hesitation before he used her name—"Fay Driver in a dark corner one night, it wouldn't be surprising if he lost his head for a moment, would it?"

I agreed that it wouldn't.

"Well, let's hope it isn't allowed to happen," he continued. "One wouldn't want to see him clapped into jug again before he's had time to do anything about the first twenty years. As long as he's free there's always the chance that a bit of new evidence might come to light . . ." He ran a hand across his forehead. "I mean, one wouldn't want it to be overlooked just because he's made another bloomer. For any reason. It would make a wow of a story. . . ."

I said slowly: "Do you mean the new evidence would make a wow of a story, or the fact that it might be overlooked, Mr. Craig?"

"Either, really." I could see the torment in the man's

4

eyes; he hated what he was saying. "I don't suppose the
police would take too bright a view of it. One wouldn't
want another Royal Commission. The police wouldn't,
anyway. Some of the newspapers might."

I felt myself colouring. "Mr. Craig, just what the hell do
you think you're saying?" He kept his eyes on his cup.
"If you have any doubts about the integrity of the police,
take them elsewhere."

"I haven't," he said.

But now I was certain he knew. He knew my wife's name
was Fay Driver. I learned later that Asprey had told him;
the sergeant who fished Davidson out of the river had
married the Driver girl, he had told Craig: follow it up.
And in his odd way Craig was trying to warn me that he
knew and that if necessary, in Davidson's interests, he
would use it.

"You can be assured," I told him, "that if any such
evidence as you hint at should ever come to light, it will
not be overlooked—for any reason at all, Mr. Craig."

Then he raised his eyes. I believe he was thanking me
less for the assurance than for putting him out of his own
misery.

4

So it came back to Davidson. We revolved about him
like spokes about a hub. And for five days he made no
move. I drove down to Morocco Bay two or three times
and talked to Bletchley, who now was extremely anxious
to do well, but I never saw Davidson once; it was to be
some time yet before I met him face to face. And because
I never saw him except through other people's eyes and
never heard him speak except with their lips, I was aware
of him only as a bulk, vague in outline and without
character, but high, towering. Indeed at that time it was
only in our minds that he seemed to exist at all, having a
different aspect, representing a different kind of threat, for
everybody involved.

Pewsey had been traced. He was living at an address in Gravesend and was in the employ of the Drewster Tug and Lighterage Co., which had an office on the Royal Terrace Pier. The local station was asked to keep an inconspicuous watch on his home.

Early in the following week Davidson made his first move.

CHAPTER THREE

I

IT WAS Bletchley who telephoned, to say that Davidson had gone out on the river in a boat. It sounded harmless enough, to be sure, but the unfortunate Bletchley, having no boat, had been unable to follow him, and, short of taking off his clothes and swimming, had been unable to keep his quarry in sight; he was in some despair.

"What sort of a boat?" I asked him.

"Well, it's got a sail, sir, and an engine."

"Large?"

"Which, sir?"

"The boat."

"Oh, pretty small."

"Was he alone?"

"No, sir, with a chap called Scotson."

"Who's he?"

"I don't know, sir. One of the people who hang about this café place." Then I remembered: Scotson had been one of the three I had seen playing cards in the corner. "And sir——" Bletchley continued.

"Yes?"

"There's something fishy about that place."

I was beginning to find it hard to take Bletchley seriously. "What do you mean—fishy?"

"There's something going on here. It's phoney."

"What makes you think that?"

"Well, to begin with, they're perpetually getting tight in the back room and they haven't got a licence. Then there's a chap who arrives in a car two or three times a week and sneaks in and out and then buzzes off again."

Bletchley was too good to lose; no organisation can afford to be without a clown; a place would have to be found for him somewhere. I told him to let me have a report.

"Right, sir."

2

Barney Scotson was a small, dapper man with a large hooked nose and shining, mischievous eyes. He was like a lizard, at once timid and audacious, which, sallying boldly from its cleft in the rocks, would then wait, poised, bright-eyed, ready to scuttle back if all was not well.

He had been watching Davidson for some time, apparently, before he slipped into the chair at Davidson's table that evening and made his proposal. He wanted Davidson to join him. "You look like a fellow that isn't going to talk much. Can't stand talkers aboard." He waited, intent and still. "Well? A third of the profits, no more, no less. Take it or leave it."

Davidson stared at him, resentful and wary.

"No? Too busy?"

He did not want another intruder, another Jackson, another obligation. He let the man talk. Scotson prattled on, darting in and out of his shelter. Davidson listened. He must teach himself to listen. He knew he must stifle the instinct to bolt every time a man spoke to him.

"What I want to know is, are you coming in or not?"

He watched Scotson's face.

"No?"

"Yes," he said suddenly. His voice was so loud that the other men, in the corner, looked over at him. His lips dried. "Yes, I'll come."

"If I could manage alone, mind you, I would," Barney told him severely. "There isn't enough for one man this time of the year, let alone two. But I can't. She's out there by the landing stage. Engine's a Handy Billy, starts on petrol, runs on paraffin—sail, when there's a fair breeze.

Boil the catch as you haul in; there's a boiling copper aboard. Ever done any shrimping?"

"No." He told himself it would get him out on to the river, into the bustle and movement and the criss-cross of trails.

"Makes no odds. Soon pick it up. The art's in the salt. Right amount of salt in the boiling. You leave that to me, takes a lifetime of experience. Ever handled a trawl?" He explained: "That's the trimtram, we call it."

"Once."

"Good. You hoist a basket to your masthead when your trimtram's down, that keeps the shipping off, means you can't get out of the way, they has to get out of yours. Sail has the right of way, no matter how small." He stuck out his sharp pointed chin. "And stand by your rights. Mind you," he went on, "there's not much to be had nowadays. Shrimps don't come in as they used to."

"No?" He was feeling easier. "How's that?"

"Oil. Oil in the water. Druv 'em away. Not so bad in summer, of course. On a summer's day I've taken a hundred gallon. Five or six shillings a gallon, boiled—that's not bad. But not now, not this time of year."

"Where do you trawl?"

"Off Leigh Middle, mostly. Right in the traffic, mind. You have to trawl on the flood, see, when the big ones is coming in and out. Pilots are all right, but there's some don't use pilots to save the dues, see? . . . coasters, tankers, Dutch and German stuff. Run you down as soon as look at you. Stand firm, that's the only way with those folk. Just as the flood's on the turn, that's the time. You get to know. It's the undertide that matters for shrimp. The undertide's high half an hour before the top tide in London River. You get to know her." He smiled as if to himself. "Lovely river. Lovely . . ."

When he looked up he said aggressively: "Just don't talk, that's all. Last fellow I had was chatter, chatter, chatter, nearly druv me mad." He sipped his tea and

Davidson saw the bright, beady eyes on him over the rim of the cup as he sucked at the sugared dregs. Barney set down the cup. "You got a name?"

"Davidson."

"Davidson. Used to be a line of tugs belonged to a fellow of that name. Mark," he remembered. "Mark Davidson. Any relation of yours?"

Davidson lied. "No."

"Well, no matter. We'll start tomorrow morning. Tide's in around seven. Should be enough water out there by six-fifteen."

He went out with a nod, buttoning his jacket.

So it was done; he had taken the first step. The radio murmured music, the stove hummed softly. Rigfold and Willie played their endless games of cards in the corner. At another table sat a man named Shaw, who was big and burly and thick-featured, sprawling in gumboots and talking to little Fryer, who came to the café two or three times a week in a car; the man's sleepy eyes moved round the room while Shaw guffawed. The lights were strong and the place had no shadows; the wind shook the wooden walls and rumbled in the chimney.

Then a curious thing happened; in itself it was trifling, but for Davidson, who told me about it long afterwards, it was like an explosion in his heart. When he raised his head he saw Elsa, the girl who scrubbed the floor, watching him from behind the counter. Alice Gedge had gone into the kitchen and silently the girl had taken her place.

She looked away when Davidson lifted his eyes, but he knew she had been watching him and, puzzled, he stared at her. But then her gaze returned and when she saw the incomprehension in his face she smiled faintly and looked down at the bread she was cutting. A trace of colour came into her cheeks. Then she raised her head again and as if with an effort looked him full in the eyes, steady and unflinching. His head swam.

But it was not yet finished. For Alice Gedge had

returned and, running an impatient hand over her hair, had been pulled up short by the manner of the girl behind the counter. For a moment she said nothing. Then she came to Davidson's table.

"Like another cup of coffee, dear?"

He felt himself trapped. "Yes."

"Elsie!"

The girl looked up.

"Another cup of coffee for the gentleman." Already she was beginning to shake with the nameless fury of which I, too, had had a taste.

Elsa fumbled with the tall shining machine at the end of the counter, raising a cup and saucer to its beaked snout in an attitude of supplication. The cup rattled in the saucer. Then she came across the floor holding it in front of her carefully, while Alice Gedge watched, arms akimbo.

It was inevitable. When she stumbled and the cup toppled and smashed and the coffee ran across the boards, she stood perfectly still and waited.

Alice's voice rent the sudden silence. "There!" she cried triumphantly. "Now see what you've done. Another cup." The thin strident voice began to rise. "I've told you to be careful, haven't I? Haven't I? Didn't I warn you?" Hysteria took hold of her. "Poles!" she gritted. "Poles! We went to war for you, d'you know that? To war!" It was absurd and childish and contemptible and she must have known it; all she wanted was to say something clamorous and provocative, something in whose extravagance there would be a little relief. "For a lot of Poles! And now you come running over here to hide and expect to be looked after . . . and . . ." She reached for the girl's shoulder and swung her round. "Say something, can't you?" She was out of control now and a stillness had fallen over the bright interior of the café. "Why don't you say something?"

I don't think she meant to hurt the girl. She struck instinctively, blindly, not at Elsa, but at a face without features, at the empty leering years, at the ache at the heart of her rage.

Davidson put out a hand to stop her. And then withdrew it. This had nothing to do with him. He was not involved, not in this. He had another thing to do. He stumbled out of the place, into the dark.

3

The day had not broken when he returned to the landing stage. Barney Scotson was already on board the little bawley. The keel was lifting gently to the incoming tide and a small bright fire twinkled beneath the copper of fresh water in the well amidships.

They started up the engine and cast off and backed away from the landing stage. The river was black. They turned in a wide circle, the Billy singing to itself with the quiet contentedness of its kind, and headed for the estuary and the Essex shore, where a few lights winked. Presently they felt the tranquil rise and fall of the swell, like a bosom deep in sleep, and as they came out into Sea Reach the water began to slap briskly at the hull. They turned east towards the sliver of limpid green light below the hem of the sky.

In the bows where Davidson prepared the trimtram the air was fragrant with salt and burning wood. He looked back at the shadow of the shore and the wind blew off the water clean and cold into his face; it still troubled him somewhat, for in prison there is no wind, and he was not yet accustomed to it. Barney Scotson sat in the stern with the tiller tucked under his arm, his face alive in the light of the fire beneath the copper. The boat's wake hissed in the dark water behind him.

So for a little while Davidson was at peace. The hatred which preyed on his mind was appeased: he was moving at last. When he stood still again, then it would return. Now it was quiet. The two names, the almost forgotten faces, floated on the surface of his mind, lightly. He was moving towards them and for the moment it was enough. He forgot the ugly scene in the café; it had left him alarmed and uneasy in the night, for he had felt the pull of the currents it had started, new and strange, flowing about him. It went with the morning wind. Somewhere, far ahead of him, there was an end; nothing else truly mattered. The bawley rose and pitched and fell.

As they approached the Chapman Shoal the sun rose above the horizon and they saw the shipping in the roads, the freighters and tramps and tankers and colliers and coasters and merchants and towering liners which had reached the estuary in the night, and so had waited for dawn and the flood tide and the mud pilots for the passage to the docks. All their lines and angles glistened in the yellow sunlight and light streamed along the lofty flanks as they followed one another in from the sea.

"Far enough," Barney called. He shut off the Billy and the boat lost way and began to roll. "Get that basket hoisted."

Davidson ran the basket to the masthead and Barney came forward and together they secured the flimsy trawl, which was like an open purse, of net, weighted on its underlip with a length of cable, and fed it into the river from the boom. They set the tiny foresail to give themselves a knot or two of way and Barney went back to the tiller.

"Keep your eye on the fire," he told Davidson.

He took the tiller under his arm and watched the leading ships bear down, close now, huge and splendid against the dawn. Presently he opened a billy-can and began to eat. A barge stood out from Shoeburyness under a tall triangle of canvas and, leaning on the wind, butted across the tide to the Isle of Grain. Barney looked at Davidson sitting alone in the bows with his face seawards and the hands hanging loosely between his knees.

"Brought a bite t'eat?"

Davidson turned. "No."

"Should have done. Here." He broke off a hunk of bread and cheese and held it out. "Bring your own next time." He waited. "Go on. 'Tain't poisoned." There was a glint of humour in the beady eyes.

So Davidson took it. "Thanks."

Barney nodded and bit into a crust and chewed, fast, like a small animal, a rodent, narrowing his eyes at the tug which had moved up under the lee of the first ship in line. Raucous voices fled on the wind.

"I knew your father," Barney said suddenly.

Davidson's bowels shrank and his mind went vacant. He should have expected it. He turned to look at the man in the stern, who seemed to be peeping from his crevice in the rocks, bright and sly.

"Seventy-three, I am," Barney said.

Davidson said: "You look younger."

"Seventy-four next."

"Really?"

"Fine man—Mark." He nibbled at the cheese in his fingers. "I knew him well."

The rigging slapped at the mast. A jet of white steam waved for a moment at the funnel of the freighter and, a moment later, the voice of the siren boomed huskily on the wind. Davidson stared across the water and Barney looked at him reflectively.

"Wouldn't worry," he said briefly. "None of my business. I go my own way." But it was too late; the thread had attached itself; he heard Barney saying: "Me, I'm what you'd call a happy man." He chewed rapidly. "Reckon it's on account of being old. All your life you fret yourself about making a mess of things. Till you get on a bit. Then it doesn't matter any more. Give yourself a bit of peace—other folk, too."

"How did you know?"

"Knew as soon as I heard the name. Just thought I'd let you know."

"Why?"

"Why did I let on? Well, I knew your father, that's why." He sucked the fingers which had held the cheese. "Fine man."

The tugboat, which had left the freighter's side, came bustling towards them throwing up small fountains of water like explosions under the bunt stem.

"Hi-i!" The skipper, whose name Davidson later learned was Stallybrass, leaned over the bridge rail and grinned down at Barney Scotson; a bell rang and the tug swung round with the water tossing under her stern and the bawley rocked violently.

Barney cried: "Ay-up!" and scowled up at the skipper on the bridge.

"Fine day," Stallybrass bawled. He had an untidy grey moustache and a generous paunch and a round, red face. On the deck, leaning against the towing-hook below the bridge, there was a deck-hand, a small man in a blue jersey, whose bald head shone incongruously in the sunlight.

"Got a present for you," Stallybrass bawled. He stooped behind the rail and then, taking aim, tossed a packet into the stern of the bawley, where it landed at Barney's feet. "Many happy returns!" he bellowed.

Barney nodded and raised a hand in acknowledgement. He threw a glance at Davidson but said nothing. The packet, wrapped in brown paper, lay where it had fallen.

Stallybrass was shouting: "The *Ranji's* due into Tilbury tomorrow. Second mate. . . ."

Barney nodded impatiently. "Get off my trawl!"

The skipper laughed and rang for speed and the tug hurried away upstream, riding a wide rolling bow-wave. Davidson became aware that Barney was watching him speculatively. The old man said at last: "Should have told you about these maybe." He touched the packet with his foot.

"What is it?"

"Don't know, I never opened one. Hemp, drugs, jewellery, watches, I don't know, I just deliver. Fellow comes down from London two or three times a week and takes them away. We get paid. Please yourself."

"Still going on, is it?"

"Oh, aye, there's a fair bit. Lot of people in it one way or another. . . ." He shrugged his shoulders.

And now one more. He heard Barney saying: "The fellow on deck there, the one with the bald head, he was the one I was telling you about. Used to work for me, same job as you. Chatter, chatter, chatter, all day long, like a bloody barber. Never took to him. . . ."

Davidson watched the shipping. The ships flew pilots' pennants, red and white, and their company ensigns and the flags of the countries they had come from, and plodded up to Gravesend where the launches scuttled out with officials who examined their bills of lading and doctors who examined their bills of health and scrutinised the tongues of the crews, the Lascars and Chinamen and Arabs and Turks and Portuguese and Singalese and grinning negroes. At Gravesend, he remembered, the tugs would put out from the Royal Terrace Pier to lead them upstream on loose bridles like fillies at a horse show, and the cutters, taking off the sea pilots who had brought them round the Goodwins from Dungeness, would put aboard the mud pilots, who would coax them up the river through Northfleet Hope and Fiddlers Reach, Halfway Sand and Gallions Reach and Bugsby's, to the Royal Albert Dock and the Victoria or the George V, or round the Isle of Dogs and Limehouse to the Indias or the Surrey, which is the timber dock, or St. Katherine's or the Pool of London.

Then of a sudden he was wishing Barney would take in the trawl so that they could move on: move: anywhere, it didn't matter, for anywhere was forward, towards the end.

It was essential to move. He hated to stand still like this, rocking gently in the wake of the passing ships. He had begun: it must continue. He had a great fear of losing momentum.

4

He forced himself into motion. He had no plan at that time, other than to run them to earth; the plan would come; first he had to find them. So he tried to translate the passion into action. He began to ask questions, to talk to people, with a pitiable attempt to appear at ease and indifferent; and feeling no doubt that he could not allow any chance to go untaken, however remote, nor any suggestion, however extravagant, to pass untried, he blundered hither and thither without system and certainly without success. He asked the station sergeant, where he had periodically to report; no, the sergeant said, he had never heard of Pewsey or Fay Driver; but was Davidson looking for a job? He, the sergeant, had a friend who owned a timberyard and, if Davidson liked, it would be no trouble . . . I know that somebody told him of a man named Dewes, living in All-hallows, and Davidson waited outside the man's house for hours to catch a glimpse of him: the names were similar. I know, too, that Rigfold, one of the two old men who habitually played cards in the café, suggested, probably as a joke, the local electoral register: if this fellow Pewsey and the woman were conscientious citizens, he pointed out, then they must surely express their opinions in political matters; and in order to do so, in order that they should be allowed to vote, their names must appear in the register of electors, together with their addresses.

So Davidson walked into Gravesend with the dogged Bletchley at his heels and, by God knows what effort of will, actually presented himself at the Registration Office and asked to see the register.

He was interviewed by a Miss Tomlinson, who was extremely kind. What she thought of the big, iron-faced man who floundered into her office that morning, I don't know. He was trembling and hardly able to speak above a whisper; when he did mouth words it was as a deaf man speaks, unable to hear and so to control the wayward groping of his own voice, blurting this and whispering that . . . he was plainly in the slough of some terrible inner anguish, and Miss Tomlinson was touched and disturbed. She gave him the sheaf of papers and watched him. The sweat ran down his face and the print slid in and out of focus as he looked at it. The names were not there. But Miss Tomlinson wanted to help; if she could not help him in this way, then there must be some other. So she asked him eagerly if his name appeared in the register yet. She wanted to inscribe it at once. This she could do. Of course he must have his vote. It was his privilege. She would hear of nothing less. . . .

He trembled on the brink of wild, idiot laughter. He had come to get the address of a man and a woman so that he might run them down and strangle them with his hands, and Miss Tomlinson tried to give him a vote. Everybody was kind. Everybody he spoke to was kind. They reached out after him with long, warm, kindly tentacles.

He went back to Morocco Bay. He barricaded himself in the cabin of the hulk in the reeds.

When he reported again to Barney Scotson, the old man said: "Where've you been, eh?" He was very angry. "I thought you was coming in with me?"

"Yes."

"Well, where have you been?"

"I have been looking for somebody."

"Oh, you have, have you?"

"A man called Pewsey, and a woman—— "

"Pewsey?"

"Yes."

"Why, bless my soul, that's the fellow I was telling you

about. Why didn't you ask me? That's the fellow that used to work with me. You saw him yourself. Bald-headed fellow, on that Drewster tug. Used to be a boxer. so he says. Is that him?

CHAPTER FOUR

I

WHEN Bletchley telephoned to say that Davidson had called at Drewsters' office on the Royal Terrace Pier I drove down from London immediately.

The uniformed official at the entrance to the Pier let me pass and I went on down the gloomy, cavernous corridor with the little offices on either side. One's feet rang hollowly on the boards. At the far end there was an arc of daylight, where half a dozen tugboats, moored to the jetty head and to one another, rose and fell slowly. Each door bore a brass plate . . . *Watkyn, Sun, Gamecock.* Drewsters was the last.

There were four tugboat skippers sitting on a bench in the agent's office, waiting for their next assignment. The agent, pleasant and dark, sat at a desk and between telephone calls and making entries on a chart of some kind, exchanged abuse with the skippers. He was very helpful.

"Pewsey? Pewsey? Yes. . . ." He scuffled among the papers with which the desk was littered.

"That's my deckhand," said one of the skippers. I learned afterwards that this was Stallybrass. He was rolling a cigarette on his vast belly, like an old woman knitting. "Gone queer," he said. "Been queer a couple of days now."

My alarm mounted suddenly. "Has anybody else been asking for him?"

The agent pondered. Then he looked up. "Yes," he said. "Now I come to think of it, there was a chap in here a couple of days ago asking for Pewsey's address."

"Did you get his name?"

"No. Big fellow. . . ."

That was enough. The local station was warned again and they set up a day and night watch on Pewsey's home. Bletchley was told and he, too, stood by. There was no object in advising Pewsey himself; he would probably have run for it and doubled the difficulty of keeping him under surveillance. When there was nothing more to be done, we waited.

2

We waited for Davidson, but what Davidson waited for he was never able to explain. For his purpose to crystallise again. Suddenly, too suddenly perhaps, he had reached his first objective—had almost stumbled over it. I suppose it was to be expected that he should recoil to gather himself. It was almost as if in the heat of the pursuit and sighting of his quarry, he had forgotten what it was he wanted Pewsey for. He sat in the cabin of the barge for two nights and a day and went to the café only once in that time. Jackson saw him and gave him a mallard he had shot. He dropped it on the table; Davidson did not even raise his head. So Jackson, encouraged, brought him mugs of tea, which he drank.

He must have been aware that he was watched; he saw Bletchley, and Craig also, several times during those days. I don't really think it troubled him, for he must have known the police were likely to be interested in his movements; indeed the governor of the prison had told him so at that last interview: "We know what you are contemplating, Davidson. Well, let me warn you . . . ." Then they had taken him to the railway station in the prison laundry van and had left him there, and the warder bouncing on the tail-board had waved through the dust and Davidson had started after them, calling to them to take him back, take him back. . . .

Another thing that troubled him was that if he made an attack on Pewsey then we, the police, would have every reason to intervene before he could move against Fay Driver. Craig, I think, in believing that Davidson would somehow make his intentions known to Pewsey and Fay and then await their impatience and curiosity, under-estimated the effect of seventeen years of penal servitude on a man of Davidson's sensibility. Davidson had in fact no such plan; he was too tired in body and soul even to contemplate such a thing; his yearning in any event was too urgent for cold calculation; it was to himself, or to the memory of himself as a boy, that he owed the debt, not really to Tim Pewsey and Fay.

Number 11 Orchard Lane was one of a row of cottages, very small and tumbledown, nor far above the river's level. There was only one side to the lane; the other was a high, tarred timber fence bordering a narrow walk. The cottages had each a tiny garden at the front, with a tiled path leading from the door to the walk.

You reached Orchard Lane by crossing an open space between the rows of dingy houses—a small area of waste land overlooked by a school. When I reached the waste land there was a constable at the end of the lane. Lower down, Bletchley stood at a street corner. I got out of the car and crossed over to have a word with the constable.

"Is there somebody at the back of the house?"

"Yes, sir."

"Good. Now, I want you to let him see you, you under-stand? Look him straight in the face as he passes you . . . you've got your eye on him: no nonsense. When he goes up to the house, follow him. Stand at the gate. If he enters the house, go up to the door. If you hear a call or a voice raised or anything sounding like a scuffle, break in. Break the window if you have to. But get in. Got that?"

I returned to the car and sat in the back seat, from which there was an adequate view.

We waited a full hour. There were several constables in

the vicinity; now and then they appeared at the street corners giving on to the open ground and then strolled away again. At four o'clock the town clocks began to strike and then there were children coming out of the school. First there was a boy, lustily shouting; then a group of little girls, very contained and demure; then many, clamorous and gay. And suddenly Davidson was among them, coming diagonally across the waste land from the street behind me and up to my left. His head was down and his hands were deep in his pockets. The children swirled about him.

When he saw the constable at the end of Orchard Lane he stopped. He looked over his shoulder; there was a uniformed man at every corner. I saw him look at the car I sat in.

Presently he went on, but slowly. He was looking at the numbers on the doors. He stopped at number eleven and, stooping, opened the little gate, which swung back juddering drily in its hinges. As he went up the path the constable moved to the gate. We heard the knocker. Then he was talking to somebody. When the constable moved up to the door we knew Davidson had gone in.

I got out of the car and at the same time Craig passed me; I recognised the greasy felt hat and called to him, "How did you find your way here, Mr. Craig?"

He turned. "Hallo. I wondered if it was you. Find my way? Well, it's not hard. Bletchley follows Davidson. I follow Bletchley." He grinned.

"Go to hell."

"Presently, presently."

The wait was almost unendurable, though I suppose it could not have been more than ten minutes. When Davidson came out and walked away across the waste land and Bletchley set off after him, I drew a deep breath of relief.

3

I knocked at the door of the cottage and Mrs. Pewsey opened it. She was holding a moist handkerchief to her eyes as if there had been, or should have been, a flow of tears from them. Possibly there had been, so she continued to make the appropriate motions. Mrs. Pewsey was a stout, shapeless woman with dishevelled grey hair and purple cheeks, but a decent soul, I think, as capacious and homely as a shopping-basket. She peered round the door blinking her swollen eyes. "Yes?"

"Is Tim Pewsey at home?"

"He's not here," she said. Her glance went uncertainly beyond my shoulder, to the gate, where the constable had been. "What is it you want?"

"I understand he lives here."

"He's not here." The tears came welling up into her eyes again. I was mystified. "He's gone away. Who is it wants him?"

I told her. "The police." Her eyes widened. "Are you Mrs. Pewsey?"

"Yes. What's he done?"

"Nothing. There's nothing to worry about. . . ." She began to whimper. "May I come in and talk to you?"

She opened the door a little wider and I stepped into the tiny hall. She followed me with her eyes. "He's got himself into trouble," she said suddenly. "I knew it. I knew he would. What's he done?" she quavered.

"Nothing wrong, Mrs. Pewsey."

"It's that other man . . ."

"Which?" I said.

She stopped. When she shuffled into the living-room I followed her. Then she faced me and I could see she had made up her mind about something. Her expression was determinedly vacuous; she folded her hands. "Mr. Pewsey isn't here," she said.

"Where is he?" I was getting alarmed.

"How should I know?" She sniffed and touched her nose with the handkerchief; but the resolution was wavering already.

I said: "You're his wife, Mrs. Pewsey. I must ask you where he's to be found."

"He's gone," she said, "that's all I know. Gone. So it's no use coming to me any more, I'm not responsible." The tears defeated her. "He's made his choice."

I tried again. "Couldn't you tell me where he's gone, Mrs. Pewsey?"

"Where?" Then suddenly she blazed as the enormity of it swept over her again. "He's gone off by his self with another woman," she gritted, "that's where he's gone."

I sank on to a chair.

"He's gone off with an usherette from the Odeon," she said. "The damned old fool."

"With another woman?"

"Yes. Didn't you know?"

"No. How should I——"

"Then you're about the only nosy parker in Gravesend that doesn't."

"When did this happen?"

"Last Friday." She sniffed and dabbed at her eyes. "I comes home from a cup of tea with Mrs. Spicer up by the ferry and there he is, gone. Gone off with a girl he's old enough to be the father of. She's got three kids of her own. So what he'll do, I don't know."

"Oh, I expect it'll all work itself out, Mrs. Pewsey," I said.

She was still talking, shifting from anger to blank hopelessness and, most touchingly, to a fine indifference. "Left a letter. My dear wife, he says, him that hasn't called me his dear wife in fifteen years. My dear wife . . . I've got it here. . . ." She fumbled in the pocket of her apron. "No, I must have put it down somewhere. . . ." She began to move about the little room, picking things up to peer beneath them, lifting the bowl of fruit and the table centre and looking behind the clock aimlessly, talking as she did so. "He's deeply in love, he says, with Gladys. Love, mind you, at his age. Makes you sick. It's downright disgusting. Love. Going on forty-nine and bald as an egg. . . ." She shook her head. "I can't find it, I must have put it down somewhere." She drew a deep shuddering breath. "I've tried. I've talked to him. No, he will do it. So I said, all right, Tim Pewsey, if you've got to make an exhibition of yourself . . . the silly fool . . ." She dabbed angrily at her eyes. "He thinks he's still a boy. He thinks he's still a boy, you see. . . ." She cried gently into the wet rag. "And her . . ." An expression of bitter triumph stole into the round, drooping face. "Her. Well, it serves her right."

I began again, as gently as possible. "Mrs. Pewsey, there was a man here this afternoon——"

"Yes, and he's another of them."

"Another of which, Mrs. Pewsey?"

"One of them that's carrying on with the shipping. I know them. They want him back. Well, he's not to go. He's stopped it." She was talking directly to me now. "You're the police. Tim's got nothing to do with it, whatever it is, so you can leave him alone. He's promised me he'd never have anything to do with it again." She must have thought Davidson had come as the agent of a gang of waterfront pilferers.

"Who is the woman he has gone with?"

"I told you. An usherette from the Odeon."

"Where does she live?"

She looked at me, blinking her reddened eyes. "What do you want to know for? He's had nothing to do with them."

"Mrs. Pewsey, your husband may be in some danger."

A little of the colour left her face. "Danger?" She began to whimper again.

"There's nothing to worry about. We'll take care of him. But we have to know where he is."

"What danger? From him?—that man?"

"Yes."

"Why? Tell me why."

"I can't tell you that, Mrs. Pewsey, not now. But we want to know where your husband is. We must have the address."

"What are they going to do? Davidson . . ."

"That's the man. Did you tell Davidson the address?"

"Yes. . . ." The handkerchief went to her mouth.

"Then surely you can tell the police?"

And at last she told me.

CHAPTER FIVE

I

IT WAS Bletchley who saw them return on the second night. He stood on the landing stage and watched the tiny navigation lights, the green and red and at the masthead the white, drawing nearer, and heard the measured drumbeat of the Billy. The bawley bumped the timbers gently and he felt the shock in his feet as the boards swayed and creaked. Far away under the Essex shore the Chapman Light winked above the shoals and the thin white blade moved serenely round the sky; you felt it must make a noise and, because it didn't, that your hearing was somehow at fault: a tenuous cutting sound, like that of a scythe, as it came and passed and died away. Bletchley withdrew and from a distance watched the dark figures climb up on to the boards and cross the open ground. For a moment they were outlined in the bright doorway of the café as they entered. A thread of music escaped and made off on the wind.

Gedge's café had, I think, a strange fascination for Davidson. It was like a shop window where fragments of life were displayed in a clear white light—the life of which he had had so fleeting a taste and which he had forgotten; the memory remained, as something seen, but the flavour had gone. And here, in the café, people came and went and talked aloud and were concerned with their own problems and loves and hates, and they left him alone. Only the girl, Elsa, intruded. She had not looked at him again since the night she had smiled. But he remembered it, and when she was there behind the counter he was taut and strained and uneasy, without knowing exactly why; it was as if something beckoned; his shoulder was stiff against the hand that seemed to touch it. But he was learning. Pewsey had taught him another lesson. You needed to be a little brazen with yourself.

Elsa was behind the counter when he entered with Barney Scotson that night. He did not look in her direction. He sat down with his back to the counter and Barney took the seat opposite. When the girl brought the cups of coffee to the table, and then the sandwiches, he kept his eyes from her face. There was laughter in the room beyond the curtained door and presently Alice Gedge's voice: "Elsie! Elsie!"

When they had finished Barney said: "I'll go and hand this in." He patted his pocket. A moment after he had gone Alice came in. She saw Davidson alone at the table.

"Oh hullo, dear," she said. "All alone?" She stood over him. "Been shrimping, have you?" She had been drinking and her breath was heavy. "Why don't you come and have a drink?" She slipped into the chair Barney had vacated. "Come on. . . ."

"No. Thank you."

"Why not?"

"I'd rather not. If you don't mind."

She studied him reflectively, smiling. "You know, you're a bit of a dark horse," she said, "aren't you?"

"Am I?"

"I've been watching you."

He set his teeth. "Have you?"

She nodded. "I'm interested in you. You've suffered." She nodded wistfully. "You've had a lot of suffering."

He put his fists beneath the table.

"We must have a chat some time." She smiled. "Then you can tell me all about it."

Barney Scotson returned and Alice got up with an exclamation of impatience and left them alone.

Barney said: "They want to see you."

"Who?"

"Gedge and Fryer. It's all right. Just to have a look at you." He dropped his voice. "Go on. There'll be jobs for you."

Reluctantly he went, through the curtained door which led not, as he had always thought, to another room, but to a dark, draughty passage. There were two or three doors giving on to the passage, but they were all closed. He felt the cold night air in his face and saw that the door at the end was ajar; it seemed to lead out into the yard at the back of the building, for he saw the outline of a little tool-shed with the stars above and, believing that this must be the place they meant, he went towards it.

As he stepped out into the yard he heard a faint cry and, this abruptly stifled, the sound of a struggle and then a man's voice cursing. It was Shaw, the burly gumbooted fellow he had seen talking to Fryer once or twice. Davidson was too surprised to defend himself; the onrush was totally unexpected. He felt a dizzying blow on the side of his head. It was not so much the weight of the fist as the weight of the man which threw him over, however, for Shaw was drunk and reeling. Bletchley, who saw the scuffle, said that Shaw was standing over the prostrate Davidson, then, kicking him viciously.

Davidson got up and as Shaw came at him again he hit out—a wild, inexperienced, swinging blow which missed altogether. Then Shaw hit him again and he went down again. He struggled to his feet and lashed out blindly and Shaw swung his fist and they both failed to connect, for Shaw was drunk and Davidson had never struck a man with his fist before, and so they reeled ineffectually against one another in the dark, till Davidson caught the man beneath the ear and Shaw went down, Bletchley said, and lay still. Davidson stood over him, breathing huskily.

Nobody saw Elsa till she moved. She was crouching among the spades and forks and hoes on the floor of the shed. She was shivering and her teeth chattered. Once, incongruously, she hiccupped.

Then in the silence they heard Alice Gedge: "Elsie! Elsie!"

The girl whispered: "Take me away from here." She was weeping soundlessly. Her voice rose: "Take me with you, take me with you. . . ."

Davidson turned and they heard him lumbering away in the dark.

Bletchley, reporting the incident, said: "It looked like rape to me, sir—attempted, anyway." He was very solemn. I remember that was the first time it occurred to me that Elsa would play a part in Davidson's story.

2

We were outside Gladys's house then. It was in the East Milton area of Gravesend. Gladys's husband had been killed in an accident at the gas works and Gladys received a small pension which she supplemented by working as a cinema usherette or shop assistant or whatever offered. She was small and neat and pert and, I came to learn, wholly unscrupulous where her own welfare was at stake. She had ash-blonded hair and a quantity of Woolworth jewellery, most of which she wore all the time. She herself was not unattractive in her way, but her children, who were aged four, five and six, were the most repellent children I have ever met; while I talked to Gladys and she told me what had passed in the house during the two days of Davidson's siege, they gathered about me and, with a kind of gloomy greed, subjected me to a selection of tortures whose ingenuity was little short of remarkable. I could imagine what Pewsey had suffered. However, Gladys was well charged with sex and it was not difficult to account for his earlier infatuation.

I saw Craig again while I was having a look round the outside of the house—it was the last in a row of council cottages and so was surrounded on three sides, as it stared

down the hill, by allotments and weed-infested open land
—and this time forbore to ask him how he had discovered
the address; I was getting somewhat fatalistic about
Craig; no doubt he had followed Bletchley again.

"Some time I've got to write something about all this,"
he said morosely. "Some time soon."

"Have you? Why?"

"Haven't we talked about that?"

"You're wasting your time."

"I spoke to Asprey last night. He says if I don't write it,
or won't, he'll send somebody down who will."

I looked at the sad face and the eyes slipped away and
narrowed defensively. "He asked me if you were around."

"What did you say?"

"I told him you were."

"You got it from him, did you?—my interest in this."

"Yes. I told him there wasn't anything to write about
and he said he knew damn well there was. The usual."

"Go on."

"That's about all really. He says I've got myself involved again." He spoke with a weary bitterness. "Told
me I've gone and fallen in love with my victims again.
Gone sloppy. Says he's getting sick of my crocodile tears
and why the hell can't I just write the bloody story without
all this messing about every time, the bastard."

"You'd better write something, hadn't you?"

It was then that we saw the woman coming down the
street. I recognised Mrs. Pewsey, stout and waddling; she
was carrying a shopping basket. She went up the path to
Gladys's house.

3

For a day and a night following Davidson's visit and my
own, Mrs. Pewsey maintained her anger against her
husband. She clung to it, feeling it to be righteous and
justified, fending off the insidious anxiety which over-

whelmed her the moment, so to say, that she turned her back. If Pewsey had run away with a hussy like Gladys, if he had got himself into trouble with the police, if another of those whom she knew to be trafficking illicitly in the estuary was on his heels, if he, Tim Pewsey, were, as I had told her, in danger, then let it be so. He would have to learn.

Such was her frame of mind when she filled the basket with Spanish onions, which are said to be good for colds, with two pairs of socks that he had left behind, with a woollen vest and a bottle of camphorated oil, and put it all by in case she should later change her mind . . . a contingency as natural and fortuitous as tomorrow's rain, and to be accepted as philosophically.

She did change her mind.

It was Gladys who opened the door, the three children crowding at her heels. "Yes?"

"Tim Pewsey," said Mrs. Pewsey firmly.

Gladys called over her shoulder. "Tim!" She went back into the kitchen. Presently Pewsey came to the door.

Pewsey had changed very little in seventeen years. He was nearing fifty now, but he still wore the white sweater and rubber shoes of his youth. I don't think he was by nature a bad man; he was only weak and volatile, trying to be bold; the ferocity of his broken nose, in the context of his bald head and childish face, was comic.

When he saw his wife his mouth fell open and the strength ebbed from his limbs. He glanced over his shoulder in the direction of the kitchen, and then back to Mrs. Pewsey.

"What d'y'want?" he whispered.

Mrs. Pewsey looked at his face. Then she nodded. "Every November," she said, "regular as clockwork." She stepped into the hall. "How much is it this time? Have you taken it?"

He wilted and gave in without a struggle. "A hundred and one and a half," he said limply.

"I thought so. Can see from the look of you."

Gladys came into the hall on high heels, jewellery flashing in the lobes of her ears and round her neck. She stopped short, frowning.

"Who's this?" she said.

Pewsey made a gesture of helplessness. Mrs. Pewsey said bitterly: "Couldn't you see he's got a temperature?"

Gladys looked from one to the other.

"It's Mrs. Pewsey," Tim said huskily. He eased the muffler round his throat and blew out his cheeks. The pale round faces of the three children stared up at him.

"Mrs. Pewsey?" Gladys whispered.

"That's right," said Mrs. Pewsey. She set down the basket and drew the pin from her hat and took it off.

Gladys exploded. "Well, really!"

"It's no good getting excited," Mrs. Pewsey said.

"My God, you've got a nerve. Who said you could come in here? He's told you he's left you——"

"Now, dear," Pewsey began.

"You shut your trap," said Gladys. "Tell her to get out of my house. She ought to be ashamed."

"I've told her."

"Well, you'd better tell her again."

"Flo," he began, clearing his throat.

"Don't imagine I've come to stay," said Mrs. Pewsey. "I'm not a one that needs telling twice."

"Then what's she hanging about for?"

Mrs. Pewsey said acidly: "I suppose you want a corpse in the house, in front of the children?" Her voice shook a little. "Look at him. Look at his face. His eyes is glazed already. He could die for all you'd lift a finger."

"Die?"

"I know your type, my girl. Yes, die."

"Either this silly old bitch gets out," said Gladys, "or I get angry, one or the other. So make up your minds before I lose my temper."

"Don't you go calling me names, my girl."

"It's all right, Gladys," Pewsey said miserably.

"It's not all right. It's disgusting, hanging about here after what's happened. I've got my morals. You know what you promised."

"What did he promise?" Mrs. Pewsey enquired.

"Never mind," Gladys said. "There's the children."

There indeed were the children. They stood among the knees and stared up expressionlessly. There was a placid malevolence in the faces of those children, I recall, such as is not uncommon in the faces of certain animals. Their noses ran and they sucked sweets as a cow sucks a cud, turning it ruminatively, and they listened.

"Well," said Gladys, "what's she come for?"

"If you want to know," Mrs. Pewsey said, "I've come to rub his chest."

Pewsey went into the living-room and sank on to the sofa and put his throbbing head in his hands.

4

I was never able to elicit from Pewsey a coherent or even credible account of his career as a boxer. I believe he had had three or four fights as a feather-weight, which he lost, but which were unimportant. He had drifted into boxing-booth exhibitions and at one time was attached in that capacity to a travelling circus: he challenged all comers, one of which, unexpectedly, broke his nose. His ring career came to an end. He continued, however, to speak of himself as a professional boxer, to talk the correct jargon, to shadow-box and click his teeth, and recall his non-existent triumphs. He lived in a dream-world of heroic come-backs, of cheering multitudes, of perfect triumph, and it was out of that world that came the things he did which, in this one, were only pathetic or ridiculous. One of these was his abandonment of his wife for Gladys.

The romance did not prosper. It had not been so bad, he told me, while he had been at work, for then he returned only in the evening when Gladys's children were either in bed or so tired that their presence, that perpetual hostile audience, was not intolerable; there was room for love.

Gladys's attitude, however, was not all it might have been. She accepted him as a man about the house rather than as a lover, and was impatient of his efforts to conjure up the romantic aura which he seemed to think proper to the affair. She was extremely matter-of-fact. And when he caught a cold and developed a fever she made no secret of her irritation; the children, moreover, taking their cue from their mother, were at pains to cause him the maximum of further discomfort; to keep himself in Gladys's favour he swallowed and laughed at their evil pranks and this emboldened them still more; they left pins and half-sucked sweets on his chair, tied lengths of cord across the doors so that he would fall headlong, and let off small bombs in the hearth.

But he had a pride and when Mrs. Pewsey arrived he did his best to conceal his wretchedness from her, making light of his disappointments and much of his love for Gladys. He was also very resentful of his wife's interference; it made him look a fool in the eyes of his beloved.

Mrs. Pewsey was unmoved. She set her basket on the table and began to take out the things she had brought. She said at last: "Tim, what have you been doing?"

"Doing?"

"The police has been."

He paled a little and sat up. "Been where?"

"Home, looking for you. They wanted to know where you were."

"What for? I haven't done anything."

She set the bottle of camphorated oil on the table. "It's those men on the river, isn't it?"

He looked at her astonished. "I don't know what you're

5

talking about," he said. "Honest. I never been near them, not for years."

"The police says you're in danger."

He stood up. "Danger? What danger?"

"That's what they said."

"Who? who was it came?"

"I told you, the police. You're in danger, they said. I thought I'd better tell you in case," she added, heavily ironic, "in case you got blinded by love."

"But what sort of danger?"

"You should know." She peered into the basket. "I brought you some onions. There's a big fellow with bushy eyebrows," she said.

"The police?"

"No, him. One of those fellows on the river."

Alarmed now and exasperated he cried: "Christ, can't you say something clear?"

"Don't you swear at me, Tim Pewsey," she told him. "You've given up the right to do that."

"Listen," he began. "There's been two men, one of them's a big feller and the other's a policeman . . . that right?"

"That's right. That's what I said."

"And the police says I'm in danger. What from? From him—the other feller?"

"Yes."

"Who is it?"

She looked at him. "Don't tell me you don't know."

"How the hell should I know who it is?"

"Where's your chest?" she said, uncorking the bottle and rolling up her sleeves. "Lie down there. Take off that jersey."

"For God's sake——"

"Lie down on the couch."

"I'll get more cold."

"Pull it up, then."

"Did he tell you his name?"

"Yes, I've got it written down." She looked in her hand-bag for the scrap of paper. "Davidson," she read out. "That was it. Davidson."

She followed him to the sofa. "Lie down," she said. "Pull up your jersey." She poured a little oil into the palm of her hand. "How did you get it this time? You'd think you'd have learned by now."

His face was grey. Mrs. Pewsey bent over him and applying the oil to his chest, kneaded the ribs, not without a certain grim satisfaction. He stared up at her.

"Love," she said contemptuously. "At your age." She ground into his chest with her knuckles. "Silly fool."

5

First came fear, small but shrill. Bluster followed like a high wind, to cover the tracks the fear had left across his heart. Volubly he talked to himself, explaining, reassuring: there was nothing to worry about. But it is always hard to satisfy one's own doubts—harder, sometimes, than to satisfy other people's. So he was glad when she asked him, "Who it is, Tim?" quietly, to tell her; if he could cope with her anxiety, then his own would cease to trouble him perhaps. He told her about Davidson. Some of it she knew already. He told her again.

"If he got a fair trial, then," she said with some per-spicacity, "what's he hanging about for?"

"'Course he got a fair trial, same as all of us. Have you ever heard me complain?"

"The police says he's dangerous."

"Okay, okay. Let them. If he comes snooping around me he'll get a dose of the old one-two one-two."

"Lie still." She massaged his chest with strong, red fingers. "What is it he wants?"

"How should I know what he wants?"

"I just thought you might. Did you tell any lies, Tim, that time?"

"Who says I did?"

"Nobody, far as I know." She looked at the bright, fevered face. "You're all of a sweat."

"I hate the smell of this stuff."

"It's good for you." She rubbed it into his ribs steadily. "She's not going to like it, is she?"

"Gladys? What's it to do with her?"

"You'd better ask her. Doesn't she love you?"

"'Course she does. Deeply."

"That's nice."

"You've took it well, I must say that. It can't be helped, Flo. When it's love, I mean. You have to do what it tells you. You'll be all right."

"Don't you worry about me."

"You'd like her, Flo, if you got to know her."

"I haven't done with her yet."

"Now don't go and start a row."

"Silly old bitch she called me. Well, we'll see. There." She stood back and corked the bottle and he pulled down the jersey and sat up.

"You didn't tell him where I was, did you, Flo?"

"I did."

He stared at her, aghast. In the kitchen Gladys was clattering the crockery. Her fury hung in the air like gas, needing only a naked spark to set it off. Presently they heard her call: "Tim!"

He swallowed.

"Tim!"

"Hallo."

"Put the cat out." She asserted her proprietorship of him. If he had walked out of the house alone she would probably have wished him good riddance, but she would not lightly surrender him to another woman. "The cat's wanting to go out."

"You stay where you are, Tim Pewsey," said Mrs. Pewsey. "Do you want to catch your death?"

"Tim!"

Mrs. Pewsey raised her voice. "He's not to go out. Do you want him to catch his death?"

Gladys came into the hall and stood at the door of the living-room. "The cat's his job," she said.

"He's not to go out," said Mrs. Pewsey. She drew in her chin. "His pores is wide open."

"I don't care if they're open or shut——"

"No, I don't suppose you do. No more do I, to tell the truth. But I won't see murder done. I've just oiled his chest."

"I know that. The whole house stinks of the stuff. But it won't do him harm to put the cat out."

"Yes, it will."

Pewsey said: "For Christ's sake . . ." The children watched him speculatively.

"You hold your tongue, Tim Pewsey. I've told you before about using language like that."

"Is he going to do it?" said Gladys.

"I'll put the thing out——"

He went into the hall and picked up the mewing kitten. He switched on the light and carried the creature to the door. When he opened the door and the bar of light fell across the path in the darkness he saw Davidson there, walking towards him. He dropped the cat and flung the door to and threw all his weight against it, slipping frantically on the mat, calling in a hoarse voice for help. The three children watched with flat incurious black eyes.

CHAPTER SIX

I

WE WATCHED Davidson a whole day, outside the house. He himself had no recollection of the passage of time. Now and then he heard the town clocks chiming. Once or twice people went up to the door; there was a milkman; then the baker; then an errand boy. He would have gone up to the door himself; he had made himself ready and was about to move. But the milkman arrived; then it was the baker; then an errand boy. And these were really the only moments of respite, because while they were at the door there was nothing he could do, and the agony let up till they had gone. Then it returned.

He tried telling himself he was waiting for a very particular moment and that he would know, would get some sort of signal, when it arrived. He would count a hundred; he would wait till that dog had gone. So he counted and waited, with a thundering heart. Each failure was more deadly than the last.

He was glad in a way to have the police at his back, watching him: it showed we were taking him seriously, at his own estimation. We lent his purpose a high, taut gravity.

He would not know what to do, he told himself, when he would get there and Pewsey would open the door. But he knew well enough: he had known for seventeen years: he knew what he had to do. So he looked inwards, to the smouldering passion in his heart and, by thinking on it, tried to fan it into bright, searing flame; it glowed, but it wouldn't erupt. Was life too precious? Hardly. He would pay with his life, no doubt; or he would return to prison;

but he would have been glad enough of either. He had never thought beyond this moment; life had always ended here; how could he begin again? The boy who had had his name had vanished; he could remember him, vaguely, but only for his absence, like a younger brother who had died many years ago, and this man, this tired effigy, had little to live for. He was not afraid of death.

So he stood beneath the street lamp in the twilight and we watched him while he watched Pewsey's door. He told me later that he could hear in his mind the stammered explanations that Pewsey would blurt out, like a man who owes you a sum of money and, unasked, inflicts on you the embarrassment of his excuses, knowing you have avoided him because you are afraid of just this: yet he must explain. But Davidson wouldn't listen, because he knew the moment of hesitation would be utterly fatal, and it was worse to try and then fail than not to try at all, because after failure there would be nothing left anywhere. Yet he must try.

Bletchley said: "We could take him in, sir, if you liked. Loitering with intent——"

Craig muttered: "I'm going to talk to him."

We watched Craig walk down the street towards the tall figure under the lamp. He touched Davidson's arm and began: "Listen, old chap," very gently; "why don't you come and have a drink?"

It must have been the sign the man had been waiting for. At all events he moved on it. We saw him leave Craig without a word and start across the street. When he was half-way up the path and we were closing in, the door opened and there was Pewsey with the cat in his arms.

2

Pewsey fought with the hall-stand, to push it against the door. Panic sat giggling on his shoulders. Mrs. Pewsey cried: "Tim, what's the matter?" and Gladys stood arms

akimbo in the kitchen and said: "Have you gone crazy?"
Against the hall-stand, and on it, he piled the chairs.
Sweat streamed down his chubby, fevered face. Then he
stood back, panting.

He muttered suddenly: "The back door. . . ."

He scattered the children and ran past Gladys into the
kitchen. They heard him shoot the bolts and then the
shrill whimper of table legs on the linoleum as he rammed
it against the panels.

Gladys began: "Now just what the hell——"

"Quiet!" he barked.

They all listened; there was no sound but the mewing of
the kitten beyond the windows, for the creature now
wished to return.

"The windows," he said. He stumbled into the living-
room and bolted the windows and attended to the blinds.
He ran from room to room, closing the windows and
latching them and drawing the curtains. Then he seemed
to expire like a punctured balloon; he leaned against the
door jamb and wiped his face with his sleeve; his breathing
was fast and murmurous.

"Tim!"

He looked at his wife and his eyes came back into focus.
"Is it him?"

"It's him." He swallowed and moistened his lips.

"That man? Davidson?" Her hand went to her
neck.

"Yep."

Gladys said: "Now will somebody kindly tell me——"

"Sst!"

They fell silent again, frowning. The children stood in a
group. The smallest of the three began to cry.

"What sort of a game is this?" Gladys demanded,
exasperated. "Cops and gangsters? As if I didn't see enough
of them six days a week five times a day?" Her stencilled
eyebrows drew together and the jewellery flashed and
glittered beneath her ears. "Take those things away from

that door. Look at the mess you're making . . ." She
started to shift them herself.

"Leave them alone!" Pewsey told her fiercely.

I think she must have realised then that this was no
game.

Gladys's version, and Pewsey's and his wife's, of the
events of that night were different in detail as their natures
and viewpoints varied, but the gist of the story, steering an
erratic course somewhere between pathos and buffoonery,
was pretty constant. Poor Pewsey. He must surely have
had, as he looked from one to the other of those two women
and the three children with whom he had shut himself in,
some premonition of the torment to come: perhaps he had:
but he could never have known what he would do at the
end of it. He had no time in which to think in any case,
for it was already upon him.

"What is it he wants?" Mrs. Pewsey said. Her voice rose.
"Tim, what have you done?"

"For Christ's sake——" The windows rattled and his
eyes widened.

Gladys said vigorously: "I want to know what's going
on in my house."

"Nothing's going on. Listen . . ."

"I'm about fed up with this," Gladys announced.

"Can't you keep quiet?"

"No, I can't. And what's more, I won't. Now is somebody going to tell me——"

Pewsey said desperately: "Oh, it's a feller I used to
know. Old sparring partner. Thinks I did him a bad turn
or something, years ago. Now he's turned up again."

"The police says he's in danger," Mrs. Pewsey quavered.

"Who's in danger?" Gladys's brow darkened. "Him?"
She looked at Pewsey.

"Yes."

"You mean the chap outside . . . where is he?"

"He was there when I went to put the cat out," Pewsey
told her.

5*

"So he's come after you, has he?" Gladys said. "Well, I don't know what you did to him, Tim Pewsey, and I don't care, but whatever it is, it serves you damn well right." She nodded, narrow-eyed.

"What's up with you?" Pewsey enquired sulkily. "I did him no wrong."

"Maybe you didn't," said Gladys, "and maybe you did. But I'm telling you this . . . whatever he wants to do to you he's not going to do it in this house, I can tell you that. So you can put that hall-stand back where you found it, and those things back in the kitchen, and tidy up this mess. And then you can let the cat in."

Pewsey moved quickly to the furniture stacked against the door. "Do you want him to break in?" he cried.

"He won't break in," Gladys said. "You'll break out. If there's going to be a rough-house, it'll be outside."

"He's not to go out," Mrs. Pewsey said; "not with his chest."

Gladys set hands on her hips and addressed Pewsey. "Just exactly how long is that silly old bitch staying here?" she demanded.

"Don't you talk to me like that," Mrs. Pewsey said. "Calling me names. . . . If he goes out in his condition he'll be on his back for a month, in hospital."

"I don't care if he's on his back for twenty years," Gladys said. "There'll be no rough-house round here."

"There." Mrs. Pewsey nodded and pursed her lips. "Well, you made your choice, Tim Pewsey . . ."

"Oh, shut up," said Gladys. "Silly old hen. If you want him why the hell don't you take him? Go on, take him! Get out of my house, both of you. I don't want the little wind-bag. Anyone would think he was a catch, the way you talk. Take him," she cried, "and for God's sake let's have a bit of peace and quiet!"

"Oh no," Mrs. Pewsey said. "Oh, no. You've got him now. It's no good trying to get rid of him that way, my girl.

I shan't take him back. He's made his choice, and I wish him joy of it."

"Then what are you fussing about his chest for?" Gladys said with fair reason.

"Do you want it to turn nasty?" said Mrs. Pewsey.

She saw nothing illogical in her reply, and indeed found nothing at all irreconcilable in the two extremes of her attitude. It was too much for Gladys, however; she could make no headway in any direction; finally, fuming, she marched her three children off to bed (where they did not stay very long), and then retired herself, slamming the bedroom door. Pewsey, who was sitting on the bottom step of the stairs listening to the rattle of the windows and the mewing of the kitten beyond the front door, raised a haggard face. As he contemplated the barricades he must, I fancy, have felt rather a fool, but having erected them he was reluctant, like a man who has clothed himself too well on a cold day, to remove them. Mrs. Pewsey came out of the kitchen.

"I've put the onions on," she said. "I'll just give your chest another little going-over . . ."

"Again? But you've done it once."

"Won't do any harm to do it again. Come along."

He was too ill, I imagine, and too distraught to offer resistance, and she led him into the living-room where once more she massaged his ribs with camphorated oil.

Then, hauling him aside, she took his place on the sofa and, easing off her shoes, put up her stout legs. She would have a little rest, she said.

"It's no good looking at me like that, Tim Pewsey. I don't want you. You've done yourself now . . ."

So presently he trailed up the stairs to join his beloved.

But Gladys seemed not to want him either. When he went into the bedroom she reared up on the pillow. "Don't think you're coming in here," she cried. "You stink of camphorated oil. Phoo! Get away . . ." She put a leg out of bed and kicked him briskly in the genitals. "Get away from me. . . ."

He slept on the stairs.

It must have been about one o'clock in the morning, he said, that he woke up and saw that the barricade at the front door had gone: the hall-stand was back where it had always been. He experienced a moment of sickening horror and then, staggering to his feet, frantically shoved the hall-stand back against the door and stacked the chairs on it. As he did so he heard a movement in the kitchen and presently the squeal of the table legs on the linoleum.

The three children, waking much refreshed after a few hours' sleep, and being aware of the tension in the house, had got out of bed and crept to the head of the stairs; below them they saw Pewsey asleep on the bottom step. They had found a good deal of pleasure in baiting the unhappy fellow on previous occasions; now they saw opportunities for surprising him again. It is my belief that Gladys encouraged the notion, but she never admitted it. At all events they filed silently past Pewsey on the stairs and by their combined efforts pushed the hall-stand back to its original position.

When he ran into the kitchen and caught them in the act of shifting the table also, they fled with small grunts of pleasure and set about the barricade that he had just re-erected at the front door. They were delighted. The poor devil had tried to curry their evil favour so long, and had managed to laugh so often at their abominable torture, that now, when he was in earnest, the game was only the more interesting for them.

I suppose they went to and fro between the hall and the kitchen three or four times. He told me that the eldest of the children, a boy, stood behind a cupboard in the kitchen and let fall a broom, so that he, Pewsey, caught it between the legs and went headlong. He got up and cuffed the boy's ear and, at once realising his mistake, had then to implore the child to hush his howling. But the damage was done. Gladys came running down the stairs tying the girdle of her dressing-gown and Mrs. Pewsey stood in the door of the living-room blinking in the light and wanting to know what was amiss.

Thereafter there was no sleep. The bitter uproar continued all night. When, in the intervals, Pewsey peered between the curtains of the living-room into the quiet street, the man was still there, always there, a lonely, desolate figure beneath the street lamp with the light falling like a pale cloak about his shoulders.

In the morning Pewsey gave himself, gladly, to the police and said he wished to make a statement. There was still a certain pathetic bravado in his manner, but he looked an old man. Davidson had gone then.

Pewsey didn't know how unexpected his move was, nor how unwanted.

CHAPTER SEVEN

I

PEWSEY'S statement—I suppose you could call it a confession—landed with a sickening thud on a part of the body I had not armoured because I had thought no blow would ever land there.

He talked for threequarters of an hour, and the station sergeant took notes. It was something to flinch from; and yet there was a solid satisfaction in it; his tongue was the clapper of the bell which tolled the end; for this was it, or its beginning.

His face was a sweaty, ashen grey and his eyes shone with fever as he sat at the desk and told his story. For my part I offered neither pity nor censure, and indeed felt none, being weary of the fellow and anxious only to have done with him. So, having nothing to play upon and nothing to protest against, he didn't know where to stop. A pause for breath was only the preamble to another version of the same events, and there was everything in his manner but guilt. What he chiefly felt, I think, was a sense of outrage that life should have done this to him. It had been quite a harmless little lie, that one about Boyd's body —he hadn't thought twice about it. It had looked like Boyd's; the clothing had been Boyd's; everybody had said it was Boyd's; the trial proved it was him: who was Tim Pewsey to deny it? He hadn't really lied; it had been a matter only of not knowing for dead sure. A mistake. Anybody could make a mistake.

And now here was Davidson threatening violence, coming back after all this time to pick a fellow up on a trifling misapprehension which anyway had happened nearly twenty years ago. It was outrageous. Life had no right to do this to him; he was plainly very aggrieved. Indeed one could hardly tell which was uppermost: panic or resentment. Mostly it was resentment, for as he enlarged he became convinced that he was not really giving himself up at all: he was demanding protection and enquiring as a decent law-abiding citizen what was being done about that maniac who was allowed to rove at will about the streets of Gravesend. When I brought him back to the point with a reminder that he had just confessed to a crime of considerable gravity he was rather indignant; not grave, he corrected me, nor, really, a crime: a misunderstanding, rather, and scarcely even that: call it a belief, a belief to which he had been persuaded to give the substantiality of fact: the difference between, "I believe that is Boyd's body", and "That is Boyd's body"—which was mere hair-splitting. Why should he ever have said otherwise?—Because, I suggested, since he denied any knowledge of Delaney in order to avoid a charge of complicity in the smuggling-out of wanted men, he could not very well have identified the body as anybody else's; and when Delaney's jacket was found later, he, Pewsey, couldn't go back on his original oath without getting himself still deeper into trouble.

He brushed the suggestion aside. No, he conceived it his duty as a decent law-abiding citizen (he developed a fondness for this description of himself and used it somewhat lavishly) to place the facts before the police—with a flourish. He talked himself into jail, and back to brash confidence.

I wondered what effect it would have on Davidson. He knew nothing of it then. When Pewsey pulled down his own barricades and fled up the street that morning, Davidson had gone. It was not a failure; he swore it wasn't a failure; he was waiting only till he had found Fay Driver also.

2

In the afternoon I returned to London and after a shave went to see Flood. He eyed me benevolently. "Come in, Lowther, come in. Lowther, I do believe you're losing weight," he said.

"I'm not surprised. It's about Davidson . . ."

"Oh yes." He laid down his pen.

A man came in with a cup of tea. Flood said to him. "Bring a cup for Commander Lowther, will you?" He went on again: "About Davidson . . ." I suggested I should wait till the tea arrived. "Oh, very well."

We waited. The big clock ticked on the wall and the traffic murmured in the street below the windows. The tea came. I took a sip and said:

"Pewsey has made an important statement."

"Pewsey?" He began to turn it over in his unfathomable mind, his face a mask.

"One of the original witnesses." He knew exactly who Pewsey was. I continued: "Statement isn't quite the word perhaps. Confession." I watched his face. "He admits that the body he identified as Boyd's might not have been Boyd's."

"Bless my soul. Has he?"

"Yes. This morning."

He pushed out his thin lips to meet the cup. "Voluntarily?" he asked, sipping.

"Entirely."

"A curious thing for a man of Pewsey's type to do, wasn't it—voluntarily? As I remember him——"

"Davidson found him."

"I see." He put down the cup.

"—A very frightened little man, I may say."

"Yes . . . Does Davidson know this?"

"Not yet."

"Does anybody else know?"

"I don't think so." He was beginning to feel his way round it.

"Well, this is very grave," he said. "This is a very serious matter indeed. Extraordinary. Good heavens. . . . He actually admitted that the body he identified as Boyd's——"

"Might have been anybody's."

"Good God. Is he in custody?"

"For the moment, yes."

"Well, if this is true——"

I said: "We have the statement."

"Properly witnessed?"

"Yes, it's in order."

I watched his finger tapping the desk. I had an idea how he felt. I had handed him his arraignment, and Fay's and my own also.

He said: "You have it in hand?"

"Good. Keep me informed." There was a faint dryness in the pursing of his lips.

For a second his face swam as if I were looking at it through clear, slow-moving water. "Naturally, naturally," I stammered. Was this all? I must have forgotten something. Inwardly I raged: one should never approach Flood without a clear idea of what one wanted.

"Did you want my advice on any particular . . ."

"No, no—perfectly straightforward."

"Well." He shifted the papers on his desk: a small polite suggestion.

Then I had it again. I had expected him to let the conversation take its course, which would have led to this thing I wanted to say. Now I had to contrive its entrance. But it would not be difficult. A few days ago he had directed me to my duty; all I wanted to tell him now—not, perhaps, without satisfaction—was that I would continue to do it. And it was a very simple one. A man had been wrongfully convicted and imprisoned. Today, evidence which would set right a little of the wrong that had been done had dropped like a rotten plum into our hands. Well, we could pass it from hand to hand as we liked; the truth was out and it was indestructible; if he threw it back to me, as he had done, he must know what I meant to do: it was no problem. The whole monstrous edifice would come toppling about our ears, and those who were lucky might crawl from the ruins and begin again, but clean then. So it all seemed; I caught the faint odour of sanctimony again.

"Perhaps," Flood was saying, "perhaps you'd like to hand over to somebody else in view of this development, Lowther . . ."

"I can manage."

"Harris . . .?"

"No." It was mine. I didn't want exposure; I wanted immolation.

"You have a family, Lowther, a son . . ."

"Yes——" I was going to heaven on Isaac's back.

"And I'm not sure it isn't highly irregular . . ." He eased his weight from one bony buttock to the other. "You have too great a personal interest, too much at stake. We are all human, Lowther."

Not you, not you.

"You can't be expected to act impartially, in the circumstances."

Yes: Fay. And Mick. "Why not?" I asked.

"My dear Lowther, since you must have it: because you might be persuaded to act in your own interests and those of your . . ."

"My family." I went cold. "You have no right to say that."

"Alternatively," he continued urbanely, "in your anxiety to avoid leaning too far backward, you may fall flat on your face."

"I shall try to do neither."

"No doubt, no doubt." He drummed lightly on the desk. At last he said: "Lowther, have you considered this matter fully? Have you any idea what the repercussions will be?"

"Yes."

"You see, Pewsey's statement is not very much use by itself. It will have to be substantiated. If it isn't, then there's really very little we can do at this stage. If it is, then of course we can act. You think the body they identified as Boyd's was—what was the other fellow's name?"

"Delaney."

"Ah, yes. Delaney. And Boyd was carried out to sea?"

"Possibly."

"Yes. You realise, don't you, that even if you do get"— he hesitated—"another confession of perjury, let us call it, you don't prove Davidson's innocence. You point out the lack of evidence, that is all."

"It's enough."

"Well . . ." He moved his shoulders. "So long as you understand the consequences."

"Perfectly."

"They will be considerable, Lowther. Not only— personal. It will cause a national uproar, I dare say."

"I hope not."

"Personally, I feel that another man on the job——"

I said: "There is only one man who can get what we need."

He looked me in the eyes and smiled faintly. I knew he was telling me: Quite so; that is why I suggested putting another man on it.

"Very well," he said at last. "Let me know if you change your mind. In the meanwhile you can count on my support in any action you may, or may not, take."

"The thing has to be put right."

He nodded. "Yes."

CHAPTER EIGHT

I

FAY HAD asked no questions; I had told her nothing. But the silence had a certain brittleness. I had not mentioned Davidson to her since the night I had told her of his release. Already it seemed long ago. He was there, of course, between us, but we ignored him by tacit agreement, as people do with explosive subjects when they have been married a long time; nothing is so important as to keep the peace. Yet I believe she knew, the day of Pewsey's thunderbolt, that something had happened; she knew instinctively that something was amiss. She was worried. She began to prompt me, not with words or innuendo, but with her silences. Slowly we reached the moment at which the silence, if not broken, would burst of its own, exploding in our eyes with a rush of wind and the tinkle of bitter fragments.

It was a Saturday night. We had driven out to a club for supper—a place on the river some way beyond Richmond of which we were, I regret, members. I detested the place and never felt myself anything but a fish out of water in its bogus luxury. There was a bar, I remember, and several lounges, a billiard room and a dining-room with, among the tables, a dance floor. The lighting of the place was brown so that people glancing at themselves in the mirrors, which appeared to be pink, had the comforting healthy tint of sun-bathers on a beach. Its members all knew one another by Christian name, especially the bald-headed dance band leader and the gay divorcees behind the bar, and were at casual pains to show themselves and one another that they were perfectly at home here and were not being taken in by all this gilt stuff. Everybody talked and laughed and used bad language a little more than they would ordinarily have done, and there was a deal of waggishness about the men and their billiards and the men and their drinking and about the girls taking their hair down to have a natter, all punctuated by the melancholy sighing of the band and the brisk muffled hiccough of the fruit machine in the gentlemen's lavatory. The owner, whose name was Vernon James, and who wore a rat-catcher jacket and suede shoes to show how informal it all was, used to go from table to table and, putting his arm about one's shoulders, ask: "Enjoying yourselves, every-body?" My bowels turned to ashes, but nobody else seemed to mind.

"You never spoke a word the whole evening," Fay said as we left and walked through the rain to the parking lot. "I know you don't like the place, but at least you can be civil to people. You snubbed poor Vernon, deliberately snubbed him."

"I don't like the man."

"Why not?"

"I don't know."

"Because he's such an old smoothie?"

"Yes." It didn't matter.

"He's only doing his job."

We got into the car. "You like coming here, don't you, Fay?" I said.

"Oh, it's somewhere to go." She looked out of the window, through the raindrops on the glass. "You never take me anywhere else."

The silence returned.

The car was an old Wolseley and I was fond of it and felt at home peering through the windscreen. The tyres hissed on the road and rain pattered on the roof and shone briefly in the headlights. The dashboard threw out a semi-circle of yellow light; Fay's legs were in it, and my own. We drove on. Then there was a car coming towards

us with big white lights and I watched the frantic sema-
phore of the windscreen-wiper to and fro across the glare
and thought, as I have thought a thousand times: now if
this fellow should swerve or if I should swerve or skid or
anything, we're all dead ducks. By the time the car had
passed, with a little rush and a sense of shock, I had
broken the silence.

"Davidson has run Pewsey to earth."

She said: "Oh yes, how's Philip getting on? I meant to
ask you."

"Very well."

"He's found Tim Pewsey?"

"Yes."

"My, he has been quick."

I thought: so this is the way it's going to be: casual
indifference: neither of us deceiving the other for one
moment, yet both of us clinging to it as if it offered some
kind of protection.

"What's he doing now? Have you found out?"

"Nothing very much. Bit of fishing."

"Fishing!" She laughed slightly. "What sort of fishing?"

"For shrimps."

"Oh . . .!" She uttered a yelp of laughter and I grinned
in the dark; hang it, it was a little incongruous. That
seemed to decide it; laughter simmered in every word
from then on, and it was only in the last minute that
we touched the knife-edge which lay just beneath the
surface.

"Was that how he netted Pewsey?" she asked, still
giggling.

"Indirectly, I think. Anyway, he's found him."

"Pewsey," she said pensively. "You know, I wouldn't
recognise him if I saw him. Wasn't that the one who was
always talking about boxing?"

"That's the chap."

"I remember. How did it happen?"

"It will amuse you, as a matter of fact. Pewsey had just

left his wife. He'd gone off with a girl from the local cinema."

"What fun! Was he living with her?"

"Apparently. That's where Davidson found him."

"Oh, my goodness. How very thoughtless. Just like Philip to crash in at the wrong moment." She laughed. "It must have cramped Pewsey's style a bit . . ." I listened to her filling in the silence with words.

"Mrs. Pewsey turned up, too."

"Oh . . ." She fairly crowed. "What a party it must have been. All three of them?"

"Four. And some children."

"My God, I wish I'd been there." She laughed delightedly. "Whatever did he do?"

"Well, Pewsey stuck it as long as he could——"

"Philip, I meant."

"Davidson never entered the house. He never got farther than the door."

"Why on earth not?"

"I don't really know. Pewsey barricaded the doors, I think." I could feel her watchfulness all the time. "He hung about outside most of the night."

"Poor old Philip. So what did Pewsey do?"

"In the morning he gave himself up to the police." Rain streamed across the windscreen and the tyres hissed on the road. She lit a cigarette and the smile on her lips glowed for a moment in the dark glass.

"Well," she said, "two women and three or four kids and then Philip . . . who wouldn't give himself up to the police?"

"He confessed to having lied about Boyd's body, Fay."

She sat quite still, staring out of the window. We were both utterly alone then. I floundered on. "He says in fact he didn't know whether it was Boyd or not."

A long time later I heard her murmur: "My God."

2

I put the car away and locked the garage doors and went into the house. Fay was in the kitchen, making tea. In the living-room the fire was grey and dead; Mick had left his jacket over the arm of the chair at the fireside; it was still damp when I touched it; he must have been out in the rain.

Fay came in with her tea and stood at the table and poured it out.

"Do you want a cup?"

"No. No, thank you."

Presently she said: "What are you going to do, Bobby?"

"Pewsey's statement isn't good enough by itself."

"What's the matter with it?"

"It has to be supported."

She was very pale. "Is that what you expect me to do?" I knew exactly how she was feeling. The desolation was in her eyes. "Who said I . . ."

"Fay, we don't have to hide it from each other any longer."

But she meant to fight. "I know your sense of duty," she said. "It's a menace." And she added: "You can leave me out of it."

"Let's get it over, Fay."

"Pewsey can make statements till he's black in the face as far as I'm concerned. What about Mickie? Do you want a statement from him, too? You might just as well—he's the one who'll suffer most." Her voice trembled. "I won't do it—you can't make me."

"I'm in it as much as you are, Fay. I've always known about it. I even tried to do something about it once—did you know? Years ago."

"What happened?"

"Nothing. I talked myself out of it."

I knew it wasn't fair to myself, put in that way; but that was how I felt, and we had reached rock-bottom.

"I don't see why it's any different now. Just because Pewsey——"

"It's enough."

"But you said his statement isn't any good by itself."

"Oh my dear, an innocent man was sent to prison for twenty years. I'm a police officer."

"Can't you forget for a minute——"

"Life wouldn't be worth living."

"Would his?" she cried. "Mickie's?"

"Fay, there are more important things——"

"All right, then—your own life. Your own career. My life. Everything we've got——"

"I know how you feel, Fay."

"I won't do it."

It was hard to blame her. Once she had all but drowned in the vortex of her own wretched youth; she had clutched at a straw to save herself; and out of that, seventeen years later, this had come. She had lied then without any true understanding of the consequences; now she looked them in the face. She was fighting for her son now as she had fought then, in a sense, for her mother.

"But Fay," I said, "if you made a mistake, then we must try to put it right. If you have to pay, well then you pay. It wouldn't be for long. I, too . . ."

"You should have done something about it before, if you thought there'd been a mistake . . . when it would have done Philip some good and Mickie no harm."

"Yes, I know. I tried and failed. I could have tried harder . . . I should have done. Oh, I'm in it just as deeply as you are. They'll pack me off, too——"

"You? Why you? What have they got against you?"

"There's such a thing as misprision."

"What's that?"

"Concealment of somebody else's crime."

"And you think I'm going to stick my neck out—Mickie's neck and your neck—just because . . ."

"Mick will understand, Fay. If he doesn't know now, he

will later on. Good God, what sort of a boy do you think
he is?"

"It will ruin his life."

"Oh, nonsense."

"It isn't nonsense. And I won't offer him up as some
sort of sacrifice. What's Philip Davidson to him? Or me,
either."

"Among other things, he loved you, Fay."

"More fool he."

"Oh, come, Fay."

"Don't expect me to behave like a saint. I'm not one. I
never was." She wrapped her bogus infamy about her like
a suit of armour.

"No, but you're not as wicked as all that."

"Aren't I?" she said. "You don't know. You don't
know."

There was something in her voice which made me look
up, but she had gone. I heard her going up the stairs.

3

I don't remember how long I sat there after she had
gone, or how long the telephone had been ringing before
it occurred to me that it would have to be answered. It
was Bletchley.

"Sorry to wake you up at this time of night, sir."

"Never mind, I wasn't asleep."

"You said I could use your private number in case of
emergency—"

"Yes. What is it?"

"Well, sir, something pretty fishy is going on down here,
and I thought you ought to know about it."

"Go on."

"Well, sir, you know the girl in this café place—some
sort of foreigner . . ."

Elsa. "Yes." I had forgotten her.

"She's moved in with Davidson."

"How do you mean—moved in?"

"Well, I rather think she's living with him."

"Well, go on."

There was a short silence. "That's all, sir. I just thought you ought to know . . ."

"Oh."

"I just thought . . ."

"Yes, all right, Bletchley. Quite right. Keep in touch."

"Right, sir."

Not quite an emergency, I thought; but very unexpected.

CHAPTER NINE

I

I DID not want to run into Bletchley and have to take
him with me, so I left the car a long way up the road and
set off across the marsh on foot. There was a great orange
sun and the wind was soft and scented. A curlew followed
me all the way.

Jackson's moustache rose like hackles when he saw who
it was. He stood in the door of his cabin with the barrel of
the shotgun in one hand and an oily rag in the other.

"What d'y'want?"

"May I come in? I'd like to talk to you."

The cabin was warm and the air alive with the odour
of ancient roots and rubble-heaps; a kettle simmered on
the stove. Through the window I could see the stern and
cabin of the hulk Davidson lived in. "Is he out?" I asked.

"Gone fishing. Nothing agin that, is there?"

"No." He began to clean the shotgun. "How is he
getting along?"

"Well enough." It struck me suddenly that something
was awry; the old fellow was angry.

"How often do you see him?"

"See him every day. Any business of yourn?"

"Well, yes, it is really."

"Then why don't you talk to him yourself?"

"He's out, you said." It was Davidson with whom he
was angry. "So I came to see you—you're a friend of his."

He dropped his eyes to the gun barrel. "That's right."
He laid down the barrel and picked up the stock. "Three
times a day a mug of tea . . . wouldn't take it if he wasn't a

friend of mine, would he?" He looked at me with a challenge.

"Does he drink it?"

It was a thoughtless cruelty and I wished it unsaid. The old man's hurt filled the cabin; he seemed to bleed quietly.

"Did do," he said. And with sudden fury: "Now he tips it over the side, thinks I can't see, but I see. I've seen him do it, every time——"

"Why does he do that, I wonder?"

"It's her," he blurted. His hands were shaking. "Things was all right till she busted in . . ."

It was comic and touching. "It will work out," I told him feebly.

So Bletchley's report was correct. It was astonishing. That a lonely man should take in a stray girl was not in itself remarkable; but this was Davidson; it was contrary to everything we knew about the man. I had thought of him as remote, single, impervious—or determined, for reasons of his own, never to embroil himself in the stream of life about him. His face had been without features—inhuman; I feared him; in a sense I had felt respect for him; but I had never pitied him. And now suddenly, this, with a jolt.

It was many months before I learned, from Elsa herself, exactly what had taken place. She, I suppose, was an ordinary little thing in most ways, yet she had a sweetness and a valour which makes it hard to think of her except as of singular beauty.

2

She stood in the light holding the bundle in her hand. Davidson had then ceased the practice of barricading the door at night, so it was open.

Her hair had been ruffled by the wind, and, though her grey eyes were wide with apprehension, she seemed bold and hard, for she had to overcome her fear and that was a good way to do it: to smile and show her small white teeth. Davidson always remembered how she stepped into his life, out of the fringe and into its tortuous pattern, with a hard, bright smile and trembling hands.

She had followed him from Gedge's café. It was dark but there were stars and the river itself seemed to hold a little of the light of the day; she had been able to keep him in sight. She had had her few clothes ready for some time —since the night Davidson had left Shaw sprawling in the door of the tool shed and Alice had found him there, and Elsa too, crouching among the spades and forks. Those three days she never forgot. Each of them, Shaw and Alice, waited on the other's absence, and then, with words or with a menacing silence, sometimes with blows, gouged into the heart of the quivering creature they hated. But at last Davidson came back, one evening when Shaw was away, and when he left she followed him.

He stared at her. Far away across the marsh the ware-house roof clanged fitfully. The wind whispered in the reeds.

"I am run away," she said with that bright, brittle smile. She spoke English rather better than Alice Gedge had thought.

He was sitting on the edge of the bunk near the stove.

She had expected recognition. "But I am run away," she said. "From that place."

He sat motionless.

"You know me?" she said desperately.

His head was a little on one side, and he stared.

"Well, I am run away."

A faint perplexity gathered about his eyes.

"I am come to you," she said. She smiled. "To you."

There was no answer.

"I will cook for you," she said. Her voice began to rise a little. "You do not pay me. I cook."

He seemed not to have heard.

"I will care for the house."

She looked into the pitiless stare.

"I will do all that you say."

And then: "I will work truly."

And then: "I will wash."

And then: "I will clean. Look . . ." Suddenly she was fumbling in the bundle with shaking hands for the worn and flattened scrubbing-brush she had stolen from Alice Gedge's kitchen, and was down on her knees scrubbing the floor at his feet, saying with that frightful brightness: "I am good. I clean well. Look, I clean truly. A little water . . ."

She looked up at him, smiling with clenched teeth. But he didn't move. She began again, scrubbing the boards with the dry brush. "Every day I clean, like this . . ." Her voice was high and thin. "I work for you, I work for you . . ." Then the muscles of her jaw snapped and her teeth began to chatter and she was crying. "You will be pleased . . ." She went on blindly scrubbing.

Suddenly he said: "Get up."

"Every day I will take care of the house."

"Get up," he said harshly.

She stopped scrubbing and sat back against the wall with her head against the door, shivering, her eyes closed. She felt herself lifted. Then she was on the bunk leaning against the wall and hearing his urgent voice.

"Listen," he was telling her. "Listen, girl."

Spasms of shivering swept up her body. "I will clean for you. . . ."

"Listen!" He took her by the shoulders and shook her. "You can't stay here, you can't stay here. Why did you come here?"

"You hurt me," she said. "Aie!"

He let her go. "Who asked you to come here?"

She shook her head.

"Why did you come? You can't stay here."

She whispered: "I am run away from that place. Do not be disturbed. I will go. In a minute I am gone."

"You must leave."

"Yes." She closed her eyes. "In a minute."

"You're not ill. You can't stay here."

"I will go."

He moved away from her. Even then he knew it was too late. "You had no right to come here," he said bitterly.

"No," she whispered. "I am sorry. I had not the right."

"You must go back."

She shook her head and her eyes closed. "No."

"You can't stay here. I . . . I don't want anybody here."

"Yes."

"Where will you go?"

"I will find a place."

"Where?"

"Do not be disturbed."

He stood in the door and looked across the dark river.

3

He rarely saw her. She cooked the food she bought with the money he would leave on the table, and then disappeared; he ate alone. She kept the cabin clean and lit the fire.

At night she slept on the other bunk, taking off her clothes in the dark with small, diminutive movements. Once when the dying fire fell in and there was a little blaze of light, he saw the white body; she turned swiftly, holding something against herself lest he should see. He was indifferent. If he saw the absurdity of the situation, he was indifferent to that, too.

He did not know where she went during the day, or what she did. But one afternoon, when he returned from the river, there was a jar on the table which contained three or four stunted red flowers standing in water. She had picked them at the foot of the rubble-dumps on the edge of the marsh, where Jackson would root for scrap iron to trundle to the yards in his old perambulator. They were bamboo blossom.

It is hard to believe that bamboo should be found in such a place, much less that it should flower there; but it does. For among the cargoes that flow into the port of London there are many from the Orient. The disposal of the packaging and cratage of these goods is quite a problem. Usually it is tipped into lighters and dumb barges which are towed down-stream to places like Mucking Flats and the marshes of the Kentish bank, and there dumped or burned or in some way rendered innocuous. The straw and hay and dried vegetation with which the goods are packed contain not only spiders and snakes such as one occasionally reads reports of in the press, but seeds, too, of all kinds.

Some of the seeds survive and take root and grow, so that in summer the rubble dumps are gay with curious oriental blossoms, among the sardine tins and bicycle wheels and rotting straw. How the bamboo that Elsa found came to bloom in that place at that time of the year nobody can say; we had had a kindly autumn certainly, and a spell of warm weather, and that may have brought it about. But there are many kinds of bamboo and it seems more likely that this was one of the type, familiar I believe in Burma, which blossoms only rarely, at long and irregular intervals with sometimes years between, and irrespective of weather or season; midwinter is lit with bright unexpected flowers.

Book Three

THE POOL

CHAPTER ONE

I

THERE were bamboo flowers on the table and the table was scrubbed as white as the floor. There was a faint smell of soap. The lamp no longer gave off an acrid black smoke. Outside the wind bumped against the walls and inside the fire throbbed. He watched her all the time. Each night when he returned from the shoals he found Elsa there. She was a perpetual reminder and her silence, her efforts to deflect attention from herself, were a nagging oppression. He knew she must go. One evening he tried to tell her.

"This is no place for you," he said. "You must find somewhere else to go."

"I am the happiest I have ever been."

"You know nothing about me."

"I do not need to know."

He shook his head. She stood across his path in a way he couldn't explain. Her desperate mute anxiety to please hung like a weight across his shoulders; wherever he went he took it with him like a shackle.

"I do not do well?" she asked piteously.

He had always known this would happen. It rose about him like a tide, like the tide of Jackson's friendship, whose cups of tea he had now to tip furtively over the beam lest he should hurt the old man by refusing them to his face and thus set him fumbling for some other crack in the wall. He hated himself for his flaccidity—for so it appeared to him.

She did well enough, he said.

"I do anything you wish."

"Then go. Don't argue: go."

"If it is what you wish."

She turned away. She understood he was forcing himself to put her out, but she had a pride; she would not angle for charity; she would argue no more.

"Tomorrow will do," he said. He could not bear to watch and listen while she packed her belongings under his eyes. She could go tomorrow, while he was away. When he returned she would have gone, and then he could begin to look for Fay Driver.

Elsa said: "If you wish it."

He nodded and was very relieved. He seemed to relax a little. He caught her eye and smiled faintly and she returned the smile. Even those few days away from Alice Gedge had made a difference to her appearance; the bluish pallor of her face had gone and there was a touch of colour in her cheeks; the scarlet weal had healed; the small breasts stood out; her movements had a certain serenity.

She could scarcely recall her parents, she told me once; they had been beautiful, she remembered, but severe, of ancient family, with a house full of servants and statues and echoes. As a child she had been herded with tens of thousands like her into camps which were moved hither and thither about the lean face of Europe like pieces in an endless ponderous chess game. She learned to accept privation, if not with resignation then as a necessary and inevitable part of life, knowing no other. She went with the rest. But in the days of the war they had heard that many people had found asylum in England irrespective of nationality, and so England became in a sense the end of every journey, for they had to believe they were going somewhere. As they grew older they grew astute and curiously wise, like tramps, childish and wise, edging their way to England. It took Elsa seven years. She wormed her way on to a ship in a Dutch port; she was employed as a kitchen hand; when the ship docked in Tilbury she ran away.

So she appeared to acquiesce in his decision. But even her submission put him in debt to her.

"There is something I have to do," he said. "It doesn't concern you." He tried to explain: it would rebound; when it exploded it would destroy not only what it was aimed at, but the thrower too, and any near him; she must understand that it was not against her that he acted. "I have something I must do."

"It is something wrong," she said. She stood under the lamp in the circle of light.

He raised his head.

"I do not stand in your way," she said.

Now she was nibbling at the decision already made.

"Why do you have to do it?"

"It's necessary."

"Somebody has done you a great wrong."

"Yes." Leave it at that; there was no explaining.

"That alone?"

He smiled. "That's all."

"And you must do it?"

"Yes."

"Perhaps you are afraid not to do it?"

He winced. She was clumsily percipient, like a precocious child. He wished he had not begun this now.

"It's not a matter of being afraid," he said.

She nodded. "I understand. I am sorry with you." She looked at the hands moving to and fro on his knees. "I would like to help you."

He shook his head.

Then she said a thing which it must have taken all her bright courage to say. The odd formality of her English lent it a kind of ceremonious elegance. With eyes averted and the hard brittle smile he already knew, she told him:

"If it is your wish, I will be your mistress."

For a moment there was a jarring stillness in the place. The wind stirred the reeds outside.

"It was for that I am come," she said. Tears were starting to her eyes. She smiled steadily.

He looked away.

"I have not before," she said. "Never."

He stood up suddenly and the table legs barked on the floor and the jar of flowers toppled and fell and water ran across the boards. He went out and the door slammed.

2

It was during the next morning, as I remember it, that Craig telephoned. I was glad; I had not seen him for a day or two and had wondered what he was up to; in any case I owed him a lunch.

"So Pewsey has come across?" he said. We had ordered the lunch and were nibbling radishes.

I asked him how the devil he knew and he grinned. "Oh, I guessed."

I watched him: this slight, soiled, inwardly despairing man who carried my fate in his hands—liking him and trusting him as I always did; the cryptic pertness of his conversation was so plainly a defence that one wanted to tell him to stop it, there was no need for it.

"Does Davidson know?" he said.

"I was going to ask you that."

"Me? How should I know?"

"You might guess."

He smiled, very pleased, and salted another radish.

"Well, what about it, Mr. Craig?"

He made a wry face. "I wish you wouldn't call me mister. Frightens the life out of me. Just Craig. I've got a Christian name, but not even my wife can stand it——" I learned afterwards it was Cuthbert—"and God knows she's patient enough." He went on: "I don't know whether

Davidson knows about Pewsey or not. I'd say not, not yet. Though I must say I think it would be charitable of some-body to tell the man."

"Do you indeed?"

"Well, I don't suppose he's feeling any too pleased with himself just now, poor old chap. Must think he's failed all along the line. Somebody ought to put him out of his misery." He threw me a glance. "Might save any amount of bother, too."

"All right, you tell him."

He looked at me under his eyebrows, turning it over in his mind. Then he said: "Too deep for me," with a shrug of the shoulders. "You'll have to explain."

"I see no reason why he shouldn't know."

"No, but why do you want him told?"

"I don't particularly. I just don't mind. I don't think it will make all that difference, myself—not to him."

"You don't think he'd drop it, then?"

"No. No, I don't. Why should he?"

We settled down to eat.

"What I really wanted to talk to you about," he said presently, "was this. . . ." I waited, aware of what was coming. "You see, from my point of view as a lowdown muck-raker . . ." He paused. "You might have the common courtesy to take me up on that," he said.

"Go on."

He began again: "From my point of view Pewsey's . . . what do we call it—confession?"

"You could call it that."

"He admitted perjury, did he?"

"More or less."

"The wrong body?"

"You're very astute, Mr. Craig."

"Just Craig, please." But he smiled. I think he believed he had tricked me into some sort of indiscretion, for the smile was a sly one. For my part, however, I was prepared to answer any question he might ask; I knew well enough

6*

that the best way to muzzle Craig was to tell him everything—to keep him emotionally embroiled. Craig would
win very few battles against his own cardinal decency. So
I piled it on. "He admitted he didn't know whether it was
Boyd or not."

"My word, he really spilled it, didn't he?"

"It was a great surprise for us all."

"I bet it was. Whatever next, I wonder?"

"You were saying——"

"Oh, yes. . . ." Then he came out with it. "Isn't
Pewsey enough? I mean, do you need any more?"

"I'm afraid we do."

"Oh. Pity. You see, from the standpoint of a bog-rat
like myself, Pewsey's confession is something of a honey as
it stands. It really is."

"I can imagine."

"It's a sort of lesser Dreyfus affair, or could be, with a
little manipulation. I'd hate to see it go astray." Again his
own distaste for the threat in his words seemed to sweep
over him; he dropped his eyes. "You know what I
mean. . . ."

"It won't go astray."

"Are things moving?"

"Not yet. Pewsey's little effort isn't much good alone."

He had his eyes on his plate. "That rather narrows it
down a bit, doesn't it?"

"Yes."

For a little while then we talked about other things. I
asked for the bill and when we got up to go Craig said:

"I wish I didn't know. If I didn't know I'd write it
now, and get the man cleared." He smiled and said again
with his queer inverted savagery: "I wish to God I'd
never set eyes on you."

3

The afternoon dragged away. I had the feeling something was happening. I felt the storm gathering, but out of sight, beyond the horizon. It was difficult to sit still. Before I left, however, I knew which direction the break would come from. The telephone rang.

"That you, sir?"

"Yes." The blithe Bletchley.

"I thought I'd better let you know, sir——"

"Fire away."

"You told me to keep you informed."

"Quite right, Bletchley, you're doing famously."

"Oh thank you, sir."

Why he, Bletchley, should have been selected by divine providence to be my particular harbinger of evil I do not know. "What is it?"

"Well, sir, there's been somebody else down here this afternoon."

"Oh? Who's that?"

"It's a reporter, sir, I think."

"How do you know?"

"Well, sir, before he went aboard Davidson's barge he called in at the café, and when he'd gone I asked Mrs. Gedge who it was, and she told me."

"Was it Craig?" But I knew it could not have been.

"No, sir, this was another fellow altogether. . . ."

I let him go on for a little while. My heart was cold and heavy.

4

I saw Mervyn Fisher only once. He came, sowed his havoc and went. I remember a narrow white face and pointed chin and bad teeth; he had a frond of red hair on the back of his head which rose and fell as he walked.

Craig described him as a ruthless little ruffian, but perhaps he did him an injustice, for Fisher was acting on Asprey's instructions; it was Asprey who told him of Davidson's whereabouts, Asprey who gave him my address. Admittedly Fisher overstepped his brief and even Asprey, I gathered, eventually washed his hands of him. But by then the mischief had been done.

For he found only Elsa, who remembered him, when she spoke of him afterwards, with a shudder. She had cleaned the cabin and prepared Davidson's meal. Her clothes were bundled; she was about to leave the place as Davidson had requested. But then Mervyn Fisher stepped into her life, indeed into all our lives. He pushed open the door of the cabin and said:

"Hallo, hallo, anybody at home?"

She swung about.

"Davidson?" he said. "Philip Davidson live here?"

She looked at him wide-eyed.

"No? Next door?" His eyes moved round the cabin. "My, I like your weekend hidey-hole," he remarked. "Fixed it up real purty, haven't you?"

"Yes," she said. "He lives here."

"Oh, he does, does he? Goodo." He stepped into the cabin. "Thought so. I'm Fisher. Is he about?"

"No."

"Oh, that's too bad. Any idea what time he'll be back?"

Again she shook her head. "He is away."

"Damn." He got out a note-book and pencil. "Oh well, I'll take a few notes anyway. By the way," he looked at her, "whom have we the pleasure . . . ?"

She did not understand.

"Who are you, missy?" he said.

Then she understood, but she did not answer. He looked down at her and a slow grin spread across his face. "Well, well," he murmured. "It just goes to show. I don't know, some chaps get all the luck."

She faced him, bright-eyed and flushing, hating him

from that moment on. "I do not know you," she said, and stood trembling in his laughter. It occurred to her of a sudden that this might be the man who had done Davidson a wrong and whom Davidson sought. And this man was surely wholly unworthy. . . .

"Met him after he came out, did you?"

She must make him leave, lest Davidson should find him here. Davidson must not die for the killing of this creature. . . .

"And love him just the same . . . ah, well."

She didn't understand. "Came out?"

"Out of the cooler," Fisher explained. "The cooler, duckie, the cooler. Prison."

"You know him?" she said.

"Me? Sure. Known him for years."

"Please go," she said suddenly. The notion took hold of her. "You must go, it is dangerous."

He grinned, showing his broken teeth. "Jealous, is he?"

"Go—please." Her alarm rose.

He looked down at the hand she tried to push him with. "What's the idea, duckie?" He looked into her face, smiling. "Trying to throw me out?"

"Go, go. . . ."

"Hey——"

"He will return. He is searching for you."

"Eh? For me?"

"Yes yes—you must leave quickly. Oh, please go."

"You've got the wrong man, ducks." He was interested. "Who is it you think I am?"

"It is dangerous——"

"I wonder. . . ." He looked down at her, narrowing his eyes dreamily. "Might be worth a try. I wonder now . . . Listen, ducks, did you ever hear tell of a fellow named Pewsey?"

"He will kill you, he will kill you. . . ."

"Steady on, steady on . . . whoa! All right, I'm

going." He stood at the door. "Listen, ducks . . . Fay Driver: does that mean anything to you?"

"No, no——"

"Tell you what, then. Give him a message, will you? Needn't say who left it. I'll write it down. . . ." He scribbled in the notebook and tore out the sheet and handed it to her.

"There we are. Just give him that, will you?—there's a good girl."

She snatched the scrap of paper and put it in her pocket. "Now go," she pleaded, "only go, quickly."

"Okay, okay. You give him that bit of paper. I'll call back in a day or two."

"Yes," she said, "yes." She was pushing him out of the door. "Oh, please."

They heard the heavy footsteps on the deck and turned. It was Davidson; he stood looking from one to the other. Elsa uttered a cry and ran between them, crying "No! No!" and holding Davidson's arm. He shook her off. "No!" she cried, and threw herself back on him.

"Well!" said Fisher. "The man himself. Practically saved my life. Where did you pick her up?"

Davidson brought up his hand and backhandedly swung at Fisher's face. The blow made an odd hollow sound as it landed and Fisher toppled against the wall and stood leaning on it, shaking his head with tears coming into his eyes.

"Christ," he muttered, and shook his head again.

Davidson took him by the lapels of his raincoat and swung him round and dragged him, protesting petulantly, out on to the deck, with Elsa leaning on his arms and beating his shoulders with her small fists and crying, "No! He is not worthy . . ." For she was certain now in her anguish that this was the man Davidson was looking for.

But he only set Fisher on his feet and let him go and Fisher slithered down the ladder and splashed away through the pools of water among the reeds in the dusk.

Then he turned to the girl. "You were to be gone," he said. "You were to be gone." Had he not told her to go? And she was saying she had been about to go, look, all her things were rolled up and ready, she had been on the point of leaving, when this man had arrived. Her voice trailed away.

"Is it true?"

"Yes, yes . . ."

"It's a lie."

She moved her hand helplessly

"You must go."

"I cannot," she whispered. "You must drive me away."

He shook his head. "I am no use to you," he said heavily, but either she didn't or wouldn't understand.

5

Their own halting account, one's instinct, acquaintance with them both, imagination prompted by a shadow of meaning, the inflection in a voice, the flush that a memory brings to the cheek, the movement of a hand, the half smile, the glance, the shining or clouding of an eye, the unanswered question: these are the only sources for this account of their love; the rest is guesswork and my own sentimentality.

It began, I do know, that same night, when he lay beneath the blankets with his face to the wall, feeling his heart in his chest like something cold and hard he had swallowed. He watched the dim firelight playing on the worn timbers a few inches from his head. Then he heard her movements, small and timid, and the faint susurration of the fabric of her clothes as she pulled them over her head. He turned his face into the pillow and held his hands over his ears, going rigid. Presently the sound ceased.

"Philip . . ."

The voice was hardly audible.

"Philip . . ."

She was standing naked, near the fire, with its light on her small, smooth limbs, with a ferocious brassy smile on her lips and her teeth chattering.

"Look, I am here."

He felt a blind, violent rage, a black murderous rage. By what right did she inflict this on him?

"I am not beautiful," she said. "I know I am not beautiful. Oh, Philip." She heard the breath rattling in his throat. "I am not beautiful enough." Her voice was rising steadily. She trembled and her teeth chattered.

In his rage there was now the feeling of being sorry for her, achingly sorry for her, with an immense choking pity for her standing there in the firelight offering him her love, understanding the jangling brassiness and the ghastly rigid smile, praying to God for her to stop, to stop it, to stop doing this to herself before him. He would not be able to stand it long. In a moment now he would get up and strangle her if she did not stop.

"Stop it," he blurted.

"I will love you," she cried.

"Stop it," he shouted.

"Philip, you must not refuse me now."

"Let me alone."

"Philip . . ."

"God in heaven."

"I am so ashamed, Philip . . ."

"No," he groaned, "no, no . . ."

"There is only to let me love you."

She came crouching to his side and then suddenly he reared up and reached out and got his hands about her neck and kicked off the blankets and put his legs to the floor, tightening his grip. He swung her to and fro blindly. Then his eyes cleared and she was smiling at him, trembling all over her body, white to the lips, her neck in the halter of his hands. He swayed and she took his head tenderly and her hands closed round it. She felt his brow between her breasts and the harsh grey hair under her chin.

"Philip," she whispered, "Philip, Philip . . ."

Then she was lying beside him quietly beneath the blankets with her face in his neck and her small hand cool on his shoulder. She felt his loneliness, and so her own, like a cold sea. She did not know what to do, and began to weep silently. "I am so ashamed," she whispered. She felt his hand rise and move over her head and through her hair, gently. She lay still under it, following its movements, closing her eyes.

"Tell me you love me," she said. She took the hand and kissed it and let it go. "It is dark. It does not matter. Tell me you love me."

She heard him a long way away. "I love you, Elsa."

She lay under his hand, and when she uttered a little sigh and moved her movement travelled through his arm and into his shoulder. Deep down inside him something seemed to stir and stretch, like a small fierce animal which has slept through the long winter and now awakes with the melting snow: something lost and fabulous. There was a wild thunder in his ears. "Philip," she whispered.

CHAPTER TWO

I

WHEN Craig was told of Mervyn Fisher's visit to
Morocco Bay he went to see Asprey and, standing at
Asprey's desk, called him a number of vile names.

"Hallo, Craig," said Asprey cheerfully.

He began again. Asprey said: "Sit down, old boy,
you're looking quite done up. How's the wife and family?"
The heavy red face was iridescent in the green light and
each lens of his glasses was a gay green moon.

"They're all right."

"That's good. Tricky time of year for kids. Nasty cough,
my youngest—doctor coming this morning. . . ."

"What did you have to do that for, George?"

"It's the devil when they get it in the throat—whooping
cough before you know where you are."

"And Fisher. Mervyn Fisher, of all people."

Asprey grinned. "What's the matter with Fisher? Nice
chap."

"I'm entitled to some sort of explanation, George."

"And you shall have it, Craig, you shall have it."

"You can be facetious afterwards."

Asprey said. "It's no use getting tough about it, old boy.
You know the form as well as I do."

"I want to know why you put Fisher on to this story."

"Somebody's got to cover it, Craig."

"I'm covering it."

Asprey leaned back. "It is now getting on for two
weeks," he said softly, "since I asked you to give me something on Philip Davidson. You have not yet shown me a
single paragraph. Nor have you condescended to tell me

why you have not yet shown me a single paragraph. What you've been doing I don't know. I don't really care. The point is that this newspaper, or any newspaper, isn't so damn rich it can afford to pay you a salary for not producing a single bloody paragraph in two weeks."

"A retainer," said Craig; "not a salary."

"Retainer, then."

Craig sat down. "When did you start worrying about this newspaper's finances, George?"

"Cut it out."

"It's as rich as Croesus."

"All right. And do you know why? Because it isn't in the habit of paying people money to frig around building up swindle-sheets and not producing a single bloody word in two weeks."

"Go on."

"So I put Fisher on it."

"Fisher ought not to be on a newspaper, not even this one. Fisher was born to blush unseen."

"A very promising journalist."

"He's about as low as they come."

"One of our blue-eyed boys, Fisher is."

"What was the idea?"

Asprey said: "You really want to know, do you?"

"Yes."

"I'll tell you then. Fisher is by way of being a kick up the bottom for Craig. Fisher is a spur, one of those Mexican affairs, with long sharp rowels. Fisher is a gauntlet. Fisher is a challenge. Fisher is an ultimatum." He nodded. "Now you know what the idea was. And is."

"He'll make a hash of it."

"I know. I tremble to think."

"Then call him off, George."

"Failing something from you, Fisher stays."

Craig said: "There's nothing worth writing about Davidson. If there had been I'd have written it."

"You're not a very classy liar, Craig."

"What makes you think I'm lying?"

"I'd put a fiver on it."

"If there's no story and he thinks it will do him any good, Fisher will write one. He's a mischief-maker."

Asprey said: "There are times, Craig, when I find you downright touching. If there was nothing to write about you would have written something yourself, just like Fisher. But you've written nothing. And yet you're still hanging about down there. So I know damn well there's plenty to write about, and I know it must be thundering good. I want it."

"For God's sake there are plenty of other stories, aren't there?" Craig cried. "The world's full of misery. Why the hell do you have to have this one?"

"This has got a bit of something extra."

"Fisher will ruin it."

"I'll put a re-write man on it."

"How much did you tell him?"

"What I told you."

"All of it?"

"Everything. Look, Craig," he said gently. "Nobody else would bother this way. Life's too short—they'd hand you your hat. I'm the only man in this city who'd trouble. But there's a limit. You've reached it."

Craig said: "George, if Fisher is staying on this job, I'm dropping it. I'm walking out—right out."

There was a moment's silence. Then Asprey said: "Fisher stays till you produce something. And you won't walk out. Never in this world."

The telephone rang and Asprey picked up the receiver. "Yes?" And then: "Put her through." His voice took on a slight urgency. "Yes, love. Yes. What's he say? What, I don't believe it. What? What are you crying about? Well, he's not, he's not going. No, I'm damned if he will. There's no reason for it. Bloody cattle pens. No. No. Then we'll nurse him ourselves. Yes. What d'you mean, the others? Oh, nonsense. But he can't do that! Who does he think he is? Yes, love. Now look, lovey, there's nothing to worry about, nothing at all, so stop crying, don't worry, it's a thing everybody's had, of course, just one of those things, had it myself. Yes, of course. No, love. Don't you worry, we'll fix it. No, of course not. Now don't cry, there's nothing to cry about . . ."

Craig heard the click of the receiver at the other end of the line. Asprey sat frowning at the desk. Presently he said: "Where were we?"

"Mine have had it," Craig told him. "Both of them."

Asprey said: "What gets you is the coughing. I can't stand seeing his face get redder and redder."

"Yes, they do."

"Where were we?"

"Doesn't matter. Mervyn Fisher."

Asprey said: "I think I'll go home and see what's going on," and stood up and got his hat and coat from the stand in the corner. "Had a flat tyre this morning," he said. "Tell Gough I've gone home, will you?" He looked about him for something. "Where's my hat?"

"You've got it on."

"Fisher, you said." He was patting his pockets.

"It doesn't matter."

2

Somewhere upstream a lighter had been in collision and had foundered. It had been loaded deep with big metal drums of oil and now these had drifted ashore and lay in the mud in groups of two or three, or sometimes alone, along the hem of the little beaches of blue mussel-shell. They were painted bright yellow and had red lettering. Davidson and Barney Scotson were among the scavengers.

The river was a flat silver-grey and a red sun overhung the mist in the west, over the purple haze where the city lay. Just off-shore, wallowing in the water, there were three or four boats, dirty, graceless craft belonging to no species at all, like backyard sheds, collecting the drums; from time to time they spurted astern with a muffled phutter of engines, when the ebb carried them too far down away from the pickings. Barney Scotson's bawley was among them.

On the dry land beyond the bank there were two trucks, one an old army fifteen-hundredweight, the other entirely nondescript but very old, loading the barrels. The competition was lively, but there were many of the yellow drums, so the quarrelling would not begin till the supply got low. The work was fast, a little feverish, for the oil would fetch good money in salvage, and the voices of the men were sharp and cheerful as they called to their crews in the boats and the trucks. They used ropes, wading ashore through the mud to get the rope round the barrels and then shout; the barrels would then be hauled out to the beam and hoisted aboard, or rolled over the mussel-shell and up the slope to the trucks. The men shone with black mud from the waist down. Davidson was among them.

He and Barney Scotson had trawled the Leigh Middle shoals on the tide and then had turned for home. Barney saw the distant activity and knew what it meant; he sailed in among the pickers. There was some opposition from those already there, but fortunately the first of the trucks trundled along the track at that moment and Barney deflected the abuse from himself to the truck and bellowed with the rest: had a man no rights? Who did they think they were? Did they not know the laws of salvage? Nobody took any action, however; there were many drums of oil, stretching away downstream at the water's limit.

When Davidson recognised Shaw he knew there was going to be trouble of some kind, and he did not want it that day. This, in a way, was a first day, and he didn't want to spoil it with a fight with Shaw. The man was

working with one of the trucks. When he saw Davidson
floundering with a keg of oil he stiffened and stood up
straight with the noose of the rope hanging from his hand.
But he said nothing.

Davidson needed only to raise his head to see the low
bank where the track went away over the blue, fissured
mud through the little explosions of stiff marsh grass
towards Morocco Bay. He could see the unevenness on the
sharp black line of the first horizon, where the hulks lay.
His heart came into his throat when he thought of it;
the uneasiness slipped away.

He heard Barney's voice across the water: "Ay-up!
What's holding you?"

All round him men were struggling to lift the kegs to get
a rope beneath, slipping in the mud, cursing happily. He
stooped and set his hands about the rim of the drum at his
knees and it came up easily; he got the rope beneath and
brought it round and knotted it. Barney leaned on the
rope but the drum wouldn't budge. So he gave the rope
a turn round the tiller shaft and started up the Billy and
the boat moved and that shifted it; the drum ploughed
across the mud and into the water and Barney windlassed
it aboard. He waved and shouted something.

They went on all afternoon. Then the men with the
trucks had the advantage, for the boats had to edge out as
the tide ebbed, till they were as much as fifty yards away,
and the drums had to be rolled or hauled that distance
across the mud-flats with block and tackle. But it was done
at last. In the twilight Davidson and a small old man
ploughed their way to the last of the drums—two which
lay together in the mud. At the same time Shaw came
over the bank trailing a rope.

Davidson took one barrel and the old man the other and
for a moment nothing was said. Then Shaw addressed the
old man.

"That's mine," he said.

Davidson knew it was a challenge. He bent to pass the

rope beneath the drum he had claimed, hearing the old man saying: "No, it isn't. I got here first. You know the laws of salvage."

"It's mine," said Shaw, watching Davidson.

Davidson said: "Let him alone," and rose upright.

Shaw came down the bank slowly. "Talking to me?"

"Yes," Davidson said.

The old man looked suddenly from one to the other. They were both big men; it would be very ugly. He said quickly: "I don't care about this one. Let him have it if he wants it."

Davidson told him quietly: "Rope it up, it's yours."

"I say it's mine," Shaw said.

They stood facing one another. Shaw swung with the rope but Davidson had been expecting that and ducked, straight into Shaw's fist, and went over with his head ringing. Shaw lifted his leg to kick, but he slipped in the mud and Davidson got up and threw out a wild swinging blow. The old man hopped round them saying he didn't want the drum, he didn't want it. Then Shaw's fist landed again and Davidson went down again with Shaw on top of him, sitting astride him, taking aim with his fists and Davidson knew he had to get up somehow; he caught the man's arm in his hands and exerted his strength and Shaw let out a bellow and toppled off. When he got up Davidson hit him once with all his weight behind the blow and the man smacked into the mud and lay groaning.

Over the bank there were voices calling impatiently for Shaw, or for the drum he must by now have roped. The rope lay in the mud waiting. So Davidson passed the noose under Shaw's armpits and shouted to them to take it away and the rope tightened and Shaw was dragged across the mussel-shell and over the bank. Then there was silence.

He wished he hadn't done that. Walking along the track in the dark he knew he had been showing off, bragging, and wished it undone. That had been unnecessary and unfunny, solving nothing. The bruises stiffened in his face and his head ached. Why had he done that? It had been enough to thrash the man.

3

The cabin was warm and clean and lived-in. Elsa was looking up at him with nervous grey eyes, hopefully, prepared either to melt or stiffen, watching for his mood. He asked for a bucket of water and she prepared it and he washed, outside on the deck. He hung up his coat near the fire so that the mud would dry. Then he noticed the rushes she had cut and stacked near the fire; he did not at once understand what they might be for, but he didn't ask. When he had washed off the mud, the bruises on his face and on the backs of his hands were red and angry. She saw them and did not understand how he had come by them, but she didn't ask. They were both very constrained and watchful, breathing through parted lips lest somehow the struggle for breath should be audible, waiting, not knowing, knowing yet not being wholly sure, and so holding back, doing commonplace things with nonchalance.

She asked him, "Did you fall?" knowing he had been in a fight with somebody, knowing it quite certainly.

Yes, he said. Yes, he had fallen. He sat on the edge of the bunk and looked up at the lamp. Then he looked at the rushes again, stacked by the fire; she caught his glance and when his eyes rose to hers the colour came flooding into her face. He understood what they were for then and he felt his lips drying suddenly. When she moved to the table he put out his hand and she came into his arms suddenly, blindly, with a whirl and a shock. She was laughing breathlessly as he held her in his arms and rolled over. Then she had his head in her hands and was holding him by the short hair on the temples, laughing and showering kisses on his face. "Oh darling, darling, darling, Philip, Philip, my Philip, my darling . . ."

He closed his eyes so that there could be nothing other than this. She lay across his chest whispering and touching the bruises on his face with her lips as though she would heal them that way. Presently she slipped off her clothes. There was nothing else then to think of.

She whispered: "Now I am hungry. You also?"

"Yes."

She laughed and looked towards the stove. "The rushes," she said. "Oh, the rushes. We did not have time to put them beneath."

He smiled. "Tell me something nice," she said. "Please. I will make it dark." She brought her face close to his so that their noses touched and then cupped her hands about their eyes. "Now tell me," she whispered.

"I love you."

"And there is nothing else, is there?"

"No." He saw it standing beyond her shoulder, waiting. "No."

"And you love me?"

"I love you."

"And I love you," she said. She kissed him. "And now we will have the dinner."

4

The next morning he found it. She had left it under the jar of flowers on the table so that she would be able to tell him when the moment came, if he found it: Oh, yes, the man named Fisher had left it and she had forgotten. She knew it was wrong and dangerous, but she knew it hadn't left his mind whatever he said, this sleeping dog; she thought that she might love him enough, and make him love her enough, to forget it and the dog would die in its sleep. She would have destroyed the scrap of paper but that Fisher had said he would come back in a day or two. If he did, and Davidson discovered she was trying to stand between him and his objective, she would have failed utterly. So she hid it under the jar of flowers on the table.

He found it. He saw the writing on the paper, down through the water. When she came into the cabin with the coat she had been brushing he said abruptly: "What's this?"

The blood drained from her face. "Oh, yes," she stammered, "I—I had forgotten. It is what he left you."

"Who?"

"The man who was here. You sent him away. He told me to give it to you. I forgot . . ." She looked at him with false, bright insouciance.

He was puzzled. "You forgot?"

"Yes." She struggled on, trying to talk inconsequentially with terror in her heart, not for what he might say about her having kept the message from him, but lest her subterfuge should merely have hardened his resolve. There were two addresses on the scrap of paper: Pewsey's and Fay Driver's. Where Mervyn Fisher had got them I don't know; certainly it could not have been difficult.

He went out without a word and presently she heard him tearing up the deck boards and sawing them into lengths for burning in the stove. Then he came to the door with the saw in his hand. She heard his deep, husky voice and turned, smiling.

"You didn't forget it," he said. "Did you?"

She knew it was hopeless then. "No, Philip . . ."

"Why did you hide it?"

"I was afraid."

"Why didn't you burn it, then?"

"I would have given it to you."

"When?"

"When it would not matter any more."

"When did you think that would be?"

She did not answer. His coat hung from her hands.

"Do you know what it means?" He flicked the scrap of paper.

"Yes," she answered. It had to do with the creature of the bitter breath that lived with them day and night, watched them over their shoulders, sat with them, ate with them, lay with them beneath the blankets.

"Did you think I would forget it?"

"I hoped with my heart," she whispered.

"You are trying to interfere."

"No, Philip . . ."

"Yes." What did she think she was trying to do? Did she think she could lead him away, dangling a carrot before his nose as if he were a donkey? Did she think she could slip a bridle over his head while he ruminated?—Tie his hands? Swathe him? How the hell had she thought she could do it?

"With love," she said dully.

He took his jacket from her and pulled it on.

"Philip . . ."

Well, she was wrong.

"Philip, where are you going?"

He folded the bit of paper and put it in his pocket.

"Philip!" she cried suddenly. She put her hand on his arm and he threw it off. "Philip! No! No! I will go away, I will go away . . ." She ran to the door and put herself across it. "No! You must not! I will go. . . ." He pushed her aside and she clung frantically to his arm. "No. . . ."

CHAPTER THREE

I COULD hear Mick padding about in his room upstairs. Fay was threading a needle and then bending
her shapely head over the stocking which she pulled up
her wrist till the toe was stretched across her fingers. All her
movements were calm and unhurried. Knowing now what
lay in her mind that evening, and indeed all the silent
evenings of that time, I find it hard not to admire the cool
determination with which she defied the enemies who were
converging on her; she shut her eyes to the flash of the sun
on the helmets and her ears to the rustle of stealthy movement, and darned a stocking. Yet in her heart she was
desperate—I realised it later; the action she took when
she felt herself finally cornered, brave and extravagant as
it was, could only have sprung from the unbearable
torment. She tried to cut the knot at one despairing blow.
It must have been in her mind even that evening, but she
went about her business undismayed.

We talked a little. There was nothing much to say; we
had said it all before; we embroidered on it. We both
waited, she, I suppose, for the moment beyond which
there could be no more evasion; and I waited for her,
miserably. We all waited for her: Flood and Craig
and I and Pewsey and an endless nameless multitude,
silently.

She drew another stocking on to her wrist. "Bobby,"
she said at last, "there's something wrong with Mick."

"Something wrong?"

"Yes. Haven't you noticed anything?"

"Is he ill?"

189

"No no. I don't think he's very happy."

"Why, what's wrong?"

"I don't know."

"School?"

"I don't know. He's avoiding us."

Yes, I had noticed. "Oh, I don't think it's anything serious." He was quiet now, in the room above. "I'll have a talk with him."

"Yes. He needs a lot of looking after . . ." Her face was hidden; she bent over the stocking.

"Yes."

"He gets colds easily."

"He'll grow out of that."

"We ought to have had his tonsils out."

"Well, it's not too late."

"They lose a lot of blood at his age."

"I'll talk to the doctor."

She threaded the needle. "He must go on with the piano," she said.

"Oh yes." Suddenly I realised she was on the edge of tears.

"Fay . . ."

"What beats me," she said with a sudden bitter vehemence, "is how you, his father, can even think about sacrificing him to—to some silly idea of—of putting something right that everybody's forgotten about years ago." Now it all came pouring out again. "How can you? How can you? Wrecking him, wrecking yourself and your career, for some stupid little thing like this——"

"It isn't little, Fay——"

"How big is it compared with Mickie? When there's no need, there's no need. Everything, not just me . . . your home, your career—what's the use of working like a slave as you've worked, spending a lifetime getting where you've got, just to throw it all away? Is it going to do any good? It's such a waste, such a waste. . . ."

She was beating her knee with the hand with the stocking on it. I didn't know what to say. I was glad in a way to have Craig behind me at that time; his threat was a support. I thought about him: if I did nothing, if I shared Fay's silence and let the whole thing slide, then Craig would shout it from the house-tops; he would weigh Davidson against me and against the police . . . the threat wasn't necessary, but I was glad it was there. We both wanted the same thing.

"I won't do it," she said. "I won't do it, I won't do it."

Mick was coming down the stairs and in a moment he was putting his fair head round the door and saying: "I say, dad, there's a chap hanging about on the other side of the street. . . ."

Mick was always reporting mysterious goings-on in our wholly blameless street, but I went with him into the dining-room where there was no light and peeped through the window. I couldn't see anybody.

"Must have gone," Mick said. "He was there."

I told him I expected it was a chap waiting for his girl, and suddenly the boy was uneasy. When we came back into the light he wouldn't meet my eyes. He went up the stairs. Then the telephone rang and I sat down at the hall table and picked up the receiver. It was Bletchley. He was very distressed.

"He's given me the slip, sir——"

"Where are you speaking from, Bletchley?"

"Charing Cross, sir. I lost him in the crowds, sir—the rush hour . . ."

I told him not to worry, and went back into the living-room. Fay said at once: "Who was it?"

"In the street? Oh, just one of Mick's games—couldn't see a soul."

"And on the phone?"

"Nothing important."

She said: "Is it him?—Philip?"

I could see no point in hiding it. "Might be."

Her eyes were wide and steady. "Who told him? You?"

"How d'you mean?"

Her voice shook. "Did you tell Philip Davidson where to find me?"

"Of course not. Good God——"

"You told somebody to give him the address . . ."

"I swear I didn't."

"Then how does he know it?"

"There's no reason to suppose he does know it, Fay."

Almost at once I heard Mick's footsteps pattering down the stairs. He put his head round the door again and said in an excited whisper:

"He's there again, dad."

I went with him into the dining-room and looked through the window.

"Oh, it's just a fellow waiting for his girl, Mick."

He was disappointed. "How can you tell?"

"I don't know—he has the look of it. . . ."

"Oh." He peered out of the window. "He's looking over here."

"Subterfuge."

"Good lord . . ."

He went back upstairs, though not, I think, altogether satisfied.

Her head was bent low over the stocking. I closed the door.

"It's Davidson."

She sat perfectly still. Up to that moment, when, for her, all the clocks in the world stopped, Davidson had never had a shape; he had been an influence, a vast anonymous pressure, beheld only in the mind. Therefore I think she was surprised, first, to find that he was a man, a person of flesh and blood and suffering, and substantial, having weight, who moved independently of her imagining, whose heels rang on the earth as he walked. She lifted her face a little as if listening. I saw the panic in her eyes; and then the hardening.

For my own part his coming made very little difference. For me he seemed to have been waiting on the other side of the street all my life, ever since I could remember.

CHAPTER FOUR

I

FROM the office I called the local station and asked them to keep an eye on my house; I didn't think Davidson would approach it in daylight, but it seemed a proper precaution to take. I had seen little of him during the night and when I left in the morning he had gone—back to Morocco Bay, perhaps, or in search of some kind of lodging in Chiswick. There was no knowing what he would do; he might try to break in; he might wait for a dark night and the chance of catching Fay alone; he might try to lure her away by some means. I was pretty sure his vigil last night had been exploratory rather than decisive. He would return.

Nothing happened till about the middle of the afternoon, when the unfortunate Bletchley telephoned again from Gravesend. Davidson had returned for a few hours, but then had set off again——

"And you've lost him . . ."

"Yes, sir. I'm frightfully sorry, sir." He was audibly upset. "He got on a tugboat."

"On a what?"

"A tugboat. Here in Gravesend, sir. I saw him."

"When was this?"

"It must have been about half-past three, sir."

"Which way was it heading, did you see?"

"Upstream, sir, towards town." He was almost in tears. "I couldn't help it, sir. I couldn't follow him on board . . ."

"Did you get the name of the tug?"

"No, sir. There's quite a thick fog down here, sir."

"Well, don't worry, Bletchley, it wasn't your fault." To tell the truth I was rather relieved, for I didn't want Bletchley to follow Davidson to my doorstep. But the tugboat was unexpected; perhaps he had been offered a lift upstream. However, he was on his way. One likes to be in touch with one's own quietus. I stood at the window and watched the mist thickening over the river.

When I got home Fay had gone.

2

The letter was standing on the mantelpiece, a square of white paper propped up against the clock so that it was the first thing you saw on entering; she had written my name on the envelope; I could see the faint blue scrawl from the door. The fire was not lit and the room was cold and cheerless, as if it hadn't been lived in for some time.

It could have been a note to say she had gone to somebody's cocktail party, or to Mrs. Thingummy's for tea and Maureen would get my dinner. It could have been about a telephone call and would I ring so-and-so. But I knew exactly what it was. It was none of these things. I knew what it was.

Maureen told me madam had gone out a little while before I reached home. She had telephoned for a taxi and Maureen had helped her to carry two suitcases down the stairs. Maureen's face was always a mixture of surprise and pure animal cunning and both were present as I questioned her; she was nervous and reluctant to look me in the face; she must have guessed what was afoot. Then madam had driven away in the taxi with the suitcases; no, Maureen had not heard her give the driver the address; yes, she had noticed the letter after madam had left.

"Where is Mick?" I asked.

"Master Mickie's out, sir, gone to the pictures."

Apparently Fay had given him the price of his ticket so that he would be out of the way when she left.

Maureen clearly wanted to escape my questions, so I let her go and she scuttered back into the kitchen.

Then I read it. I got up to get a drink, not truly because I wanted one, but because it was something to do; people in plays and films and books always seem to tinker with drinks in moments of duress. So I did too. It was all extremely self-conscious. I lit a cigarette, drew on it, and stubbed it out. There were all kinds of things to do, and I did them all. I acted a little parody of the man whose wife has left him. What does he do next? Another drink, gulped down; so I had another and, in trying to gulp it, choked. I felt curiously light-headed. I contemplated putting my fist through the window . . . the mirror, perhaps, would be better. It seemed rather extravagant, however, and there would be all the bother of getting a glazier to come and put in a new one. When there was nothing left to try I sat down and I remember saying aloud: "I wonder why it never occurred to me." Of course that was what she would do. "Oh, good God."

I read the letter again:

Bobby dear,

By the time you get this I shall be on an aeroplane. Its no use trying to stop me, I am leaving you and that's that, because sooner or later it would come out, and I know what you are. I won't let you make a mess of your life and Mickie's, no matter what, which is what it would mean, there are things I know that would come out that I can't tell you. I don't know how you will explain it to him. It might all blow over, but I don't think so. You'd better tell him I've just got fed up, but he's not to think badly of me, I shall find out. If you see about his tonsils he's not to go into hospital, now I can't write any more.

Fay.

It is difficult to remember what one has thought in moments of utter catastrophe. I don't really think you feel anything much. One's head is plagued by a lot of inconsequential flummery which will not get out of the way —a popular tune, the opening line of a limerick, an urge to straighten that picture which is askew and at the same time a resolve to resist the urge. You wonder how the devil you will explain this business to your mother, till you remember, oh yes, she's dead. You assure yourself you will never get over it, and this is rather saddening, because you have an idea you will, a mistaken idea; you won't, you won't. You've got it for life. And so one thing after another begins to stick like a pin-point through the veil of numbness, and you know that presently you will find the ends of this wall of desolation; just now it is still up against your nose and its features are blurred by proximity; but already it is drawing away and the questions become visible one by one. You stop swaying to and fro and asking yourself: "My God, what have I done? Oh, Jesus, what have I done?" and instead you begin to think: "Where has she gone?" and "Where did she get the money?" and "How can she be stopped?" You begin to realise the monstrousness of your own part. My God, what she must have suffered to do this, to take this way out, after seventeen years!

I heard the clock striking and looked up at it and almost immediately the doorbell rang and Maureen made a dash across the hall and opened the door and then scuttled back into the kitchen. Mick was saying: "Anybody in yet? . . ." But the kitchen door slammed. Then he was coming this way and I thought: now it begins.

"Hallo, Dad," he said. "You're home early. I say, what's up with Maureen?"

"I don't know." His hair shone with the moisture of the fog. When I looked at him his eyes moved away. I thought: I wonder if everything is all right with him? "Is there something up with Maureen?" I asked.

"Dashing about like mad." He considered the phenomenon and then decided: "I expect she's burnt something."

"Yes, I expect that accounts for it."

"Where's Mummy?"

"She's gone out, Mick." He's going to hate me, I thought, he's going to hate me for ever. He might forgive, when he understands, but he will never forget. You don't waste any time, do you? Suddenly it swept over me.

CHAPTER FIVE

DAVIDSON stood in the bows of the tugboat. There was nothing to be seen but the fog, and nothing more to hear than the pushing of the water against the hull and the beat of the turbines like a heart under his feet, and every two minutes the frantic bellow of the siren.

When he had left the bay Elsa had called his name and he had felt it settle over his shoulders like a lasso. But he went on and the rope stretched; he could feel it all the time. He had found Barney at the landing-stage.

"Little job today," Barney said with a bright glance. "Swedish ship. Timber. Passed the Nore an hour ago, so we'll be looking slippy. Start her up."

Davidson filled the carburettor from the flagon of petrol and started up the Billy. They turned out and away across the shining river. Barney stood amidships and peered downstream into the estuary through the old binoculars with the crack in the left lens.

"Can't see her yet." And then, over his shoulder: "They want a man to take this lot upalong right away. Told 'em you'd do it. That so?"

"Upalong where?'

"Don't know. Lower Pool, I think. Special delivery, wanted tonight. You get paid extra. Seems there's a tug going up. Join him at Gravesend. Take you all the way up, find your own way back. Are you on?"

Davidson nodded. "Suits me." It would be on his way to Chiswick.

Barney called: "There she is. That'll be her."

The ship was low in the water, her decks stacked high
with timber, butting through the mist off Canvey. She was
flying a pilot's pennant. Barney frowned, looking twice,
carefully, through the binoculars. "Blast it," he said. "I
don't like jobs with pilots aboard." He watched the ship
with a sour face.

They bore across the river and approached the ship.
"I don't like it," Barney repeated. "Wouldn't have taken
the job on if I'd known." He came aft. "We'll have to
slow her up a bit, never get close enough else. Give me
the tiller."

He took the bawley straight across the freighter's bows,
watching the big blunt stem, and then, waiting till the
siren whooped and he could hear the distant shouts from
the bridge and the tinkle of the telegraph and the ship
began to lose way, he put the bawley about. It was very
close. The great rusty cliffs slid past with a distant thud-
ding of engines, so near that Davidson could almost have
touched the plates. Heads came over the rail above and
angry voices bawled abuse from the sky. Barney shook his
fist and mouthed his defiance.

Then he grinned at Davidson and wiped his nose with
the back of his hand. "Only way to get close enough,"
he explained. He held on his course and the long flank
glided smoothly past. In the stern a man leaned out over
the rail and, taking aim, dropped the package into the
well of the bawley, then nodded and raised his hand. The
bawley tossed wildly in the hissing grey wake.

Gedge and the man named Fryer were waiting. Gedge,
small and neat, looked at Davidson through thick glasses.
"Are you going to take this up?" he said. He had the
package in his hands.

"Yes."

"Do you know where to go?—Pickle Herring Road?"

"I'll find it." He had a dim recollection; Pickle Herring
Road ran behind the wharves along the south bank of the
Pool.

"You'll be put ashore at St. Saviour's. Then you walk, along Shad Thames and under Tower Bridge. Just this side of Pickle Herring Stairs you'll find Longman's Wharf. That's it. Find the office, there will be somebody waiting. Say you come from me."

Davidson nodded. Fryer was watching him with melancholy eyes. "And give him that," Fryer said; he touched the packet in Davidson's hands and looked into his face with a sad smile.

He had reached Gravesend at about three-thirty in the afternoon. A grey mist hung over the water. He boarded the tug at the Royal Terrace Pier; it was Stallybrass who stepped out of the little cabin. Davidson had looked about him for Pewsey, for he remembered that it was on this ship he had first seen the man; Pewsey was not aboard; it was a relief—he didn't want to return to Pewsey yet. Stallybrass nodded affably and bawled to the mate to let go the head and stern ropes; he went up on to the bridge and the bell jangled and the tug moved out. Davidson went forward into the bows. He saw the bright lights of the Tilbury ferry-boats and then the tug gathered way, leaning back a little on the slope of its own bow-wave.

In Halfway Reach the fog came down in earnest. It was like a khaki blanket, blinding, deadening, silent, brown, acrid in the nostrils. Stallybrass slowed to half-speed and began to tug at the siren lanyard. But the fog was absorbent of sound and seemed to throw back an echo from a high wall a few yards away all round the ship. The mate came forward into the bows where Davidson stood and peered into the murk and strained his ears to the silence. "Proper bastard, isn't it, eh?" he muttered. Davidson knew how it was; you had nothing to steer by but compass bearings of the river's reaches, which you never really trusted, and instinct and your own knowledge and the smell of the factories and power-houses along the banks. It was bitter cold. Once they heard the muffled bass boom of a siren and then the rumble of big engines

7*

and the tug pitched in the wake of a vessel they had not even seen. Later, as they came up into Woolwich Reach, they heard the clangor of beaten iron bars and frying-pans, forlorn and eerie in the fog like the din of some ancient, dreamed-of battle; there were barges at anchor somewhere, and nervous.

They sidled into Bugsby's and round the point to the West Indias and the Isle of Dogs and then the sirens began to bray all round them, calling and answering on a crescendo of alarm. Suddenly the mate let out a yell. The wall of the freighter's flank loomed above, high, vast, spouting condenser water. Stallybrass cursed and sent the wheel spinning; bells jangled and the tug heeled over, striking the freighter a glancing blow on the curve of the stern. Davidson and the mate went sprawling on the wet boards and there was a distant crash of crockery in the galley and a muffled wail of abuse from the ship's rail, above and unseen, already lost in the fog. The trumpeting began again, deep and slow and solemn, or high and staccato, till the fog itself seemed to have a thousand voices, like a lowing herd. The night fell.

He was glad to be moving. The moisture settled on his face and he felt the thrust of the heavy air. Now he was on the way again. He would deliver the package and then go on, to find Fay. There was nothing else. He told himself a thousand times: there is nothing else, that is all I have to do. This time there would be no failure, by whatever name. This time it will be done. There is no freedom without it, nor ever will be. I know nothing other than this: this is what I am.

He heard at last the rumble of the steering engine and the tinkle of the bell and presently a mooring dolphin loomed up and slid past. They were close in; in a moment now they would see the yellow haze of lighted wharves. The mate muttered and let his breath go with a hiss and a street lamp came out of the fog towards them. The tug sidled in to the steps.

He walked along Shad Thames behind the granaries and warehouses. They were silent, dark, deserted. The lamps were few, and of gas, clinging to the walls, whispering in the fog, and the gangways running from building to building over his head were like laces in a boot, or branches in a bowered hell. His footsteps echoed dully. At the end of Shad Thames there were dim yellow lights across the sky where the ramp of Tower Bridge climbed from the land to the span; a bus ground its way up the slope. He went into the tunnel and, beyond, came into Pickle Herring Road.

Close to the wall of Longman's Wharf there was a big car. The main doors were closed, but beyond the car there was a narrow alley. A few yards down the alley, beneath a single naked light, there was a door, and a man stood in it, reading a newspaper. He looked up when he heard Davidson's footsteps.

"Is this Longman's?" Davidson said.

"Yeth." The man, who wore the uniform of a chauffeur and was hardly more than a boy, had a pronounced lisp. He folded up the newspaper.

Davidson said: "I've come from Gedge."

"Oh, yeth. Will you wait?" He went inside and Davidson heard him calling.

It occurred to Davidson as he waited that this would be the clearing house of the organisation of which he had drifted into membership, and that this man he was about to see was either very near the head of the business, or even the director himself. Then there were quick light footsteps on the stone floor and the door swung back and a stout man of middle age stood under the light fumbling with a wallet.

"Where the hell have you been?" he said, but he didn't seem to expect a reply. He took the package from Davidson and thrust a couple of pound notes towards him. Well, no doubt they would be useful if he had to pay for a room somewhere and he took them. He looked into the man's flaccid face and the man also glanced at Davidson, and for a moment their eyes met.

When he had gone a few paces up the alley towards Pickle Herring Road he stopped and looked over his shoulder. As he did so the door closed quietly. But the features of the man's face . . . there was something familiar in them, and in the set of the eyes. He knew that man. He groped in his memory for the name. It was there, it was there. Yes, of course, he had it: it was Spenser Boyd. No doubt about it.

When he swayed and bumped into the wall and grazed his knuckles he stood looking down at the beads of blood on the back of his hand. He toppled against the wall again, rolling, turning his face to the bricks.

CHAPTER SIX

I

AFTER a while I folded up Fay's letter and put it in my pocket. I went up the stairs.

He had a table and a chair and a little electric fire in his bedroom so that he could do his homework there. He was writing laboriously when I opened the door.

"Hallo, Mick." He had got ink on his face again. "How's it going?"

"Oh, it's just geography," he said. "For old Bertie."

"Bertie?"

"Chap with the tin behind."

"Has he really?"

"Oh, yes. Everybody knows."

"What happened to his real one?"

"Got it shot off in the war."

"That's not very respectful, Mick."

"Oh, he's not a bad chap."

"Tell me," I said: "how do you know he has a tin behind?"

"Somebody saw it in his tent at camp, hanging up on the tent-pole. Every time he sits down you can hear it go clank."

I said: "What's the essay about?"

"Oh, the usual tripe. Isobars and isotherms and all that stuff."

"It will be useful to you in after life, Mick." All the time he avoided my eyes. Fay had been right: there was something amiss. I looked down into the quiet street. "Mick, is there something worrying you?"

He flushed suddenly. "No. No . . ."

"How would you like to go to the pictures?"

He sat up. "What, now?"

"Yes. You and me."

"By Jove . . ." He swallowed and looked at what he had written. Then he said: "Yes, rather."

"We'd better not. We'll go some other time, Mick. Not tonight. Better get on with your homework." His sports bag lay on the table against the wall, open. I could see the muddied boots and jersey and the scrum-cap.

"It's only for old Bertie . . ."

"We'll go some other evening." There was a book among the clothes in the sports bag. "We'll save it up." I turned the book over, idly; it was only a pamphlet. I remember wincing at the title and very carefully, so that he should not know I had seen it, pushed it back beneath the boots. "We'll take the car and go together one evening." But I knew now what was wrong.

"But I could easily manage it, Dad."

"Some other evening."

"Honestly, I could wangle it——"

"Don't wangle things, Mick."

"Oh, Bertie never believes you, so that doesn't matter."

"And suppose he believed you?"

"I suppose it wouldn't be fair if he did, not with Bertie . . ."

"Decent chap, is he?"

"Oh, he's all right."

I stared out of the window. I wondered if Davidson would come tonight, and stand under the lamp on the other side of the street.

"That book in your bag, Mick . . ."

I knew what I wanted to say: you don't have to read that sort of thing. What the hell do you want to read that sort of stuff for? He had looked up and his face had flooded bright red and his eyes fell.

"Where did you get it?"

"A chap lent it to me last term," he whispered.

"Do you understand it?"

He shook his head and said in a high whisper: "I only read the first two pages."

"Give it back to him."

"He's been expelled."

"I'm not surprised. What happened?"

"The Reverend made a speech."

"What did he say?"

"He said the reproduction system was not a laughing matter . . ."

I thought: the bloody fool. The boy was crying without a sound. I didn't know what to do. I knew I must not put my arm round him or ruffle his hair: he would hate it. "Mick," I said, "you're not one of those, are you?"

He knew what I meant and shook his head.

"Well, you'd better not let your mother see it." Then I remembered. "Get rid of it. Get rid of the thing."

He nodded.

"Drop it down a drain."

He said: "I never thought of a drain."

So I asked him: "Mick, for just how long have you been trying to get rid of that book?"

"Months," he whispered. "Oh, months."

"Well, we'll do it now. Come on."

We took the book downstairs and I waited on the step while he ran down the path and into the street. Presently he came back. It must have been a great weight off his mind. I was very pleased; it stood up like an island in the desolation.

In the bedroom the wardrobe doors were open; it was empty. She had left her silver brushes on the dressing-table. Her slippers were beneath the bed. I stood and looked at everything.

When the bell rang at the front door I thought it was Philip Davidson. Maureen pattered across the hall to open it. I heard something heavy set down on the floor.

Then there was a movement in the living-room and I went downstairs quietly.

Fay was searching frantically, on the piano, under the cushions, on the table, but always returning to the clock on the mantelpiece, to look behind it and beneath. I saw her push it too far and it toppled over the edge and fell with a crash and a hideous jangling of chimes and the silly whir of a broken spring, into the hearth.

2

She turned blindly to look for the couch, like an old woman venturing a journey, and presently, wavering a little on her high heels, moved towards it and crumpled up in the corner and put her head back. Her face was perfectly white. There were mauve shadows under her eyes and deep lines on either side of her mouth. It was almost unbearable: she had aged twenty years.

"It's all right, Fay," I told her, "it's quite all right."

Time passed. It seemed an hour before she spoke: then it was scarcely above a whisper.

"You're home."

"Yes."

"I thought you might not be. There was a chance . . ." A slight frown passed over her brow and the gloved hand in her lap moved as if to make a gesture of some kind—of hopelessness and defeat and submission.

I told her I understood. "Don't worry. It doesn't matter. I understand."

"Was I much too late?"

"I was home quite early."

She nodded. I think she was pleased, in a way. It had not been by mere minutes that she had arrived too late. There had been no element of chance. She could not yearn for the wasted moments that might have made the difference.

"What did he say?"

"Mickie? But I haven't told him, Fay."

"Then he doesn't know?"

"No."

She drew a deep breath and closed her eyes: the relief must have been overwhelming. "Well, that's something," she said.

I had to keep reminding myself that this was all real, that it had happened, however fantastic it seemed, and was happening, to Fay and to me, that she really had run away, or tried to, from home and from me and her son and everything she loved, in order not to destroy them. I didn't know she had so much love.

"What went wrong, Fay?"

"He didn't turn up." She laughed soundlessly; an expulsion of the breath through the nostrils. "He just didn't turn up."

I looked down at her, not understanding. "Who didn't turn up?"

"The man with the ticket and the money."

"Oh."

"I waited hours. I thought it was the fog."

"Wasn't it?"

"No. I telephoned. He was there. He picked up the receiver and when he heard my voice he just put it back."

"Fay," I said, "I don't quite get it. Who was going to give you what money? What ticket?"

"The aeroplane ticket," she said wearily. "He said he'd get it for me, and lend me some money, some dollars."

"I see." That I could understand; I knew she hadn't more than two or three hundred pounds of her own, saved from the cheques and birthday presents I had been able to give her from time to time. "Where were you going?"

"Paris, first. Then . . . I don't really know." She moved her shoulders.

"You were going alone . . ."

"Did you think I was hopping off for a naughty weekend or something?"

"No."

"I believe you did. You funny old thing."

In despair there is a greater store of action than one ever dreams. She was like a trapped and tethered animal which, in its pitiable panic, will tear its own limbs asunder to escape the rope, thrashing wildly hither and thither, never dead till killed, always dying, still with a tiny reserve of strength to spend in another twitch.

"I'm so sorry, Fay . . ."

She opened her eyes. "You?" she whispered. "What have you got to be sorry about?"

"To have driven you to this."

She smiled. "It wasn't only you, Bobby."

"I'm very sorry."

"Oh, it's all over now."

"Don't worry about it. You needn't worry about it." I couldn't bear to see her huddled on the couch like that; her defeat was more than I could stand. "You've no need to worry. Not any more."

"Why, what's happened?"

"Nothing's happened."

She considered me under her eyelids. "You're such an old duffer," she murmured. "Such an old duffer."

"We'll keep out of trouble somehow."

"Not you," she said.

"Yes, we will."

She shook her head, smiling. "I know you, Bobby. I know you so well."

"We'll say it was a mistake . . ."

She went on shaking her head.

"Who was it, Fay?" I asked her. "Who was going to lend you the money?"

"Nobody you know."

"I'd like to know his name."

"I can't tell you."

Something in her voice brought me round. I saw again in her face the slight hardening I had seen before. Not altogether defeated, then. Another twitch, another spurt still to come, perhaps, in another direction. I was glad, it was a relief, I could have cheered.

"Fay, you really can't walk out on me and then come back and expect me to be content with that." I was delighted.

"Where's Mickie?"

"Upstairs. Fay——"

"Is he all right?"

"Of course he's all right. By the way, I've found out what's been the matter. Nothing very serious . . . just growing pains."

It was several minutes before I saw the tears which were running down her face.

CHAPTER SEVEN

I

I WOKE up with all my promises gathered about the foot of the bed; they followed me into the bathroom on silent feet; when I sat down to breakfast they also sat down, and waited . . . the promise I had made to Fay, that she need worry no more, it would be all right, I would see that it was all right, somehow we would lie our way out of it; the promise I had made to Davidson—had I spoken it? Written it? I couldn't remember, yet it was there; the promise I had given Craig, that nothing would stand in the way, nothing, till justice was done; the promise I had given Mick because he was my son; and the promise I had brandished at Oswald Flood. I took them to work and they sat on my desk and dangled their feet.

In the afternoon I went back to Chiswick. There was no sign of Davidson yet. A few minutes later, however, Bletchley telephoned.

"I'm speaking from Tower Bridge, sir."

"Where?"

"Tower Bridge."

"What are you doing there?"

"It's Davidson, sir. I think he's taken a room here, off Dockhead."

"Dockhead?"

"You know, sir—Tooley Street. South bank."

"Are you sure you haven't made a mistake, Bletchley?"

"Quite sure, sir."

"Give me the address." I jotted it down on the telephone pad: 7 Crocker's Fields. "What sort of a place is it?"

"I don't know, sir—looks as if it might be some sort of lodging house. There are people going in and out."

"All right. You'd better keep an eye on it and let me know if he moves again."

"Right, sir."

It was a relief to know where Davidson was. But Dockhead? I knew the district. That is where St. Saviour's, the barge dock, thrusts a muddy tongue through the huddled wharves to Tooley Street and Tower Bridge Road. It is not a pretty place; on one side of the dock are the wharves and warehouses of Mill Street and the grey jungle which was once called Jacob's Island, and on the other those of Shad Thames. St. Saviour's itself is scarcely more than a creek, too small and shallow for powered craft. The walls which lean out over the blue mud are like the raddled, white-powdered, gaunt-eyed faces of brothel mommas, for they house mills and granaries, and the ancient, sagging bricks are splashed with flour. But I could think of no reason why Davidson should have taken a room there.

Fay was pouring out the tea. We looked at one another.

"Where is Dockhead?" she asked. She had heard at least that, then.

"Near Tower Bridge."

"What's he doing there?"

"I don't know." I watched her adding sugar to the cups of tea. Her face was tense.

We both started when the telephone rang again. I put down the cup and went into the hall. It was Craig.

"I'm speaking from Gravesend," he began. The line was bad.

"Yes."

"I've just seen Davidson's girl, you know, the little girl from the café. . . ."

"Yes."

"I was going to tell him about Pewsey. . . ."

"Yes."

He said then: "I think Boyd's alive."

"What?"

"I gather Davidson has found Spenser Boyd."

For a moment I couldn't speak. "Really, Craig——"

"The fellow he's supposed to have murdered."

"Craig, are you tight?"

"'Fraid not."

"Who told you this?"

"The girl. She says Davidson has found the man for the murder of whom he went to prison. Could hardly be anybody else, could it?"

"She's pulling your leg. Really——"

"Oh, I don't think so."

"I'd like to hear more about it," I said.

"Well, you probably will," he answered drily.

The joke was a little grim, I thought, but I said: "I'll meet you on the south ramp of Tower Bridge."

"Tower Bridge? What on earth for?"

"Because that's where he is, or near it."

"Who?"

"Davidson. And if you're right, Boyd, too."

I heard him say: "My God." And then: "I'll be there at five," and rang off.

I sat and drew circles on the pad. It was like being ushered from a dark night into a brightly-lit hall. I blinked owlishly in the glare, too dazzled yet to see the furniture, but knowing at last beyond any doubt that it was all here, and that beyond the hall the doors of all the rooms I had never entered were wide open.

After a while I went into the living-room, pulling on an overcoat. When I saw her face I knew how much she had heard. She said in a high, taut voice: "Do you want another cup of tea?"

"It was Boyd, wasn't it, Fay," I said, "who failed to turn up with the money?"

"It's quite hot."

"How long have you known him to be alive?"

"Oh, years . . ." Suddenly she bent her head and put her hands up to her face and I was down beside her and all I remember saying was: "My dear, why didn't you tell me, why didn't you tell me?"

The yellow mist gathered in the streets. It was not yet dark, however, and driving was not difficult.

2

It was months before I learned exactly what had taken place, and some of the story is hardly more than conjecture even now. Why, for instance, didn't Spenser Boyd run for life the night Davidson appeared at the door of Longman's Wharf? One can only guess at the reason. We can't be quite sure that he recognised Davidson. Perhaps it was his own uncertainty which deterred him from flight. And he was no fool; he knew well enough that nothing is so damning as to run from mere suspicion. He couldn't even be sure that Davidson would go to the police; if he did, would it not be better to greet them with amused and slightly irritated surprise as George Berry, wharfinger, which had been his name for seventeen years, than to be picked up in flight and ignominiously hustled back to England—a virtually self-confessed Spenser Boyd? What had he to fear? Only one person in the world knew him by any other name, and that was Fay. And she was hardly likely to give him away; she would condemn herself out of hand if she did; and she had already made it clear she had too much to lose. So—to guess at his line of thought—he wouldn't bolt, not yet; he would wait, for a little while, and see.

And he would keep the money he had been about to hand to Fay. It would have been better, certainly, to get rid of her with two or three thousand dollars and a ticket to France, but then it was too late; for it was David-son who delivered the consignment of currency intended for Fay. Gedge, knowing no better, had sent him straight to Boyd's door. So he made no attempt to keep his appointment with Fay that night; instead he kept the money and when she telephoned an hour later, put back the receiver without a word; the currency would be useful if he himself had to take to his heels—it was not too easy to find at short notice. He waited. The police did not come.

I have always wanted to know more about Spenser Boyd. I would have liked to understand him better, to find out what moved him, to get the texture of his particular brand of evil, for stock villainy does not suffice. But he remains elusive, a stout, balding man with a heavy brown moustache and protruding eyes, capable of a crime at whose prolonged coldbloodedness the ordinary mind baulks. The picture is not quite complete. Davidson almost completed it, but the outline is still a little blurred.

I called at the station on Tower Bridge and arranged for a couple of squad cars and some men to stand by, keeping out of sight. Bletchley pointed out the house in Crocker's Fields, a small, bleak, Victorian building of three storeys; some children were kicking an old tennis ball about in the dingy street, though it was nearly dark. Then I went back to the car and waited for Craig. Presently the old Austin drew up behind me and Craig got out; he came round and opened the door. "Better get in," I said. We drove on to Dockhead and pulled up twenty yards short of Crocker's Fields; I could see Bletchley on the corner beneath the street lamp.

"The fog's thickening again," Craig said.

"What happened?"

He told me. He had driven down to Morocco Bay that morning. On the road to High Halstow he had passed a girl whose face, glimpsed through the windscreen, had been vaguely familiar. But he had gone on, left the car, and walked across the marsh to the bay. There had been nobody in the barge. Jackson was watching him from the reeds, his shotgun across his arms.

"Want something, mister?"

"Where's he gone?"

"Went off by hisself, early. She's gone, too."

Craig had remembered the girl then. He went back to the car.

She would run for as long as she could, and then walk; then she would break into a run again. He had seen her a long way ahead on the narrow black road, running and walking. He passed her and pulled up and waited, watching her approach in the mirror above the windscreen and hearing the patter of her heels on the shining wet road. As she came abreast he called: "Like a lift?"

When she stopped he opened the door. "You'd better get in," he told her, and when she hesitated he added: "I'm a friend of Philip Davidson, it's all right." She stared at him wide-eyed, her lips moving. "What seems to be the trouble?" he asked gently. She was shivering. "Listen," he said, "I'm afraid you're going to have to trust me or we'll never get anywhere at all." Her eyes were fastened on his face, searching it, trying to read it. "Where is it you want to go?" he said, and then: "Listen. My name is Craig. I know Philip Davidson quite well, and he knows me . . ."

"Please, I have to go," she said. "It is very important. Excuse . . ." She left the car and began to run. He started up and drove after her and she ran faster and faster, down the road beneath the trees. He stopped the car and got out, to run after her and take her arm. "Let me go!" she cried, struggling to free herself. "The police . . . I must find the police . . ."

"I'll find them for you. What do you want them for?"

"I must tell the police."

"What's wrong? What has happened?"

She went limp and began to cry hopelessly.

"Tell me." He shook her slightly. "What's going on?"

"He is gone to find a man . . ."

They heard the clip-clop of hoofs down the quiet road

and then there was a milk-cart coming towards them. He led her back to the car and in a little while, in broken phrases, she told him what Davidson had told her, that Davidson had found the man for the murder of whom he had gone to prison for many years, and that he was bent on that man's destruction. He listened, staring out of the window.

He drove her back to the marsh and left her there. He would drive fast, he promised her, and find the police and tell them and see that they did as she wished; she could do no more; now she must go back and wait.

She waited. She sat in the cabin all that morning. She told me how the horror of what she had done grew in her mind. Davidson, when he knew, would cast her out utterly. She had lost even so little as she had of his love. But she had saved him, perhaps. She told herself she had done what a woman in love would do; she had offered her love for his life. He would hate her for it, always; but she had done it for him. She must be glad . . .

And when, in the early afternoon, she heard the heavy footsteps on the deck, she felt only panic. She should not be here; she should have gone, have gone. But when the door opened it was Shaw, looming big and dark against the square of light. She shrank back against the wall with her hand to her mouth.

He shut the door, smiling. "All alone," he said.

She could not speak.

"Well, I came for him," Shaw said. "But you'll do. You'll do just as well."

She threw herself towards the door but he put out an arm and caught her in it and she let out a brief scream. He clapped a hand over her mouth. "Shush," he murmured. "What's all the fuss?"

He dragged her to the bunk. She fought with him silently. When she bit into his hand he uttered a yelp and let her go and she fell back against the wall.

"Little bitch," he said. He took hold of her hair.

Neither of them heard Jackson till the old man said: "Leave her alone."

He was standing in the door with the shotgun across his arms. Shaw let go of her hair. "What the hell do you want?" he said.

"I know you, mister." He jerked his head a fraction, over his shoulder. "Get off this ship." He lowered the shotgun and took it in his hands. Shaw looked at it.

"What's she to you?" he said sulkily.

Jackson replied: "Belongs to a friend of mine." He lifted his head again. "Get going, mister." He stood back a little to give Shaw room to pass, and moved the muzzle of the shotgun. Presently Shaw shrugged his big shoulders and went. Jackson watched him go. Then he half turned to the girl, his eyes watering profusely. It took him a long time to get it out:

"You can sit with me," he said, "if you like."

3

Craig had telephoned first to my office, and then to my home, from a petrol station.

"There's no proof that it's Boyd he's after," I said when he had told me the girl's story. "None at all."

"None," he agreed. "Do you think my car will be all right back there?"

"Yes." Bletchley walked to and fro. "We might sit here all night."

It was then something after five o'clock and the shops and offices and factories were closing and the streets were thronged with shadows in the fog; it was thickening; I prayed it would hold off. Bicycles passed us in shoals like minnows in muddy water, with bells tinkling and lights like single, roving eyes. Trucks rumbled homewards with the clatter of bouncing tailboards and cars shone beneath the lamps; now and then a tall bright bus set the earth trembling and cast a square of golden light over the shrinking shadows that flowed along the sidewalks. The fog was smoky and pungent. " 'Hell,' " said Craig, " 'is a city much like London' . . . wouldn't think that was Shelley, would you? 'A populous and smoky city; there are all sorts of people undone, and there is little or no fun done; small justice shown, and still less pity.' " He offered his cigarette packet. "I wonder," he said, lighting the cigarettes, "if Davidson has realised it . . ."

I thought I knew what he meant. I had been turning it over in my mind, too.

"Extraordinary," he murmured. "To be able to kill with absolute impunity."

"I'm not so sure of the impunity," I said.

"Fair's fair. Having paid the penalty, he may now commit the crime. Why not?"

"It's still murder."

"He's done his twenty years in advance, that is all."

"I don't think he'd get away with it."

"You can't try a man twice on the same charge."

"I agree that's the theory."

"But you don't think it would work in practice . . . I do. Tell me: what would they do to suppress the uproar there'd be about hanging a fellow who has already done twenty years on a miscarriage of justice? Show me the Commissioner that would want to face it—or the Home Secretary, either. What about the reputation of the courts? Don't you think so much noise would be considered more damaging than so little silence?"

"That isn't the point." I didn't know what else to say.

"Are you so damned sure the police would press the charge?"

"You've been thinking about it quite a lot, haven't you?"

"I don't mind telling you," he went on, "—and I'd put money on it—that I think the worst he would get would be a rescinding of the probationary period, or whatever they call it, and a return to prison to complete the original sentence. A nice, face-saving little compromise."

"There might be something in what you say."

"Then what are we doing here?"

"It must not happen."

He cried: "For whose sake? Whom are you protecting—Boyd?"

"We aren't protecting anybody, Craig. Come to your senses, for heaven's sake. There will be no murder done if the police can help it. Who appointed Davidson to dispense justice?"

"Well, the courts didn't make too good a job of it, did they?" he said.

"We are here," I told him slowly, "to get Boyd. With any luck Davidson will lead us to him. Then Boyd will be arrested and charged with, among other things, the murder of a man named Delaney. If he is found guilty, he will be hanged. And that's all there is to it."

"And suppose Davidson gets there first?"

"He will have to be held pending a full enquiry."

"I see. Really very simple, isn't it?"

"Quite straightforward."

"There will have to be an enquiry in any case," he said, "won't there?"

"Probably." I knew what he pointed to.

For a few minutes we said no more, but sat watching the jostling shadows on the side-walks. "By the way," he asked at last, "—curious how unimportant it's become —have you any idea how it all happened?"

I had my own theory, as familiar to me as the back of my hand. "Not really," I said. We had been quarrelling: why should I now forget it and confide?

Yes, I had my own theory about what had happened in the cabin of William Driver's spritsail. It credited Boyd with a capacity for quick thinking, cold nerve, and a good deal of luck, but really whatever took place between

the moment Boyd struck Davidson on the side of the head
with the poker and the moment Davidson, recovering,
staggered out of the blazing cabin and dropped over the
beam into the river, can never, now, be more than guesswork. I believe Boyd changed places with the dead
Delaney, ripping off Delaney's outer clothing and sub-
stituting his own, down to the last detail. It is hard to
believe that a man in mortal danger should stop to carry
out a plan of that kind, but it could be done; we had
it tried out; our two constables managed it in a little less
than two minutes. At all events we never reached an
explanation which seemed either as feasible or as likely
as this one. And then I believe he took Delaney's place
on the freighter with whose skipper he had arranged
Delaney's escape, sculling himself away from the barge
in Davidson's dinghy, which he then cast loose. It is
possible that he got rid of Delaney's jacket, which would
be incriminating, on his way out, or perhaps he simply
dropped it over the freighter's side; when the coastguard picked it up and returned it to the police it was
identified as Delaney's.

This, at any rate, was the theory I had drifted towards
during those early years, the one I had been trying to
verify when I went to Rotterdam to find Captain Schrey
—I thought the man a liar then, and still think so now—
and the one I turned my back on when I could get no
further with it.

There was no evasion; whatever I tried to think about
led back to the same abominable merciless truth: if
Boyd were dead, if I now allowed Davidson to kill the
man, there would be nobody, not a soul in earth, to say
that Fay had ever known he was alive. Only Boyd himself could give that evidence — and doubtless would.
The rest of her crime we could probably lie our way out of;
really, I told myself, it was very trifling: a matter of
mistaken identity—grave enough, God knows, in its
consequences, but not in itself felonious.

I stared out of the window. Was there never to be an escape from this hideous circle? I tried to thrust the idea away, to forget its smell, to grind it into the earth like a worm; I tried to blot out the picture in my mind of the woman I had left sitting on the couch in the living-room. Dear God, I whispered, help me now. . . . .

And as if he knew what I was thinking—knew precisely what was going on in my heart, Craig said: "We haven't a description of the man, have we? We don't even know what name he is using, do we?"

No; I hadn't asked her.

We sat and watched Bletchley, who watched the house in Crocker's Fields.

4

Davidson stood in the window of a bedroom on the second floor of number 7 Crocker's Fields, and waited for nightfall. He watched half a dozen boys kicking an old tennis ball about in the dusk. When it got too dark they broke up and went off in pairs, or singly; one of them came into the house and he heard the boy's voice calling and then a woman answering. The young man in the raincoat moved into the circle of light beneath the lamp on the corner, turned idly, glanced at the house, and then strolled away again out of sight; Davidson had seen him before, several times, in the marsh: the police he supposed. It didn't matter.

He was sorry the boys with the tennis ball had gone. He had followed their game with interest, fascinated by the movement: just the movement; he remembered how he used to stand on his chair in his cell on a Saturday afternoon, to watch a leaf rolling across the yard in the wind; any movement was attractive, a source of entertainment, of interest, of distraction; the leaf would scuttle out of sight and Saturday afternoon returned, and the grey nightmare of the weekend, when there was no work and so no sleep for any man in that prison, where you slept only from exhaustion, and if you slept you would be woken by the screams of the man in the next cell, who screamed in his sleep, out of the anguish of his mind; he would keep on waking you, till presently you realised that the scream was in your own throat and that you were waking yourself. He remembered the rich farce of church parade on Sunday morning, when they were allowed to sing; that was the only time in the week when a man might raise his voice above a murmured "Yes, sir," or "No, sir," and so you took this moment of sweet release for all it was worth, and bellowed till your throat was raw: hymns; and the foolish parson, moved by the prodigious fervour of the singing, beamed on his flock, believing the voices to be lifted in praise. He smiled faintly, remembering it, and wished the boys with the tennis ball would come back. He shivered; it was cold in the bedroom. When the buses went past beyond the lamp the knobs on the brass bedstead rattled distantly.

He was cool now, cool and detached and able to see very clearly. He remembered how he had been last night, when he had got back to the marsh; then he had been like a bird that had flown into a wall—stunned and broken, flapping aimless wings. Elsa had been waiting for him. She had welcomed him and tried to enfold him with love, believing he had returned for her sake. And then when he cruelly rebuffed her, her patient acceptance of his mood oppressed him like a dead weight.

"I cannot live each day in terror that you will not return," she had cried.

Who had asked her to? Had he hounded her to his bed? He had taken a waif, a stray dog which now, under the banner of love, assumed rights—rights! Her love was like a voracious plant bent upon his suffocation which, when he took a step, winced like a quivering naked nerve and cried out. She bullied him with her love, flourished it over his head like a whip.

"Today I saw the man," he had told her as if merely voicing the problem for his own better understanding of it, "—the man for the murder of whom I was sent to prison many years ago." He set it up like a schoolboy with a sum to do, repeating it coaxingly as though to wheedle the answer from its hiding-place in his own tired brain. And Elsa, he remembered, had been on her knees in front of him, her face twisted in the effort to make him go on talking till she should understand. He shook the tendrils off his wrists.

"Why will you not go to the police?" she begged him. "They will do it. It is their duty. . . ."

How could you explain? It was his alone. He wished she would be silent. Without this he could neither live nor die.

5

We sat in the car and the torrents swept past on either side. It seemed a long time before they lost momentum. Then they slowed quite suddenly, as if a tap had been turned off, and by seven-thirty the side-walks were peopled only by a few hurrying stragglers. The lights of a milk bar shone a bilious pallid green across the kerb. The fog was closing in. I watched Bletchley under the lamp.

When Bletchley moved, I planned, and Davidson set off, we would close in behind. When we saw which direction he was taking, I would try to seal off the area with a net of men, a sack to catch Boyd in when he should bolt. And we would follow Davidson closely.

While I was thinking about it Bletchley signalled and moved away from the lamp. I thought: now. Then we saw Davidson coming round the corner and crossing the road about twenty yards away. I left Craig in the car.

I followed Bletchley into the black abyss of Shad Thames and the fog dropped behind me like a curtain. One's footsteps had suddenly an echo. The lonely gas lamps hissed softly and somewhere far above, up beyond the gangways and motionless cranes and towering walls, the city murmured; perhaps there were stars. I kept Bletchley in sight and prayed he was hard on Davidson's heels. I remembered these wharves. Their interiors are timbered, warped and crumbling; you could hide an army in the wandering passages; on the other side the river flows and sometimes you can catch a glimpse of it along the narrow alleys, where steps go down to the water's-edge among the chutes and cranes and dolphins and huddled barges.

When we came to the tunnel beneath the ramp of Tower Bridge I caught up with Bletchley and told him to run up to the station on the bridge and get some men and seal off the exits from Pickle Herring Road, which lay at the other end of the tunnel, and to tell the station officer to contact the Thames Division and arrange for a patrol along the south side of the Pool. Presently he had gone and I went into the tunnel; I heard Davidson's footsteps far ahead of me and I broke into a run. At the other end of the tunnel, in Pickle Herring Road, I stopped and listened. There was no sound. I went on, right to the end, to Morgan's Lane, but there was no sound anywhere. He had gone. I ran back to the tunnel, looking in the doorways and down the alleys, but I neither heard him nor saw him. I remember whispering: "Oh, God . . ." I hadn't meant to lose him. It wasn't deliberate. I swear I hadn't meant to lose him.

6

Very briefly, in the wry, half-sardonic way he had of telling his own story, he told me the rest.

The chauffeur was sitting on a chair at the foot of the sagging timbered stairs reading an evening newspaper. On the wall behind him there was a board which read:

George Berry & Co. Enquiries, with an arrow pointing up the flight of stairs. On the left there was a door, beyond the banister. A single naked light hung from the ceiling.

When Davidson pushed open the door the chauffeur lowered the newspaper and said: "Oh, it'th you. I thought I heard thomebody." He smiled. "You can go on up." And Davidson had at once the feeling that he was expected.

He looked up the stairs to the dark landing at the top and then again at the smiling boy on the chair. The place smelled of grain and timber and, unexpectedly, of vinegar.

"It'th quite all right, you can go on up."

Davidson looked at him vacantly.

"I thay," the boy said, "you're in a bit of a thtate, aren't you?" The smooth round face twitched.

Davidson's eyes cleared. Then he was climbing the stairs and his feet were coming down heavily on the frayed timber, climbing up towards the dark landing at the top.

He heard the chauffeur calling: "Thecond on the left," and then, giggling: "No, that'th the lav. The thecond. That'th it."

He took the handle in his hand. For a moment he waited. He felt as if he were about to vomit. Then he turned the handle and leaned on the door and it opened.

In the far corner of the little office there was a desk, under the shuttered windows, and Boyd sat there in the light of the desk lamp with the centre drawer of the desk open in front of him, leaning forward with his elbows on the arms of the chair.

He had changed really very little. He was heavier, of course, and his hair had thinned a good deal; a thick brown moustache disguised his upper lip—indeed the whole face, for its nakedness now seemed clothed; but the flat glassy eyes were the same and the skin, though looser and twinkled with tiny purple stars, had the same dull sheen.

He sat forward with his head a little on one side and an expression on his face of bland attentiveness, like an employer about to interview a disgruntled foreman whom it would be a pity to lose. His plump hands were folded along the edge of the open drawer.

"Come in, Philip," he said gently. "I have been expecting you."

A rat shuffled in the skirting-board. Davidson leaned back against the door, not to seal it off, nor really out of deliberate negligence; he felt ill and dizzy. There was a faint odour of incense in the room.

"Sit down, Philip."

He sank on to the chair by the desk and slumped forward with his elbows on his knees and pressed his thumb and forefinger against his eyes. He heard Boyd begin to talk.

He did not remember, when he described the scene to me, how long Boyd talked for; perhaps half an hour, he thought; nor did he remember much that Boyd said. He heard the voice at a great distance, soothing, soft and sweet and furry with pity, like a drug, dissolving pain. Life, Boyd said, picked out its loved ones and its victims, but really there was so little to choose. He understood, he understood all there was in earth; he was glad and humble that Davidson had come to him at last. For this, now, was the end of suffering, for both of them. Now they could join together, as it had always been intended they should, and he, Boyd, could prostrate himself as he had longed to do for so long, and kiss the wounds he had inflicted . . .

"Then I began to listen," Davidson told me.

To suffer in the mind, as Boyd had suffered, was no less, he said, than to bare one's back to the scourge, as Davidson had done; perhaps it was more, even more. He had nailed a man to the cross, but the flesh which had bled had been his, Boyd's, and the scars were in his heart and in his soul. But he had come to understand. In seventeen years of torment you learn much, much.

He had learned. Sooner or later you must surrender, for there was no escape. Davidson had not suffered in vain. He had not hung there spread-eagled for nothing. Out of his hell the light had come. A soul was saved. God had relented, God had forgiven. So now there was only to kneel hand in hand, tyrant and martyr . . .

It was amazing. But he went on rather too long. And Davidson, sitting with his head in his hand, forgot his astonishment. He was trying to remember when exactly it was that his fever had spent itself. Not now; certainly it wasn't now; now was only the moment of realisation. It must have been a long time ago that the dregs of the passion had flowed away. He listened to the lilting voice and realised with an odd sense of shock that he was not only disgusted; he was bored and that was the end of it.

When Boyd left the desk and went to the cabinet against the wall and took out a bottle and two glasses, Davidson stood up and leaned across the desk and took from the open drawer the gun that he knew Boyd had had there while he was talking. He released the catch and broke it and dropped the rounds into his hand. Boyd turned as he put the gun back in the drawer and one of the glasses fell and broke.

Boyd stood with his back to the wall and the bottle in his hand. His face shone a little in the light. When Davidson moved towards him he drew a sharp breath and swung the bottle. Davidson took the blow on his forearm, which it numbed somewhat, but the bottle fell and rolled away across the floor to fetch up against the wall. So that at last there was nothing left, no bottle, no gun, no penalty, no impediment whatever between Davidson and the execution of the deed; he was free.

The chauffeur looked up and smiled as he came down the stairs. "All thettled?"

"Yes."

"Good."

"Is there another way out of here?" He didn't want to run into the police; they had nothing to do with it. "A door on to the quay?"

"Over there." The boy nodded towards the door beyond the banister. "It'th open."

He went into the dark warehouse. The air smelled of fog and copra. Presently he saw the tall sliding doors, which were slightly ajar; the night was luminous beyond, and he had a sensation of a vast presence, which was the river, flowing stealthily by. He moved towards it.

Almost immediately the door behind him was flung open and Spenser Boyd was in the square of dirty yellow light with his shadow falling far out across the wide floor and the gun in his hand. He was calling.

"Philip! Philip!"

Davidson turned. "It's all over," he shouted. His voice echoed in the gaunt, empty building. Why was the man following him like this? "It's all finished!" Surely there was no need to explain?

"Where are you?"

"Here . . ." He saw the flash of light and felt the shocking blow in his forearm at the same time; he was dizzied by the crashing explosion. But now he understood. He turned and ran, out through the doors and on to the timbers over the flowing water.

Boyd was calling: "Philip! Philip!"

Book Four
THE ESTUARY

CHAPTER ONE

I

WE WAITED till dawn. With a heart like lead I went back to the office, having arranged for the cordon round Shad Thames and Pickle Herring Road to be maintained. In the office I asked to be informed of the discovery of any murdered man in that area—information which would not normally come my way—and for a note of any bodies fished out of the river below the Pool. A description of Davidson was circulated among the squad cars and stations of the Metropolitan area and on both banks of the Thames as far as Sheerness; he was to be held for questioning. I asked for a check to be made of all persons, employers and employed, working in the Shad Thames and Pickle Herring Road area, and applied for the search warrants. I wrote a note to Flood, telling him briefly what had happened and asking for an interview, and left it on his desk so that he should see it as soon as he should come in.

Then, when I could think of no more to do, I wrote out my letter of resignation, or rather, since one cannot lightly resign, a letter requesting release. After that, while I waited for Flood's arrival, I went through the accumulation of old papers in my desk. It was a wretched job.

It was ten minutes to eleven when Flood sent for me. I went along to his office. "Good morning, Lowther." He looked at me with his heavy-lidded buzzard's eyes. "I have your note. How is it he gave you the slip?"

"That was my fault."

"Didn't you cordon the place?"

233

"So far as possible, yes. It's a big area."

"Have you applied for search warrants?"

"It's being done now."

"Tell me——" he leaned back—"how do you know it was Boyd?"

"We found out from Davidson's girl."

"By name? Did she give you the name?"

"No, not the name."

"So you don't really know that it was Boyd he was after —or even that Boyd is in fact alive . . ."

"I'm pretty sure."

"But you don't know whether Davidson found him——"

"No. There are no reports as yet."

He tapped the desk with his finger. "Well," he said, "what is it you want to do, Lowther?"

I told him what I had already done . . . "And," I concluded, "I'd like to hand over. I think it should be treated as a matter of the highest importance. I'd like to hand over to the Divisions or C.I.D.—where it always should have been."

"Come, Lowther——"

"Every available man should be put on it." I was in no mood for Flood's obliquities. "Have you thought what the consequences would be if Davidson has to be charged with the murder of that man?"

"I have. I take it you have considered the more—shall we say personal?—consequences?"

"Yes."

"Really, you know, Lowther, I have been trying to help you . . ."

And yourself, I thought. But he had dropped the notion now. I believe he had tried it out, very tentatively, for a little while.

"Yes, I know," I said, "and I'm very grateful. Now it's time it was taken out of my hands."

"Well, if that's what you wish . . ." He drew a breath. "Perhaps you're right."

"Thank you, sir. I'm preparing a report. It will be ready this afternoon." So it was done; there remained the letter; I laid it on his desk. "I am asking to be retired," I said. "There is my letter—perhaps you would be good enough to pass it up to the Deputy."

He frowned and picked up the envelope. "Retired?" he said. He turned the envelope over.

"Released, if you prefer."

"But my dear fellow—what on earth for?"

"On the grounds of ill-health." I had no stomach for the kind of self-abnegation he wanted to hear.

"Nobody else thinks you've failed in your job, Lowther," he said at last. "I suppose that's what is behind it?"

"I'd be grateful if you would give it to the Deputy Commissioner."

"Well, I will, if it's what you want," he said, "but I may as well tell you now: it is unlikely to be accepted."

"I don't see why not."

"In the first place because I, for one, will do my best to see that it isn't," he said. He looked up. "Lowther, have you any idea what the Commissioner thinks of you? Well, it doesn't matter. The point is that the police don't axe a man they think of as highly as you, simply because his family happens to be in trouble."

"Then they're very unwise."

"They will be grateful to you for making it easy for them to do so, I dare say, but I doubt very much if they will avail themselves of your offer." He smiled and nodded, not displeased with his little speech. "However, I'll see that your letter reaches the Deputy. For the rest . . ." He blinked thoughtfully at the ceiling, showing the loose red dewlaps beneath his chin. "For the rest, we'd better have a chat with Waverley. He'll probably want you and Harris to handle it together." He picked up the telephone and asked to be put through to the Assistant Commissioner, C.I.D.

I was bleakly thankful. There was an end of it.

2

After a long talk with Harris I drove home; I had placed myself at his disposal, but begged a few hours' respite; I was very worried about Fay. Harris promised to keep me informed by telephone. Dear Harris, stout and sandy-haired and twinkling; if anybody could set things on their proper course, Harris could, with a warm, friendly, remorseless precision. The rest would follow.

As I opened the door I had suddenly the feeling that something frightful had happened to her—that she had run away again or put her head in the gas oven. The house was quiet.

I called: "Fay!"

"Is that you, Bobby?" The voice came from the living-room. I closed the door, relieved. She must have been waiting since last night, when I left to meet Craig; I should have telephoned; I should have done something.

Her face was lined and pale and her voice, when she spoke, strained and expectant, unnatural with the effort to hold it at a normal level.

"Where's Mick?"

"Upstairs." She dropped the thing she was sewing. "Bobby, what's happened?"

"I'm sorry I didn't ring up or anything, Fay."

"You would have done, I suppose, if you could . . . well? Something has happened, hasn't it?"

"Well, no, not really, not yet." I sat down.

"You didn't sleep last night," she said.

"Not very much."

"Your face looks like a ploughed field. You're a fool. You know what you're like if you don't sleep . . ."

"Davidson has disappeared," I told her. "We lost him." She stopped. "What does that mean?"

"We don't know yet."

"Did he find——"

"Boyd? That's what we're not sure about."

"So . . ." She made a little gesture. "So everything is just as it was."

"No, I wouldn't say that." How was I going to tell her? "We have some more people working on it now . . . get it straightened out in no time." She was watching my face with her tired, hunted, defiant eyes; I felt a wave of pity for her and was glad of what I had decided and done. I asked her: "How did you know Boyd was alive, Fay? Did you run into him?"

Her face hardened; she shook her head.

I got up and began to move about the room. "It isn't only curiosity on my part, Fay. We have to be ready. If Boyd is found—I mean, alive—then he'll probably try to implicate other people. He's pretty certain to say you knew he was alive. So we have to have our answer off pat."

She put a hand to her throat and I saw the puzzlement and then the slow dawning of hope in her face.

"How did you know, Fay?"

"From my father. Bobby . . ."

"Your father?"

"When he died."

"When you went to see him? Good Lord, I never dreamed——"

"Boyd had been giving him money."

"I see. I suppose I should have guessed." I remembered how silent and constrained she had been, for weeks after her father's death. "Well, we'll come back to that."

"Bobby, tell me, what are you trying to do?"

"Did you ever see Boyd?"

"No——"

"You never actually met him till a few days ago when you went to borrow some money—is that right?"

"Yes."

"What made you pick on him?"

"He was the most likely one. I could have given him away . . ."

"Yes. Yes, of course. Did you go to his office?"

"No, I telephoned and then met him——"

"Did you write any letters?"

"No. Bobby darling——"

I sat down beside her on the couch. "It needs thinking out."

I felt her hand slip into mine. "Oh my dear," she whispered, "—that I should have done this to you!"

"Oh, nonsense——"

"You'll hate me for the rest of your life."

"Rubbish." Then I plunged. "As a matter of fact, Fay, I'm thinking of retiring. It's not just this—this business. It's been at the back of my mind some time. We have some money saved up, and there'll be a pension, you know. I've been thinking about that fruit farm—not too much digging in a fruit farm, just a few acres."

"Oh no," she cried. "No. No . . ."

"It's always been in the back of my mind, as you know. Devon would be the place . . ."

And then, mercifully, the telephone rang. I had not expected it so soon.

It was Harris. He thought I would like to know, he said, that he had picked up the trails. They were both alive, he said, both Boyd and Davidson. They seemed to be sticking to the river and it looked to him as if I had got hold of the wrong end of the stick . . . either that, or the pursuit had gone, so to speak, into reverse, for it was Davidson who was running and Boyd who was hunting. Surprising. Anyway, he, Harris, had got a pretty good description of Boyd, for in the check of the Shad Thames and Pickle Herring Road areas he had netted Boyd's pansy chauffeur and, by dint of frightening the boy out of his wits, had obtained all they needed, including the name; the fellow was calling himself George Berry . . . "We'll have him in the bag in no time," Harris said. He wondered if I would like to meet him at Gravesend.

I kissed Fay good night and told her I would be back soon and not to wait up.

It was freezing hard outside, but clear and starry.

CHAPTER TWO

I

BOYD WAS somewhere behind him calling his name, Davidson said. His arm swung against his side, but there was no pain as yet, beyond a dull ache. He wanted to stop and explain, to make it clear to the man that it was over and that there was no necessity for this, to reason with him and allay his fears. But Boyd was still calling and, reluctantly, Davidson fled, knowing that if he stopped he must either kill or be killed.

The parapet of the wharf came up out of the fog; he ran its full length till he found the steps. He heard Boyd's voice. "Philip! Philip, where are you?" He turned down the steps. There were lighters on the campshed in ranks three or four bottoms deep, nudging the slippery green timbers. He jumped from the steps down on to the flat boards of the nearest craft and, slipping, fell heavily on the wounded arm and the pain leapt to his throat. There were sirens booming out across the water. He jumped from barge to barge, out away from the wharf, till there was no further he could go, except into the river. The barge was empty and he slithered down the ladder into the cavernous well among the tarpaulins and sacking and crawled into the dark cave of the prow.

He lay listening; there was no sound but his own hoarse breathing and the caress of the river against the iron stem of the lighter. He tied his handkerchief about the oozing wound in his arm and drew the knot with his teeth, and then nursed the arm in his lap; the bullet had passed through the muscle, he thought; the hand was useless. He ground his teeth against the flowing pain.

Mostly awake and listening, sometimes unable to fight off the nausea that rose in waves from his stomach, he lay among the sacking all that night. He dreamed a little and woke himself with his own voice. In the morning he would go back to the marsh, to Elsa. He was full of love for her; he opened his heart and let it in. The city murmured in the sky.

Towards daybreak the fog lifted and the next time he woke the barge was moving.

From the ladder he could see. The tug scrambled round in a circle like a terrier on a slippery floor—he could have laughed aloud with the familiar delight of it—and headed downstream. The shore began to slip past and the barge rolled and trembled on the straining ropes: he caught the bitter-sweet stench of the smoke that rolled from the tug's funnel, casting a swift shadow in the cold bright sunlight. He had an intoxicating sense of homecoming. Her voice whispered in his head and her lips touched his ears.

So the journey began. But when they came up into Gallion's Reach and the tug slowed and went close inshore and sounded a peremptory call, he knew they were going to lock into the Royal Albert basin and he must leave the barge. They rumbled into the lock between the high black walls and presently he felt the inrush of water and the slow rise of the level. When the beam of the barge came up to the crest of the lock he clambered up the ladder and jumped. There was a shout from the bridge of the tug but he ran across the clinker towards the group of small buildings on the water-front. He was surprised to find himself staggering. But nobody followed. He leaned against the wall of the hut. His arm throbbed as if his heart itself were in the wound. High against the white sky the cranes nodded and dipped and swung like a herd of giraffes, feeding.

"Hallo, what's up with you?" the man said.

He wore the blue serge trousers of a uniform, but the shabby jacket and cap of a man going off duty; he was wheeling a bicycle. "What d'you want?"

"Nothing." He stood away from the wall, shaking his head.

"Nothing, eh?"

"Looking for a lift down . . . Gravesend."

"Well, you won't get it here, chum. Say, you look bad. Like a cup o' char?"

"Yes. Yes, I would."

"Well, see my mate. He's in there." He jerked his head towards the door of the little building. "Jim!" he called. "Got any tea left? Feller here would like a cup." He nodded to Davidson. "There you are, see my mate," and he called: "Be seeing you, Jim!" He nodded again and got on his bicycle and pedalled away.

"You're very kind," Davidson said, but the man had gone. He took the damaged arm and pushed the hand into his pocket; the hand was bloody and swollen. Then he went into the hut.

"Shut the door," the man at the desk told him. He had a small wizened face like a walnut, and drooping lips. "Saw you jump out of that craft. You from Longman's? Shouldn't do that, you know." He nodded at the jug of tea on the floor by the stove. "Well, help yourself now you're here."

"Thank you." He poured the tea into a mug unsteadily; it slopped over the floor. The man watched him. Beyond, through the window, there was the lock in the pale sunlight. The tea was strong and sweet and the spinning in his head slowed and cleared.

"How's George these days?" the man said.

Davidson looked at him.

"George Berry." The man shook his head. "You never heard of him, did you? Well, no matter. Sit yourself down a minute. No hurry." He went into the adjoining office.

"Got a little job to do," he said. He closed the door and Davidson heard the tinkle of a telephone and then the man's voice talking softly.

He stumbled out into the open air.

2

Boyd, we learned later, told his associates that Davidson had attempted to inform against them—that he had been to the police about the smuggling in which they were all engaged. It was an intelligent move; in this way they were induced to act quickly and ruthlessly on their own behalf as well as his; I doubt if any of them, with the possible exception of Shaw, would have contemplated murder for Boyd's sake alone, much less had they known the whole story. As it was they were alarmed and angry, they were many, and there seemed small risk involved in pushing a lonely jailbird over the side of a boat in the Thames estuary.

The chauffeur knew little of Boyd's movements beyond the fact that there had been a telephone call at about eight o'clock that morning, after which Boyd had left. It could not have been difficult to slip through the loose cordon we had thrown about the area—if indeed he was conscious of it at all; it is more than likely that the constable at the end of Morgan's Lane, armed only with a description of Davidson, touched his helmet when Mr. Berry passed and wished him a very good morning; he had probably known Mr. Berry for ten years. Mr. Berry had thus a start of at least an hour.

There was no trace of Davidson. Harris's men found spots on the floor of the warehouse which might have been bloodstains, but that was all. Nothing came to light till a check was made of the movements of the craft which had been standing empty on the campshed during the night. They were followed to the Royal Albert basin.

The lock official, under questioning, admitted he had seen a man answering Davidson's description.

Harris's argument was sound, I suppose. He was after Boyd; he used Davidson as the decoy. Once he had picked up Davidson's trail he was content to let the man run, keeping him in sight if possible, but with no intention of intervening till Boyd should try to pounce; I was too deeply embroiled to see it quite so technically; I would have held Davidson on some pretext, for his own sake, and looked for Boyd after: a fair enough reason why Harris was a good policeman and I a bad one.

He traced Davidson as far as the Anglo-American Oil jetty in Long Reach. That was in the late afternoon, and it was nearly dark and bitterly cold. Where Davidson had been during the hours of daylight nobody knew— trudging along the waterfront of the north bank, he told me later, looking for a passage downstream, hiding when he thought he was followed, stowing away in empty lighters, plodding through the nightmare towards the sanctuary which must surely lie at the end.

At the A.-A.O. pier he picked up a small craft whose destination appeared to be Sheerness, a long way downstream. There was a possibility he might prevail on the master of the vessel to set him ashore at Gravesend, and Harris warned his men there to watch for him. But it was by no means certain. The tide was on the ebb and already there would be half a mile, in some places a mile and more, of impassable mud-flats along the south bank; if Davidson were not put ashore at Gravesend, therefore, he would have to go on to Sheerness.

Harris saw two alternatives open to him: either to hope to pick up the trail where and when Davidson should again set foot on land, or to abandon the idea of using him as decoy and stop and search all small craft heading into the estuary. It was not an agreeable decision to have to make, for if he picked up Davidson he was almost certain to lose Boyd, since Boyd would undoubtedly drop the pursuit and bolt as soon as he realised what was afoot; on the other hand he might be letting Davidson go to his death. Knowing what it cost him, I have always liked Harris the more for the decision he made: he asked the Thames Division to stop and search all small vessels east of the Chapman Light and, if they found Davidson, to hold him.

It was then, having done that, that he telephoned me at home.

3

When I drove into Gravesend it was ten minutes to eight. The streets were quiet; a few lost souls huddled together to form a queue outside a cinema. I turned into the narrow street down to the ferry station and pulled up a few yards short of the open lamplit space at the river's edge. A man detached himself from the shadows and strolled up the hill towards me. It was Bletchley.

"Nothing doing here, sir, not yet."

"Are you alone?"

"Oh no, sir—men all over the place."

"Where's Superintendent Harris?"

"At the station, sir. He left the message, sir, in case you turned up here. He wondered if you'd like to go on to Morocco Bay . . ."

Going up the hill I saw two constables in a shop doorway and then, further up, two more. At the top of the hill there was a squad car. It was a great comfort to see it all, and to be a part of it; there were no tortuous problems here; one did one's job. And then I thought: but he should have reached Gravesend: if he means to come ashore here he should have done so by now. I tried to remember the configuration of the shore. But Harris would have covered every yard; wherever it was possible to land he would have a man.

I drove on out of the town. The moon was rising and a gusty wind sent shreds of cloud hurrying across the sky. It was freezing and the fences at the narrow road's side were white in the glare of the headlamps.

I remembered the boom, the old war-time defence obstacle that stuck out like a bony finger from the mud-flats of St. Mary's Bay to the dredged channel, just before I reached Halstow.

4

First you would see the winking green eye at the end of the boom, and then, a mile and a half further on, down-stream, the light over the shoals. I knew how it would go. There would be very few small craft on the river at that time of night: nondescript little hulks carrying chalk or cement or clay or old oil-drums to and from the Med-way and the factories upstream. Their navigation lights would be visible quite a long way away, but curiously disembodied, for the hulls would have no outline against the dark water, and the patrol boats would know there was a powered vessel under way only by the muffled throbbing of an engine, carried hither and thither on the wind.

They would move up alongside and tell the master to cut off his engine, and he would, rolling a little and rubbing shoulders with the launch like an old billy-goat against a wall. The patrol men would throw a light along the greasy deck and ask the skipper if he had put in at the A.-A.O. jetty in Long Reach that afternoon and picked up a man wearing a cap, a tall man, gaunt, with a gun-shot wound of some kind. No and no and no. Till at last the thick, testy, old man's voice in the wheelhouse would hesitate and then answer yes, yes he had; he had put him off at the boom in St. Mary's, no harm meant, feller never said nothing . . . but back, back upstream, way upalong.

And the sergeant would signal by radio and Harris would get the message.

But Davidson used the boom quite without guile: it was the skipper of the craft he picked up in Long Reach who suggested it, first asking where Davidson wanted to go and then offering to run up alongside the obstacle as near inshore as the tide would allow. Davidson was grateful.

He heard the engine gather speed and the little boat moved away. He set off along the frail gangway that loped from gantry to gantry towards the invisible shore, his shadow in the moonlight stretching out like a ribbon across the whispering mud. The wind shoved at him and whipped away the white smoke of his breath. His arm was a burning weight at his side. It was a long way.

Then he felt the soft, rubbery earth beneath his feet and the sibilance of the turf against his boots. He began to run, swaying. A duck went up from the reeds a little way ahead of him with a whir of wings and a wild, liquid cry. The hulks loomed up out of the darkness, solid against the stars, and he saw the light in the cabin. Once he called her name: "Elsa!" But when he threw open the door there was only Spenser Boyd sitting on the edge of the bunk, smiling at him.

5

When he could go no further he toppled into the reeds as if they were water and lay among the stiff stalks and opened his mouth wide to get the air down into his lungs, which were never deep enough. When he could hold his breath he heard them over to his left calling to one another with clipped, urgent voices as they beat the frozen pools and reeds and islands of marsh grass. Then there was silence.

After a time he took hold of his left hand gently with his right and began to pull it from beneath his weight, a few inches at a time, resting between each effort, wincing and whispering to himself. It came free. He could not see it except as a shape in the gloom, but he could feel the tremulousness of the fingers; they were curled inwards and strangely hot to the touch.

He listened to the hiss of the wind in the reeds above his head and the wild soft rattle of the blades one against the other; far away across the river a buoy tolled querulously. There was no other sound. He dropped his head to his hand. Where was she? Where had she gone? Why had she left him like this when he needed her most? For Christ's sake why hadn't she waited? Boyd had waited . . . "I've been waiting hours for you, Philip," the man had said. And Davidson had stood gaping in the doorway. "What have you done with her?" he whispered. And Boyd with a shake of the head had answered: "But there was nobody here, Philip," and looked round the cabin. "Nobody . . ."

Then as he turned Boyd had begged him: "Don't go, Philip, please don't go," and Davidson, exasperated beyond endurance, had told the man he wanted nothing but to be left alone: why couldn't Boyd leave him in peace? It was all finished. Finished. Yes, he forgave him—forgave him, if that was what the man wanted. It was ended, could he not understand?

"Oh, Philip, Philip . . . " He had shaken his head piteously. "Come with me. Come with me, Philip. Let us go hand in hand . . ."

He had shut the door and crossed the deck to the ladder. A cloud sprawled across the moon. And as he went towards the hulk that Jackson lived in, two or three men had risen from the reeds, tall shadows, armed with staves or clubs of some kind; and beyond there were others, coming towards him.

He had broken into a lumbering run, veering to his

right towards the flank of the advancing men, straight at the nearest. The man had lifted the stave and swung with it and they both fell, rolling over and over on the edge of the reeds. Davidson had left him there and the others must have thought this was Davidson, for they gathered over the fellow and struck at him. Davidson ran into the darkness, round the rim of the bay till he could go no further and then had thrown himself into the reeds.

Now suddenly he knew he was trapped, for he heard them behind him; they had moved across the open country and now were beating the reeds systematically to drive him before them, back towards the hulks where the other men would be waiting for him. He heard them slashing at the reeds and then a voice and then the squelch of a boot in the mud. So he got to his feet and ran again. They must have heard his pounding feet on the soft earth.

His eyes were misting. The spittle on his tongue was thin and metallic and each breath was a muffled explosion in the pit of his heart. His knees were wobbling and he stumbled over the rotting timbers among the pools of water which, freezing now and covered with a frail crust of ice, wheezed and crackled under his weight. The moon shone out and he saw the ancient ribs all about him, white with frost, in ranks, high and smooth and glittering. The wind stirred and the reeds rattled and distantly across the flat land the roof of the warehouse clapped its iron hands.

"Philip, Philip . . . this way . . ."

He saw the man standing on the edge of the reeds below the stern of Jackson's home. He was calling. His coat was open and he wore no hat and wind ruffled his thin hair.

"Philip, come . . ."

Davidson stared at him stupidly.

"There is no escape . . ."

And suddenly Davidson screamed: "Then if I must——"

He was plodding towards him, reaching out with his hand for the throat, and Boyd, seeing his face, was crying: "No, Philip. Not that, not that. No . . ." and was pulling the gun from his pocket.

I heard the hollow booming of the old shotgun from where I was on the track, and a moment afterwards the girl's high, cut-short scream.

We all seemed to reach the place at much the same time. One of Harris's men had covered Boyd's head with a small white handkerchief; it was big enough. I had a word with Harris. Craig was there; I don't know how he had contrived it, but he was there; he smiled and nodded as I passed him. Everybody seemed ready to smile; there was a rare, overt gladness in the way we all moved. Jackson hung about on the fringe of the little gathering with the shotgun still in his arms; nobody took much notice of him. When he was warned and told he would have to come along with us he just nodded and sniffed; he was very pleased with himself; he wanted me to tell the girl to ask his friend Davidson if he would like a mug of tea; it was hot, he said. She was sitting on the ground with Davidson's head in her arms. I couldn't tell what she was saying; she was whispering to him in her own language; not that that made any difference: whatever tongue she used would have been foreign to us.

6

There is little else to tell. When I saw Flood he told me the Commissioner wanted a full report, a history of the whole case, for the Minister; various decisions would have to be made on a ministerial level (I always loved that resounding, Olympian flourish) and a policy decided upon before the business could be made public and Davidson formally cleared. "The Commissioner thinks you might prepare the report, Lowther."

"Me?"

"Yes."

"Oh. Oh well, I suppose it really makes no odds."

"And incidentally," Flood continued, opening the drawer of his desk, "the Commissioner isn't very interested in this." He tossed me the letter in which I asked for my retirement.

"Has he seen it?"

"Yes. He says he doesn't want Commander Lowther's head now or at any other time."

"Nevertheless I would prefer to be released."

"Well, you'd better talk to him about it yourself."

"I will."

He looked at me, blinking his small, red, intelligent eyes. "Lowther," he began presently, "just why is it you want to go? The affair is virtually over—settled. Davidson is cleared and will be recompensed. There will be a lot of mud thrown, no doubt——"

"You know that's not the reason."

"Of course not. I'm simply saying that though it will be very unpleasant for everybody . . ."

"Not least, Davidson," I reminded him. "I'm damned sure Davidson doesn't want it. He wants to be left alone."

"Yes, I dare say. However, it is no longer a matter of merely putting Davidson right in the eyes of the world, it's the world, now, putting itself right in its own eyes. Nobody gives a tinker's curse that Davidson doesn't want it, we may as well face that. The point is that as far as you personally are concerned the thing is finished. Why do you have to go?"

I drew a breath.

"You and I have worked together a good many years."

I tried to sum it up: "I have to go," I told him, "because I have to write that report."

He fiddled with his pen. Then he leaned back in his chair—"Yes," he murmured, and folding his hands behind his head, stared at the ceiling. "You know, Lowther," he went on, "we all get a little corrupted by our obligations. We take on too many, perhaps—we can't ever hope to fulfil them all. But it's not so terrible a crime—is it? Where do we acquire them, after all? Out of pity, surely. Or love. Something of the kind. Because we feel sorry for somebody, or perhaps because somebody feels sorry for us or loves us or befriends us or trusts us. Not in itself a bad thing, is it?" I hadn't heard Flood in this vein before; I knew there was something in what he was saying, yet I mistrusted it: because it came from him; I had a suspicion he had learned it somewhere, by heart, and now repeated it. "But you can't fulfil all of them," he said. "You have to compromise. You can call it corruption, if you must. Or you can call it compromise."

After a while I said: "I think I'd better get on with the report."

He sighed. "Very well." He watched me as I went to the door. "By the way," he said, "the fellow who shot Boyd . . ."

"Jackson."

"Yes. We're hoping he'll get off, or at any rate get a very nominal sentence. I was thinking: do you suppose he has a licence for that shotgun of his?"

"I shouldn't think so."

"Then what do you think about getting him one? He'll be in trouble without one. You might even have it ante-dated."

"I'll do that."

"——Just by a day or two."

"Certainly."

"We wouldn't want the police to catch him without a licence."

"Naturally not."

He smiled sourly and nodded and said: "We'll drag you down yet," and I laughed. Afterwards, curiously light of heart, I went home.

THE END

Printed in Great Britain by
Billing and Sons Ltd., Guildford and Esher
G4971